DARCY'S DOWNFALL
Wild Kings MC: Dander Falls

ERIN OSBORNE

Darcy's Downfall
By: Erin Osborne

Copyright 2018© Erin Osborne

All rights reserved. This book, or any portion thereof, may not be reproduced or used in any manner without the express written permission of the author except for brief quotations used in book reviews.

This book is a work of fiction. The names, characters, places, and incidents are products of the writer's imagination or have been used fictitiously and are not to be construed as real. Any resemblance to persons, living or dead, actual events, locales, or organizations is entirely coincidental.

Photographer: Reggie Deanching at R + M Photography

Cover Model: BT Urruela, Victoria Stone, and Zachary Michael

Cover Design: Graphics by Shelly

Editor: Jenni Copeland Belanger

Dedication

I want to dedicate this book to my mom. You have taught me how to be a strong woman, to follow my dreams, and to love with my entire heart. I watched you work multiple jobs in order to make sure we had food in the house and a roof over our heads. Since my writing career began, you have been nothing but supportive and encouraging. When it comes to your kids and grandkids, you are our biggest cheerleader. I love you to the moon and back!!

Note to Readers

Hey everyone!!

    I want to thank you all for reading my first series, the Wild Kings MC. This is the first book in the Wild Kings MC: Dander Falls. I will tell you all now, this series will not have as many books in it as the Clifton Falls one did. However, you will still see characters from the first series and the Phantom Bastards in these books. I hope that you enjoy this series! Thank you for all the support that you have shown me so far in this amazing journey!!

Sincerely,

Erin

Character List

Full Patch Members
Brock 'Gage' Wilson: President
Brent 'Crash' Evans: V. President
Dominic 'Trojan' Martin: SAA
Ethan 'Steel' Stone: Treasurer
Chris 'Tech' Stevens: Secretary/IT

Old Ladies
Darcy Quinn: Crash and Trojan

Prospects
James 'Shadow' Patrick
Wayne Anderson
Mike Evans

Kitty Kat Lounge Dancers
Addison: Manager
Harley
Alyssa
Kaitlyn

Club Girls
Sally
Karla
Red
Tina

Club Businesses
Kitty Kat Lounge – Strip Club
King's Bar – Bar and Grill
King's Ink – Tattoo Parlor
Country Corner – Diner

Table of Contents

Darcy's Downfall
Dedication
Note to Readers
Character List
Table of Contents
Prologue
Chapter One
Chapter Two
Chapter Three
Chapter Four
Chapter Five
Chapter Six
Chapter Seven
Chapter Eight
Chapter Nine
Chapter Ten
Chapter Eleven
Chapter Twelve
Chapter Thirteen
Chapter Fourteen
Chapter Fifteen
Epilogue
Darcy's Downfall Playlist
Acknowledgments
About the Author
Other Books

Coming Soon

Prologue

Darcy

FOR THE LAST FEW MONTHS I've been receiving packages at my house, my salon, and on my car. There have been notes and pictures of me doing random things too. Including pictures from inside my home. I honestly have no clue who is doing this or why, it's starting to freak me out though. Especially since it's been going on so long and now the pictures, packages, and notes are becoming more personal and sexy.

Crash and Trojan know that something is going on and they are trying to figure out what it is, but I'm not giving anything away. I don't want, or need, their help. Not with this or anything else. If I know them at all though, they're going to keep digging until they figure out why I get scared and jumpy so easily. At one point, I pulled a gun on them when they came knocking on my door. If that doesn't tell them that something is wrong, then they are two of the most clueless men I have ever had the displeasure of meeting. The only reason I say displeasure is because I don't want them to be in my life the same way that they want to be in my life.

I met the two men a while ago when a few of the old ladies came in to get their hair done. They started showing me attention and I can't figure out how to get them to go away. The more that I push them away, the more that they seem to insert themselves into my life. It's annoying because I feel that I'm better off alone than with anyone else. I've learned that nothing good can come from being in any type of relationship with a man. Let alone two men.

After a few failed attempts at trying to be with someone, there was one man that made me believe in the happily ever after. That all changed about a year into the relationship though. He got demanding, possessive, controlling, and the final straw of laying his hands on me. One night going as far as almost killing me. It was like all of a sudden, a switch flipped and the man I was falling in love with became someone else entirely. I can't give anyone else a chance. I'm too scared to even attempt being with someone again.

Now, my only concern is making sure my salon is successful, I have good friends surrounding me, and getting rid of this stalker. I know that Crash and Trojan would have no problem getting rid of this person for me, but that means letting them in. Hell, it means I would have to figure out who was doing this shit. I have racked my brain for days trying to figure out who it could possibly be, and I can't figure it out.

I'm already getting feelings for the two men and I don't need to get any more. They don't need to know that they star in all my nightly fantasies. No one will ever know that part. So, I try to stay as far away from them as I possibly can. That doesn't work out when I go to Clifton Falls for get togethers or when they just decide to stop by and pay me a visit though. I'm beginning to lose all the barriers that I've been carefully erecting since meeting Crash and Trojan. They're one or two small gestures away from blowing any resistance I have to pieces.

For now, I have to focus on my salon and trying to figure out who is coming for me. This isn't something I typically have to deal with and I don't know who it could be. I mainly cater to women at the salon and the few guys that come in are old enough to be my grandfather. So, in my mind, that rules them out. Maybe this person is losing interest in me though. At least I hope they are. I mean, a girl can dream, can't she?

Chapter One

Darcy

I'VE MANAGED TO GO THE LAST few days without getting anything from my stalker. Honestly, I don't know if the person can be classified as a stalker because they're only leaving things at this point. At the same time, I don't want to relax my guard too much, not when I don't know if they're going to strike again. This has been going on for so long that I know it's only a matter of time before I get something else from whoever is doing this. When it first started, there was once when I went a week without getting anything. I relished the break and thought naively that it was the end of it, that the person got tired of stalking me. That didn't last too long though and they started up again.

Pulling up to my house, I park in the garage and make sure the door closes behind me. I grab everything I need from the front seat before I make my way inside. The only thing I want to do right now is change my clothes and wait for my Chinese food to get here. Today was a long one and I can't wait for Riley to get here so I can have some help. A few more days.

Walking into my living room the first thing I notice is my lamps on the floor. I immediately stop and look around. The room is completely trashed. My pictures are on the floor, the couch is tipped over, knick-knacks are smashed all over, and my house phone is ripped from the wall. That's what I see just from my first glance around. The way that I'm starting to panic, I'm surprised I realized all of that was done. I guess part of me knows that I'm going to have to give as much detail as possible to Gage, or the police. Not that I want to bring them in since they haven't done anything to help me yet.

I know I want to walk through the rest of the house, but I don't know if anyone is still in here. So, I quickly make my way back to the garage and get in my car. Pulling out my phone, I call Gage and wait for him to answer. Silently pleading that the person is gone, and I'll be safe in my car until Gage tells me what to do.

"'Lo?" he answers.

"It's Darcy. I need help. Please, Gage, I'm scared," I tell him, letting the panic fill my voice so he knows that I'm serious.

"What's goin' on Darcy?" he asks, placing his hand over the phone as he talks to someone.

"Someone's been in my house. I don't know who or when. I don't even know if anything other than the living room has been damaged," I say in a hushed tone.

"How long has this been goin' on?" he asks, his tone telling me that he's pissed off I haven't said anything to him before now. "I'm guessin' this isn't the first thing that's happened."

"No. Can we please talk about this when you get here?" I ask, tears streaming down my face.

"Yeah. We're on our way now."

"Don't tell them please?" I plead.

"Too late babe. They're already gone."

Gage hangs up and I just hang my head. This isn't what I wanted to happen. If I wanted them to know, I would've called them myself. I wanted Gage to come help me. After that, I would have worried about the two Neanderthals that insist on inserting themselves in my life. Now, I have no choice but to deal with whatever they're going to say tonight. Fuck my life!

I'm trying to stay calm and not let my imagination run wild when someone bangs on my window. I scream and hit my head on the ceiling of my car when I jump from the shock that I was so far in my head I didn't realize anyone came into the garage. Looking out the window, I see Trojan standing there looking equal parts pissed the fuck off and concerned. Slowly, he opens the door and pulls me out. Before I can say a word, his strong arms are wrapped around me and I lose what little control over my emotions I had.

"Baby, why didn't you come to us for help? You need somethin', you come to us," he tells me, leaving no room for me to argue with him.

"I don't want your help, Trojan," I tell him. "I wanted to take care of this on my own."

"You can't take care of everythin' on your own babe. Crash and I are more than willin' to handle the things that you need help with. All you have to do is open your mouth."

"I can't do this Trojan. Nothin' can happen between us. I'm not the girl you need me to be," I tell him honestly. "There's things you don't know that I won't share. I can't be with you, or anyone else."

"You can. We'll find out what's holdin' you back. Then we'll get you past it, so we can move on together."

I don't even bother responding. Crash and Trojan think that they can get whatever they want. Well, I hate to burst their little bubble, but that doesn't include anything to do with me. Yeah, they're hot as hell and I'd love to explore things with them. Unfortunately, I don't want a man in my life. I'm good hanging out with the men from the clubs, but that's as far as it's ever going to go.

Gage comes out and I hear some whispered communication going on between the two men. On one hand I want to know what's going on, but on the other I don't want to know. However, I know that I need to get everything cleaned up and my house put back together. Eventually, I'm going to have to see the mess that was left inside.

"Was it just my living room, or are other rooms trashed too?" I ask, needing to know before I get surprised.

"Your bedroom was the worst Darcy," Gage tells me. "Crash is in there startin' to clean the mess up. I think he's in the livin' room right now."

I nod my head and pull myself from Trojan's arms. There's no point in delaying the inevitable. Walking to the door leading inside, I bypass Crash cleaning up the mess and make my way into the bedroom. Before I can hit the floor, Crash is catching me and holding me to his chest. He's whispering to me to get me to calm down. I can't even understand what he's saying over the pounding in my ears.

My bed is ripped to shreds. Not just the sheets and blankets, the mattress and box spring are shredded as well. The clothes in my dresser are flung haphazardly all over the room, clothes from my closet are torn and cut to pieces, pictures are smashed in the carpet, and my television is overturned. What had me dropping to my knees though is the picture of me on the wall behind my bed. I'm standing outside of my salon between Crash and Trojan. They're trying to tell me something and I'm arguing back. I can tell just from the look on my face. There's a knife holding the picture to the wall and writing surrounding it. *Your time is coming bitch. You're mine!*

"We've got you babe. Nothin' is goin' to happen to you on our watch," Crash tells me, finally breaking through the fog.

"No!" I shout, needing to get out of the warmth and safety of his arms. "Please, just leave me alone."

About the only thing I don't see in my room is any of my panties. So, I walk over to the dresser and open my top drawer. It's empty. Looking around the room, I try to find any pair of my panties that I can. There's none here though.

"What the fuck?" I ask aloud.

"What's the matter?" Gage asks, coming up to stand next to Crash and Trojan.

"Whoever did this, took every single pair of panties I own," I tell them, not turning to look at them.

"What?" Trojan bellows.

The two men start looking around my room deeper. They're not going to find anything at all in here that's not already in plain sight. I don't have a lot of cubby holes to stash things away in. Crash flips my mattress up on to my box spring to see if anything is under it. Nothing's there.

Walking in to my bathroom, I see that it's just as bad as my bedroom is. Not only is everything trashed, but half of my bathroom necessities are missing. All of my favorite lotions, body wash, even my shampoo and conditioner are gone. What have I done to make someone do this to me? How am I going to get them to stop? Where do I go from here? These are the questions running rampant through my head right now.

Trojan

When Gage told us that Darcy was on the phone and she was scared to death about something, I didn't wait to find out what was going on. My only thought was getting to her and protecting her from whatever is scaring her. Crash and I knew something was going on with her. No matter what we did, we couldn't find anything out though. We can't protect her if we don't know what's going on.

Crash is hot on my heels as we hop on our bikes and get ready to get our girl. She needs us right now no matter what she says. Since she called Gage and not us, I know that she doesn't want us to know. Too bad everyone around here knows that Darcy is ours. She just needs to get used to it and accept that fact. When it comes to her, no matter who she called, we would have been notified about something happening to her.

Walking into my woman's house, I'm floored. Her normally neat and orderly house is turned upside down. Whoever did this is going to regret ever looking in Darcy's direction! Crash and I will make sure of that. We'll make sure this stupid cocksucker pays for what he's done; he's destroyed her sanctuary and her sense of being safe. That's not something that we're going to take lightly or accept.

I look over at Darcy and see the torment and how scared she truly is tarnishing her beautiful face. Our woman is curvy with long blond hair shot through with streaks of red. Her usually clear sky-blue eyes are filled with unshed tears and her face is flushed with anger. Someone has destroyed her sanctuary and invaded her privacy. Anger and rage like I've never known before fills me.

I walk over to my girl and know that she's not going to let me get close to her right now. She didn't call Crash and I for a reason. Darcy still isn't ready to let us in and I don't know what's going to help make that possible. All I know is eventually, Crash and I will get tired of waiting. We'll make her see that we're going to be perfect together.

Following her into her bedroom, I hear her tell Gage that whoever was in her house stole all her panties. What the fuck? This is some sick fuck if they're taking all her panties. Not to mention that now, he's really going to pay for going after our girl. In my experience, there's only one reason a man would steal a woman's underwear. He doesn't have good intentions when it comes to Darcy. We'll have to catch him before he does something worse than destroying her house.

"Firecracker, why don't you come with us tonight?" I ask, knowing one way or another she'll be coming to the house with us. "Get your mind off what happened here, and we can do surveillance to make sure no one comes back while they think you're sleepin' here."

"And where do you think you're going to take me?" she asks, the fire inside coming out to show how strong she truly is.

"We'll take you to our house," Crash answers. "There's an extra room and you can sleep in there."

"I don't know," she says slowly, weighing her options.

"We're not goin' to try anythin' firecracker," Crash tells her. "When you come to our bed, you'll be ready and willin'. Not scared because of somethin' happenin' at your house or thinkin' that's what we're expectin' you to do."

"Okay. Are you sure my house will be okay though? I don't want anything else to happen while I'm not here."

"I'll make sure there's a prospect and full patch on your house at all times. I'm sendin' someone to the salon too. Tech is going to come in and install a security system including cameras. For now, you've got two shadows on you at all times. I know Crash and Trojan are goin' to be with you as much as they can. When they can't be, I'll make sure two other full patch members are with you. Is that understood?" Gage asks her.

"Yes," she says, not putting up the slightest fight about what's going on right now. This is not our Darcy.

"Get some things packed up and we'll head out," I tell her, looking around to see if there's anything she can salvage.

"I don't think I have anything left," she whispers, the first tear slipping from her eye.

Nothing is going to stop me from going to her now. She needs comfort and to know that we're going to protect her. Crash and I surround Darcy and wrap our arms around her. Darcy actually lets us hold her together for the first time. Having her between us is so much better than I ever dreamed it would be. Granted, I hate the reason that she's letting us hold and support her. But, I'll make sure she knows we're here for her more than just when she needs comfort and a feeling of security and safety.

"We'll stop at a store on the way to the house," I tell her. "Please don't cry. We'll get who did this. Tomorrow, you're goin' to have to tell us everythin' though."

"I know. I didn't want it to get to this point, I thought I could handle it on my own. This is the last straw though."

Darcy lets us lead her to her car in the garage. Since Gage, Crash, and myself were the only ones here, someone managed to get in and flatten all four tires on her car. I'm thinking this is the last straw for firecracker. She lets her ass hit the garage floor and puts her head in her hands. I can see her body shaking as she silently cries. Crash goes to her this time and lifts her up. There isn't even enough fight left in her to resist being in Crash's arms right now.

"How the fuck did someone get in here with us here?" Gage bellows.

"I don't know. It must have been when Crash was vacuuming, and we were tryin' to start cleanin' the place up. Probably when we were all headed back towards the bedroom," I tell him, wanting to know who would be stupid enough to get past us and pull this shit.

This person must have a death wish if they would come back while the three of us were inside. Especially not knowing if more men were going to be coming as back-up. Or, maybe they don't know who the fuck they're messing with. I'm not sure what this person's damage is, all I know is that they are a crazy motherfucker. Now, we'll have to have Tech come in and make sure nothing is on the bikes to try to track Darcy to our house or wherever else we take her.

I follow him out to the bikes and watch as he puts her on the back of his. While I'd love to be the one she's riding behind, I know there will be time for that later. When she can actually enjoy the ride. Watching, I see my brother put a helmet on her head and make sure it's secure before climbing on in front of her. He's talking in hushed tones to her and I'm sure he's telling her what she needs to do when riding. As far as I know, she's never been on the back of anyone's bike. We wouldn't know anyway, given the state of almost shock that she's in right now.

Crash

Pulling away from Darcy's house, I have so many thoughts going through my head. The first one is that I don't ever want to see the fear and utter desolation on her beautiful face again. Second, I want to maim and torture the fuckwad that put that look on her face to begin with. Darcy is an amazing woman and doesn't need to feel the way she's feeling right now.

Knowing Trojan the way I do, I know that the same thoughts have to be going through his head. We're closer than most brothers and can read one another better than most. I'm not sure why we have the bond we do, all I know is I wouldn't change it for anything in the world. Having Trojan at my back brings me back to the better memories of serving in the military. I know without a doubt that there will always be someone at my six. And I'll always be at his.

We pull off to take our girl to a store so that she can get some clothes. I'm sure it's going to be a fight when she goes to cash out and realizes that one of us will be paying for her things. She's ours to love, protect, and make sure she has everything she needs. I'm hoping that she just goes with the flow though and lets us take care of her.

Trojan pulls out his phone as soon as we get off our bikes. I'm sure he's having a prospect meet us here to take whatever purchases she needs back to the house. Plus, he's going to have to stop at the store for us. Hopefully it's Shadow. I know that he's close to patching in and we like him being around. He does what we ask without whining, talking shit, or putting up a fight. Shadow has done some pretty shitty jobs and has done it without a word.

"Got Shadow comin'," Trojan lets us know. "He'll be here in twenty."

"Sounds good. Let's get goin' firecracker. You get whatever you need and take all the time you want."

Darcy nods her head and moves as if on autopilot. This is definitely not our girl. I can't stand to see her like this. We need to figure out a way to snap her out of this, so we can have our firecracker back. The girl that has no problem putting us in our place, the one that does what she wants when she wants, and the girl that fights us at every turn.

Trojan looks at me and I see the same thoughts swirling through his mind. We keep Darcy between us as we continually scan the parking lot looking for anything suspicious or out of place. It's a public parking lot and there's a thousand different places for someone to hide and watch us. I'm not getting the feeling that we're being watched, but that doesn't necessarily mean anything. It could just mean too much of my focus is on Darcy.

Walking in the store, Darcy comes to a stop and looks around. It's like she's a lost little girl and doesn't know which way to turn first. So, I take charge and grab a cart before heading over to the clothing section. We stand there and let her wander through the racks to pick out some clothes first. Then, we'll worry about the other necessities she'll need.

We watch as Darcy looks at all the clothes on the racks before her. She picks barely anything up and I know that she's thinking of the money in her account and not that we're going to be paying for this trip. Trojan discreetly looks at her sizes and goes to pick more of the things that she's already put in the cart in different colors. Along with a few items that are a size or two smaller than what she's chosen. He also adds some things that I know we'll like on her and not necessarily what we've ever seen her in before. This includes a few dresses, jeans, tank tops, and dress clothes so we can go out.

Darcy wanders over to the health and beauty section of the store in a daze. She grabs a few things and I ask her if she's got everything she needs. Nodding her head, we make our way to the front of the store. I'm hoping when she notices our extra purchases that some of the fight will begin to come back to her. Looks like I'm right.

"What the hell is all of this?" she asks, throwing her hands on her hips and glaring at the two of us.

"What do you mean?" I ask, making sure to look as innocent as I possibly can.

"There's a ton of extra clothes in here that I don't remember putting in the cart," she says, pulling a handful of hangers out of the cart and holding them for closer inspection.

"You were obviously pickin' things that you need and not enough to last you a full week at our house. So, I added a few things to make sure that you have everythin' that you need," Trojan tells her, like it's an everyday normal conversation between the three of us.

"Whatever! If you want to waste your money on things I'll never wear, that's on you," she tells us, picking up the original items she put in the cart and separating them out.

"We're payin' for it all," I let her know, taking the items from her hands and placing them on the conveyor belt.

Darcy gives us a final glare and storms to look at the shelves in front of the checkout we're standing at. I'm glad she's not walking away from us and storming away when there's still a threat out there. We'll give her the space she needs right now until we get home. Then, she can't run very far. And we sure as hell aren't going to let her hide in her room every single day.

We're finally pulling up to the house and I can feel Darcy tense up behind me. It's finally dawning on her that she's really going to the house Trojan and I share. She's going to be staying with us without a car and she's actually going to have to depend on us. I don't want her to hate being here, so we've got to figure out some way to make sure that she's as comfortable as she can possibly be. We want our house to become her new sanctuary. It doesn't matter if she wants to change everything about the house, decorate it to look like a chick house, or anything else her heart desires. As long as she's comfortable and with us, we're not going to give a shit what she does to it.

A few years ago, we found a house in the country. We've got more than a few acres surrounding the house so that no one can move in too close to us. We like our privacy and wanted somewhere to come that's away from everyone else. The only ones that know about our home are the members of the club, and a few guys from the Clifton Falls chapter, and the Phantom Bastards. They're lucky they know where we live since we didn't even want them to know. However, prospects helped us get our shit in here and we figured Gage needed to know in case something happened. The rest kind of figured out by accident.

We like it that way. No one can bother us when we're not at the clubhouse. Plus, no one is going to know where Darcy is. That reminds me that we need to let her know that she can't tell anyone where we are. Gage already took her cell phone and reminded her that someone can use it to track her. She gave it up real quick after being reminded of that fact. I trust the girls from Clifton Falls, but it's not them I'm worried about. This unknown person knows her schedule enough to get in her house and do all that damage while she was still at the salon. The less people that know her whereabouts the better.

"Firecracker, the prospect will be here soon with your new stuff and some food. Why don't you relax, and we'll get you when dinner's ready?" I ask her.

Without a word, she follows Trojan to the room she'll be staying in. It's right between ours so we can both hear her. I know that we'll both be up listening for her throughout the night. I'm not going to complain about it though. I want her to know that she can trust us and that she can count on us when she needs someone to have her back. I've had to stay up for days when I was in the military, this will be heaven to watch over someone that I'm learning to love.

There has only been one other time that I've given my heart over to someone. We were high school sweethearts and I thought that we would spend the rest of our lives together. Candace stayed by my side through boot camp and when I got stationed a few states away. The plan was for her to finish school and then move down with me. As often as I could, I made the drive back to see her. She made the trip a few times. After a few months of making the trips, I proposed, and she said yes. Just before we were set to get married, I got deployed.

While I was deployed, we wrote letters, emailed, and I called her as often as I could. Apparently, it wasn't enough for Candace. She sent me a Dear John letter just before I was due to be shipped back home. Not only did she break my heart, she took all my money, and got married to someone that was supposed to be one of my good friends. I vowed never to let a woman get to me again. Darcy is different though. She would never pull the shit that Candace did. Instead, she goes out of her way to avoid a relationship with anyone. I don't think I've ever seen her go out on a date in the time that we've known her.

I walk in the kitchen and pull out a beer. If there's one thing we always have in the house, it's that. I'm sure that will change with our girl being in the house, but for so long it's been just Trojan and I. Now, we need to have things in here for her. And, we'll have to start cooking again. Honestly, I love cooking. I used to do it all the time. Now, we mainly get our meals at the clubhouse or we get takeout. Those days are over though. There will still be times we go out to eat, but we need to start eating at the house and make use of the amazing kitchen we had built when we started renovations.

Trojan meets me in the kitchen and I can tell this is taking its toll on him. He wants to fix everything for her and he can't right now. I hand him a beer and watch him down it in one gulp. Yeah, he's taking this hard. I wait until he grabs another one and sits at the island before I start talking.

"We need to make sure she knows not to tell anyone where we're keepin' her. It's for her safety," I tell him.

"I know. She's not goin' to like it, but she'll understand it. We should let her talk to the girls from Clifton Falls though. They'll want to know what's goin' on and that she's okay."

"I was thinkin' the same thing. Should we bring her out here to do that before Shadow gets here? Or should we let her relax for a little bit?" I ask Trojan, debating internally as to what the best decision in this situation is.

"Let's let her relax and adjust to bein' here. I'm glad that we got her here finally, but I wish it were under better circumstances."

"I know. We'll just take it a day at a time and let her lead us in this. I know we're not waitin' much longer though."

"Nope. Not now."

Trojan and I sit there and wait for Shadow to show up. It's not long before the security system alerts us to someone coming up the driveway. Taking a look, I see the car Shadow was driving. We make our way to the door and open it, so we can help him carry everything in. I don't want more people here right now to overwhelm her more than what she already is. Darcy doesn't need to be around more than us until she calms down. She knows Shadow, but she really hasn't interacted with him.

It doesn't take us to long to unload everything. I take the bags into Darcy. She's laying on the bed, curled up in a fetal position, rocking back and forth. Getting closer to her, I see the silent tears falling from her closed eyes. Seeing her like this is breaking my heart, so I climb in bed behind her and wrap my arms around her. I tell her that dinner will be ready soon and she nods, relaxing into my embrace.

Chapter Two

Darcy

I'VE BEEN AT CRASH AND TROJAN'S HOUSE for a few days. Other than going to the salon, followed by them of course, I haven't left the house. The only other thing that I've done is make a phone call to the girls from the other club. There were tears, fear for my safety, and the promise to get together soon. Crash and Trojan are on board with taking me to Clifton Falls because it means getting out of town for a while. Hell, despite their hatred of Wood, I'm sure they'd take me to Benton Falls too. There just really aren't any females I talk to there. Slim is about the only one that's close to taking an old lady.

"You know that you're not a prisoner here, right?" Crash asks me.

"I know that. I just have nowhere I want to be right now. We don't know where this asshole is," I tell him, looking up from my e-reader. Keira may have sent me a copy of her new book and I'm loving the hell out of it.

Crash and Trojan look at me and a strange look covers their face. I'm not sure what it means, and I don't know that I want to. They exchange a look between them and sit on either side of me. Apparently, we're not done talking and they have a few things that they need to say to me. So, I put my tablet down and settle in for their talk.

"We know that somethin' is holdin' you back from bein' with us. We're done waitin' for you to get over it firecracker," Crash tells me, while Trojan is nodding his head.

"I can't do it," I tell them, putting my head in my hands and looking at our feet.

"You can. We're not goin' to hurt you," Trojan says, pulling my head up to look at the sincerity in his eyes. "Darcy, you may not know it, but every emotion you feel, every thought you think is written all over your face."

"What he's sayin' is that we know you want us. So, what's holdin' you back?" Crash asks, turning my face towards him.

"Every time I open up and give some guy a chance, they fuck me over. I'm too fat, I'm too greedy, I don't give them enough, I don't let them do what they want to me." I answer, not wanting to go down the road that we're about to go down right now.

"What do you mean that you don't let them do what they want to you?" Trojan asks me, the rage clearly written on his face for all to see. I'm sure he's thinking the worst right now.

"I don't want to go down that road right now," I tell them. I want to keep the fact that I'm a virgin to myself as long as possible.

"You sayin' what I think you're sayin'?" Crash asks me.

"I don't know what you're thinking so I can't answer that."

"You're a virgin, aren't you, firecracker?" Trojan asks, getting on board with what Crash is thinking.

There's no need to answer when my face heats up. I can feel the blush covering my upper chest, my face, and my neck. Both men look at me, and I swear that their eyes are about to pop out of their head. It's almost like I'm watching some cartoon movie where the characters have outrageous animations for their emotions. If this wasn't such a serious topic, I would probably be laughing my ass off right now. Unfortunately, they don't understand where I'm coming from and I'm embarrassed by the fact that I'm in my mid-twenties and I still haven't had sex with anyone.

"It's not a big deal guys. It just hasn't happened for me yet," I tell them, trying to get off the couch so I can put some space between us.

"Not so fast," they both say at once. "I don't know what the fuck else these men were thinkin', but they missed out on an amazin' woman. You're not fat, you've got amazin' curves in all the right places. Why are you greedy? Because you won't give them your money? That's not greedy, that's makin' the right choices for yourself. We're goin' to prove to you what you mean to us," Trojan tells me.

"You're going to find that I'm boring and all I do is work and spend my time at the house. The most I've gotten out of the house is since I met the old ladies in Clifton Falls. There's no one here that I associate with outside of the salon."

"I don't care if you're the most borin' person on this planet," Crash tells me. "You're the sweetest girl, you care about those around you, you take the awkward moments you find yourself and make it funny, you can laugh at yourself, and you don't put up with our shit."

"You two are cavemen and you think you can control me," I sass back.

"We don't want to control you," Trojan says, making sure I'm facing him, so I can fully understand what he's telling me. "There's a difference between controllin' you and protectin' you. I don't care what you do as long as you come home to us at the end of the day and you don't cheat on us. You're our woman and we want to make sure that every stupid fucker knows that."

"If I'm yours, then I expect you to be faithful to me. There won't be anyone else and I don't know that you two can do that. And you lose your shit every time Wood and I are in the same room together," I tell them, thinking of the trouble that poor man has gotten into because of me.

"That's because of the circumstances," Trojan tells me. "What if every time you saw one of us, we were face down in some bitch's lap? You wouldn't like that too much would you?"

"Not to mention that we haven't been with a club girl or anyone else since we met you. Neither one of us want to fuck this up. We want you to give us the chance to seriously be with you. I'm not talkin' about a night or a week, but for good. You have somethin' that we want, somethin' that we crave," Crash tells me, pulling my face towards him so I can see the sincerity in his eyes.

"No, I wouldn't," I admit. "But, it's not his fault I'm a total klutz. I lose my shit and he just happens to be the unfortunate victim when I do."

"Rationally, we know this firecracker. It doesn't help anything though when we see it firsthand," Crash tells me.

I can honestly see where the guys are coming from. Even though I don't want to admit it, I would hate having to see them all over some girl. Thinking back, the few times we've been around club girls, they haven't paid them any attention at all. They're too busy following me around. Can I honestly trust them not to cheat on me if it did last more than a night? But, I still know that this isn't going to be more than one night for them. Do I take that one night and expect nothing else from them?

"What's goin' through that head of yours, firecracker?" Crash asks me.

"That I know anything with you would only last one night. I'm just not sure that I want to take that as what happens my first time. I think I'd rather be in a relationship with someone when I lose my virginity."

"What makes you so sure that all we want is one night?" Trojan asks. "You're livin' in our house for the time bein' and I want to make it permanent. Crash, I'm sure, is on the same page as I am."

"I am."

I can feel my jaw drop in awe and shock at hearing these two gorgeous men want more than one night with me. So, I take a minute to truly look at them. Crash is tall and built from his time in the service. I don't know much about it, just that he's done his time and still gets called out from time to time. He's got short dark hair that he keeps shaved close to his head and eyes that look like the color of warm chocolate with the hint of golden flecks sprinkled throughout them. Trojan is taller and bigger than Crash by a little bit. I'm not sure if he was in the military, but he's got the attitude of someone that has served. He also has dark hair that's a little longer than Crash's and eyes the color of melted chocolate. You could drown in his eyes and still be left wanting more. Both men have tattoos for days and I've often found myself wanting to trace them with my tongue.

These two could have any woman they want, and I'm sure they have. Why they want me is something that I'll never begin to understand. Part of me is tired of fighting it and the other part of me wants to keep running. The voice in my head continues to tell me that I'm just setting myself up for heartbreak and to run as far away as I possibly can. I'm tired of running from them though. Honestly, if they break me after giving them one night, I have no one to blame but myself. I think I'm ready to take that chance though.

"What are you thinkin' right now firecracker?" Trojan asks me.

"I'm thinking that I'm tired of fighting what I feel for you two. I think that there's still going to be issues that creep up for me, but I don't think I can keep pushing you two away," I tell them honestly. "I will just protect myself and guard my heart when someone you truly want to be with turns your head."

"Not gonna happen, firecracker," Trojan tells me. "There's no one else we want. Hell, it's been a long ass time since we've even looked at a club girl or any other woman. You're the one we want. Only you!"

Trojan leans in and places a hand on each side of my face, whispering that I don't know how happy I've just made him. Before I can register what he's about to do, he places a gentle kiss on my lips. I give him a small opening when I gasp, and he deepens the kiss. Crash doesn't give me the chance to catch my breath as he turns me and gives me the same treatment as Trojan. Man, these two men know how to kiss and make a girl lose her breath completely. Fuck, I've been missing out. The few kisses I've had in the past have been nothing like this.

Crash

Even though Darcy has finally, after months and months of waiting, agreed to be ours, nothing is going to happen tonight. We can't push her since we found out that she's a virgin. The only thing that's going to do is make her run the other way. I'm wondering if we should arrange for her to spend a day with Skylar. Not all the girls, just Skylar. She's used to being with two men and can open Darcy's eyes as to what's going to happen between us. I don't want our girl to go in this with a blind eye. She's going to be more comfortable hearing it from another woman first. Then Trojan and I can talk to her.

I look at my brother and communicate that we need to talk later when she's gone to bed. Before I can do anything else, my phone rings and I pull it out seeing Skylar's name on the screen. Is she reading my mind now? I answer it before handing it to my girl. Now, I can pull Trojan aside and tell him my idea. The sooner we get this in motion, the better it will be.

We're still going to take this at Darcy's pace, but at least she'll have an idea of what to expect and it will be one less thing for her to get in her head about.

We both head into the kitchen so Darcy can have a little bit of privacy. I pull out steaks, stuff to make salad, and two beers. Trojan stands behind me, waiting to see what I'm going to say.

"I think we need to let Darcy have a day with Skylar. Just the two of them. Now that she's agreed to be ours, I don't want her runnin' scared. Skylar can gently let her know what to expect with bein' with two men," I tell him, sitting down at the island to hear his thoughts.

"I was actually thinkin' the same thing. The sooner the better, but I still don't want to rush her into anythin'."

I nod my head in agreement and we hear Darcy heading our way. She hands me the phone back and lets me know that Skylar is planning a trip down to see her in the next few days. Trojan and I look at one another and smiles form on our faces. Skylar doesn't need any convincing to help our girl out. I'm sure she jumped right on talking to her as soon as Darcy told her she finally stopped pushing us away.

"Um. I don't know what I can do about it, but Riley is going to be coming down with her. She's going to be working in the salon and I need to find her an apartment, or house, and make sure that she gets settled in," she tells us, completely unsure of herself.

"That's fine firecracker. I can talk to Gage and see if we have any place that will be suitable for her. I know she's got some shit goin' on that he's already neck deep in," I tell her, pulling her in between my legs. I breathe her in and get the familiar scent of hair products and something that is uniquely her.

Darcy looks back and forth between us. I'm sure she's wondering how this is supposed to work. Right now, I'm guessing that she feels like Trojan feels left out. Based on the look on his face, he doesn't feel that way at all. He's happy as fuck that we can do this with her. Finally. He'll get his turn when I'm on the patio grilling the steaks and potatoes. The salad is for Darcy. She had potatoes last night and I've noticed that she'd rather have a salad a few days a week with her dinner. So, that's what she's going to get.

"Help me make salads while Crash is outside?" he asks her, pointing towards the salad fixings on the counter.

"Sure. Is there anything else I can do to help?" she asks, pulling away from me.

"Not right now. We're pretty much set until we need to set the table. Do you want to eat outside tonight?" I ask, grabbing what I need for outside.

"Yeah," the two answer in unison.

Trojan and Darcy get everything they need to start making the salad while I make my way out to the grill. It's peaceful out here and I'm glad that we decided to eat outside tonight. The air is warm enough and the only sound around are the birds chirping in the distance. There's always been a peaceful quality to our house, today it seems to be even more peaceful. I'm sure that it has to do with Darcy being our woman now. The day just seems brighter now. She truly is the light to our darkness.

I can hear the sweetest sound coming from the kitchen through the open door. Trojan has Darcy laughing her ass off about something and I wish I were in there with them. If I'm honest with myself, I want to be the one to make her laugh like that. And I'll spend the rest of my days striving to make her laugh and be as happy as we can possibly make her. Trojan will be the same way. We've waited so long for her to be ours and we're going to make sure that nothing ever takes her happiness away from her.

Trojan

Working in the kitchen with Darcy has got to be one of the best things I've ever done. She's wormed her way into our hearts and now we don't know what to do without her in our lives. Thankfully, she put us out of our misery and finally agreed to be ours. This has been a long time coming. I know that we're going to have to work through her fears and the thoughts that run rampant through her head, but we'll do that.

We're preparing the salads and she's making some fruity drink while I grab another beer. I go to turn back to the island we're working at and almost knock her out of my way. Darcy starts giggling and the sound is music to my ears. I have my hands on her hips, to steady her, and letting go is the last thing I want to do right now. But, we need to get the food ready when the steaks are done. So, I guess we go back to work.

"Are you sure that you guys know what you're getting in to with me?" she asks suddenly, the shyness and trepidation written over her facial features.

"What do you mean, firecracker?" I ask, intrigued, and confused at the same time.

"Well, all I do is work and read. I never really go out and do anything. I'm sure you guys are used to going out and being around a lot of other people. I'm nervous and we all know I'm really clumsy when I'm around a group of people."

"We can deal with your clumsiness as it comes up. As far as bein' nervous around large groups of people, you'll get used to everyone the more that you're around them. We'll take it a day at a time and at your pace. Just knowin' that your ours at the end of the day is what we care about. Everythin' else will fall into place. And don't even worry about anythin' happenin' until you're ready. Talkin' to Sky is goin' to help you get ready for that," I tell her, making sure she's looking at me the entire time.

"Okay," she responds hesitantly. "I don't know when I'll be ready to give you guys what you want though."

"For now, it's enough that we get to go to bed every night holdin' you. Because you will be in bed between us each and every fuckin' night," I tell her, meaning the words coming out of my mouth.

Darcy gives a slight nod to acknowledge what I'm telling her. Other than that, she puts her entire focus on what she's cutting up for the salad. I take her lead and get back to work on what I'm putting together. She's cutting up the cucumbers while I work on cutting up the eggs and cheese. I've never been one for eating salad, but I'm going to suck it up for Darcy. She's already getting us to do things we've never done before. I wouldn't change anything about it though.

Dinner has been a huge success. We've got our girl sitting between us and she's laughing and eating. At first, she was shy about eating in front of us, but we assured her that we like our woman to have an appetite. Crash may have also told her that when we get to that point, she's going to have to eat to keep her energy level up for us. I swear he has no filter sometimes. Darcy didn't go running for the hills though, she took it in stride and continued eating.

"What's the plan for tonight?" she asks, shyly.

"What do you mean?" I ask, even though I have a pretty good idea.

"I know you said that we'd take this a day at a time and at my pace, I just know that you two can't go very long with waiting. And I don't want to lead you on," she answers, repeating what she told us earlier.

"We're not goin' to cheat on you, firecracker. You're in our bed and we're goin' to sleep. After you talk to Sky and you decide you want to take that step, we'll figure out the best way to go about it. Until then, we're goin' to climb in bed, wrap our arms around you, and go to sleep," I tell her.

Crash nods his head in agreement, while finishing off the last of his beer. I can see that there are more questions floating around in her mind, but I'm not going to push her. My brother might not feel the same way, but we'll find out soon. He's only going to hold his tongue for so long. If he doesn't push her away and gets her to start opening up without us prying the information from her, I'm all for it.

"Ask what you want to ask," he says suddenly. "You can ask us anythin' you want, and we'll always answer you as honestly as we can. The only thing we won't talk about is club business."

"What happens if this person finds out I'm here? I don't want to bring this shit to your doorstep," she answers, looking down at her lap. I want to kill the person that took all her confidence away from her.

"If this comes to our doorstep, we deal with it," I tell her. "You're not bringin' this to us when we're steppin' up as your old men. It's our job to protect you."

"We'll do whatever we have to in order to find this fucker and make him pay for what he's doin' to you," Crash adds in.

"We'll do whatever we have to in order to find this fucker and make him pay for what he's doin' to you," Crash adds in.

"And what if it's a female?" she asks, thinking of all the possibilities.

"Then we call in a female to deal with her," Crash says matter-of-factly. "There's one in Clifton Falls. I'm not sayin' who, but she has no problem takin' care of females that are causin' shit."

"Okay. Well, I'm going to clean up and get ready for bed," she tells us, standing up and starting to grab plates.

"I'll help," Crash tells her. "Then we'll all go to bed."

"Um, I usually read for a while before I settle down," she tells us.

"That's okay. We can get a hold of Gage and find out what's goin' on for tomorrow. I know that you have to look at a few places for Riley. We'll get the information you need and meet you in the room," I tell her, following her into the kitchen with an armload of dishes.

I go out to finish gathering everything up and make sure the grill is off, leaving her with Crash. They're talking and I'm glad that he gets to have a little bit of time with her. I may not be the most sensitive man, but she's bringing that side out in me. Crash is softer when it comes to females. There's going to be times he can give her what she needs, and I'll have to step back. At least for now. Eventually she'll get used to both of us and decide which one she needs more in that moment.

Chapter Three

Darcy

TODAY IS FINALLY THE DAY THAT RILEY gets here. She's riding here with Skylar and a few guys. I'm not sure who all is coming, but I'm excited. Skylar already told me the rest of the girls are pissed that they don't get to come on this trip. That tears me up because I don't want anyone mad. Sky assured me that once she told them why, they were happy. I know that eventually I'll be getting grilled by them, but for now, I'm happy keeping this semi quiet.

"We're meetin' them at Riley's new house. Gage is goin' to be there too," Trojan tells me, coming in the bathroom attached to the room we all share now.

"I figured he'd be there," I respond, getting a smile on my face.

"Why is that, firecracker?" he asks, leaning his delectable body against the counter as I finish my make-up.

"He's liked her since he first met her. You watch them together and you can tell," I tell him, like it's some big secret. In reality, these men just can't see what's in front of their face when it doesn't involve them.

"And you're goin' to stay out of it," he answers. "Let them figure out their own shit."

"Is that an order?" I ask, letting my sass come out to play. "Didn't we already establish that you can't control me?"

"We did. I'm askin' that you let Prez figure his own shit out. They've both been through some shit and I want them to make their own decisions."

"I know. I won't meddle. Much," I respond, brushing past him.

Crash is in the bedroom, pulling on a pair of jeans that fit him just right. I swear these two are trying to kill me. They take their shirts off almost as soon as they walk in the door every day. When we go to bed, Crash sleeps naked and Trojan only wears a pair of boxers. I don't need to have any more visuals than I already get!

Trojan plasters his front to my back as I watch Crash finish getting dressed. Even though he hasn't turned around, I know he can tell I'm watching him. Feeling Trojan's warm breath on my neck is making my lady bits warm up and a shiver to course through my body. He's not even touching me, and I respond to him. This shit isn't fair at all. They definitely know what they're doing to me too. That's what makes it even harder to resist them when half the time I just want to jump in bed with them and let them have all of me. there's just an irrational fear that's holding me back from doing that.

Finally, Crash turns around and I see the smirk playing on his lips. I let a groan escape and quickly cover my mouth. The two cave dwellers start laughing and I know that the comments are going to start any minute. Crash doesn't disappoint.

"You think you don't kill us every day? I've taken more cold showers than the human body should ever be subjected to," he tells me.

"Yeah. Especially when you go to bed wearin' nothing but a tiny pair of panties and a tank top. I want to rip that off you and have my way with you."

"So, this is just payback?" I ask.

"Not at all," Trojan responds, walking to stand in front of me. "Just know that you're not the only one sufferin'."

I take this information in and make my way out of the bedroom. Grabbing my drink from the island, I wait by the front door for them. My excitement is starting to get the best of me and I want to leave now. Neanderthal one and two have different ideas though and take their sweet time. I swear, they are worse than women sometimes.

"I'm leaving!" I finally holler out.

"Not without us you're not," one of them call back.

"I will put you over my knee if you step one foot out the door," Crash says.

"I'd like to see you try," I mutter under my breath.

"Oh, that can be arranged, firecracker," Trojan tells me, scaring the shit out of me.

I slap his chest and my hand lingers on the hard, tight muscles there. Looking up at him, I see his eye darken. There's no choice but to stare into the melted chocolate as I'm mesmerized. Fuck! Why can't this be easy, and they be ugly as fuck instead of hot as hell? Finally, I pull my eyes away from his and remove my hand from his body. I grab everything I'm going to need for the day and follow Trojan out the door.

Crash is behind me and this is how it has been since the day my house was trashed. One stays in front of me to shield me from any oncoming threats and the other one stands guard from behind. I don't question what they do, I've just been going with the flow as much as I can. It's been extremely hard for me, but I don't want to give them too much trouble. It's bad enough that they've been waiting and waiting for me. By now I'm sure they have blue balls and I can't blame them if they decide they don't want to wait for me any longer.

Today, we decide to take Trojan's truck. I'm not sure why they made that decision, but it has to be for a reason. I've discovered that everything they do is because of one thing or another. I quit questioning it. Crash sits in back while I sit up front with Trojan. If we take Crash's car, Trojan sits in back. It's funny as hell considering the backseat is almost non-existent. He looks like some scrunched up giant with his knees in his chest and that's when I put my seat almost completely forward. They won't let me sit in back though.

We're finally pulling up to the house that Gage found for Riley. She told me that she didn't have that much stuff anymore, and she wasn't exaggerating. Everything she owns fits in one small trailer that might haul two bikes. My heart breaks for her. She's lost so much more than any of us know, but that's her story to tell.

I'm not sure why Gage picked a two-bedroom house for her to rent, but I'm sure I'll find out eventually. Maybe it's for when Keegan comes to visit? Once she's settled in, I'll have her over for a girl's night and we can talk about it. Shit! I can't do that when I'm staying at Crash and Trojan's house. I'm not sure if that's something they would go for. Maybe we'll do it here instead.

"Riley!" I call out. "I'm so happy that you're finally here!"

"Me too! I miss Keegan and her little family, but I need to move on with my life," she tells me, with a sadness filling her eyes.

"What am I, chopped liver?" Skylar asks, stepping out of the van.

"Of course not!" I tell her. "I'll be spending the afternoon with you though. Riley, I'll be back by in a few hours to see how you're doing."

"Sounds good. I'm going to get this stuff set up and then relax for a while," she responds, looking in Gage's direction.

Skylar and I climb in Trojan's truck and he heads towards town. I'm not sure where he's taking us, but I'm sure he has a semi-private location in mind for the talk Sky and I need to have. I can feel her excitement bubbling up from the backseat and it's contagious. I ask about the kids and the rest of the girls. She talks all the way to the small diner in town. This is not a place I want to have the conversation we're about to have.

"Relax, firecracker," Crash tells me, leaning over the front seat. "We're gettin' takeout and heading back home. Sky already knows where we live."

"Okay," I breath out, relieved that we're going to be in a comfortable area.

We wait in the truck until the men come back out with the food. They're carrying so many bags that my eyes bug out of my head. We're only feeding the four of us, at least that's what I thought. Crash tells me that we're dropping some of to everyone else before making our way back home. Yes, I'm slowly coming to think of their house as my home. I'm not sure if I'm ever going to be able to go back in my house again. Especially not with the memories that are now tainting the small sanctuary I created for myself.

"So, are we going to be talking about what's really been going on along with the other stuff we have to talk about?" Sky asks me once the guys exit the truck.

"Yeah. I didn't mean to keep it from everyone. I just didn't feel the need to involve anyone else. At first, I just thought it was something harmless. Now, I know that's not really the truth," I tell her, staring straight ahead and fighting back the tears.

We're finally back at the house and tucked away in the bedroom. Skylar has made a picnic area on the floor, so we sit and talk while we eat. Deciding that we're better off eating first, I tell her everything that has been going on with my stalker before starting 'the talk'. I'm truly dreading what we're going to be talking about, but it needs to happen. I find myself in my head more times than I can count, trying to figure out how this is all supposed to work. How I'm supposed to give two men attention when I've apparently never been able to do it right with one man.

"So, you finally put them out of their misery?" she asks me, once we have everything cleaned up.

"Yeah. It's been long enough and I'm tired of pretending I don't feel anything for them."

"You know it's not going to be like it was with just one man, right?" she asks.

"I know that. I think," I answer hesitantly.

"In some ways, it's going to be better. In other ways, it's going to be more annoying."

"What do you mean?" I ask, confused.

"Well, when one is being a dickface, the other one will probably be acting like an asswipe. They'll gang up on you when they think they're right. And they'll play off one another with every dirty trick in the book to get their way," she begins. "But, you'll have twice the love, twice the protection, and the sex is out of this world!"

My face heats at her last statement. I can't imagine being with two men. Hell, I can't even imagine being with one since I'm still a virgin. Skylar chuckles at me until she realizes that something more is going on with me. I'm not sure what tips her off, but something does. Maybe the panic in my eyes.

"Are you a virgin, Darcy?" she asks suddenly, the laughter fleeing from her and a seriousness taking over.

"I am. No one has ever made me want to go that far. The one time I almost did, the guy ended up almost killing me. So, needless to say, he didn't get my virginity."

I can see the anger in her eyes. She's been to hell and back, and knows what I've been through with a man putting his hands on me. Even if I don't go into detail about the situation. A man has done far worse to her from what I understand. So, I'm sure she can understand why I've been so hesitant to let these two men in my life. It's one thing to hang out with them while with the clubs. It's another thing completely to have them in my life on a personal and intimate level.

"So, I think we need to have a talk, so you're not surprised when it gets to the point of you guys becoming intimate," Skylar tells me. "I know that they don't want to scare you off when it comes to that. Do you have any questions?"

"I have a ton of questions, but I don't even know where to begin," I tell her honestly.

"Okay. Well, you know that no matter how it happens, it's going to hurt the first time you're with one of them. Or both of them," Sky tells me. "They're going to make sure that it's as painless as possible, but no matter what they do, it's going to hurt."

"I know. That's not what scares me. It scares me because I've never been with one person and they want me to be with both of them."

"It won't always be with both of them. They're going to each have days or nights with you alone. If they're anything like my men anyway. It's important to the relationship for you to spend time as a unit and then as a pair," Sky tells me. "I love seeing what the guys plan for our individual dates. They don't let me plan one. Or know in advance what we're doing."

"How do you make sure that they each feel like they're getting your attention? That one isn't spending more time with you or anything like that?" I ask, wanting to know how to balance my time between the two men.

"You'll know. Once you get in the swing of things, you'll figure out how to spend time with each of them. Since it's so new, they'll want to spend time with you as a unit. Then, they'll start planning ways for you to see them on a one-on-one basis. I'm sure that they'll talk to Cage and Joker about it too."

Skylar tells me that this is going to be new for all of us. Even though they've been sharing women, it's just been about finding a release and that's it. They've never done a relationship sharing a woman and we're all going to have to learn as we go. She tells me that they're going to be pissing me off more times than I'll be able to count and that I'm going to frustrate them to the point of exasperation. It's all part of a 'normal' relationship. I know that I won't ever have to worry about them putting their hands on me in anger. Crash and Trojan aren't like that at all.

"How do you really be with two men at one time?" I ask, my face heating at just the thought of how that works.

"There's a few different ways that works," Skylar begins. "One way is you giving one a blow job while the other one is fucking you. One could be in your pussy while the other one is in your ass. I mean, you'll have to try different things and see what works for you."

"I don't know that I could have one in my ass," I let her know, not knowing if I like that idea at all or not.

"They'll take their time and work you up to that. If you don't like what they're doing, then that will never be an option for you and they'll have to accept that," Skylar tells me matter-of-factly.

I let all the information sink in that we've talked about so far. It may not seem like much, but when it comes to never having had sex before, it's a lot to digest. In order to fully understand what she's talking about though, I think I'm going to have to talk to Crash and Trojan. They'll be able to fill me in on the details she left out. What an awkward conversation that will be!

Trojan

Skylar and Darcy have been locked in the room for a while now. I'm not sure if this is a good sign, or if she's scaring our girl away. But, I'm going to trust my gut and believe that she's going to help us with her. I have no choice but to believe that. Crash and I know that at some point we're going to have to do the same thing and talk to Cage and Joker. They've been in a relationship with Skylar for a while now while this is still new to us. So, we're going to need to get advice from them as to the best way to handle things that might come up between the three of us.

"You think they're goin' to be in there the rest of the night?" Crash asks, starting to pace the living room.

"No. Skylar has to start headin' back home soon. You think Darcy is good?" I ask, my nerves getting the better of me.

"Yeah. Skylar isn't goin' to chase her away. She's tryin' to help us out brother," he tells me. I'm not sure who he's trying to convince more of that; himself or me.

"I know. It's just nerve-wracking when we don't know what's truly goin' through Darcy's head."

"We know. She's just got to get over her past and we're goin' to help her with that. And, we have to figure out who is after our girl," he tells me, sitting down on the couch just as we hear the door opening to the bedroom they were in.

I head into the kitchen to grab a few beers while the girls finish up their talk. Pretty soon we're going to have to head back over to Riley's house. I know Darcy is going to want to spend some time with her. So, we'll have even longer to find out what was said earlier. If we can get her to talk to us at all about it. We still have a long way to go before we earn her complete trust. I'm more than fine waiting on that. I don't want a part of her, I want all of her.

Skylar is one her way back to Clifton Falls and we've been hanging out with Riley for the past few hours. Darcy is nervous about her being alone her first night in a new town. I'm sure she'll be just fine since Gage hasn't left her side as far as we've seen. I see him falling hard and fast for our newest resident.

Darcy is sitting on the couch, down from Riley, trying to hide a yawn behind her hand. I know she's been stressed about the stalker and not hearing anything more since she moved in with us. Add in things with the salon and our new relationship, and she's had more stress on her plate then she's probably had in a long time.

"You ready to go?" I ask her, standing and walking to put my glass in the kitchen sink.

"Yeah. Riles I'll see you at nine tomorrow morning," she says, standing and hugging her friend before turning towards us.

"Sounds good hun! Thank you again for everything," she gushes, as Gage and her walk us to the door.

We tell our President bye before heading out to the truck. Darcy is once again in the front while I ride in back this time. Crash can drive us home and try to start the conversation we need to have on the way there. We both know it needs to happen, he'll be able to start it easier than I can. It helps that most of the time he doesn't have a filter and just blurts out whatever he's thinking in that moment. Sometimes it gets him into trouble, but with Darcy, it will help get the conversation going that we need to have with her.

"Did you have a good time with Skylar today?" he asks, turning her attention to her for a split second.

"Yeah. She let me in on some, um, interesting things."

"Like what?" I ask, wanting to know what was said.

"About how this is supposed to work between us. That we'll have our time together, but we also need time one-on-one. And some things that will happen when we reach *that* point," she says, the blush noticeable even in the dark interior of the truck.

"Care to share what she told you?" Crash asks, stifling his laughter at the fact that our girl seems to have a hard time talking about sex.

"Um…Just how it's supposed to work when we have sex. I mean when it's the three of us together. Like giving one of you a blowjob while the other one is fucking me," she begins, turning an even brighter shade of red. "Or one in my pussy while the other one is in my ass."

Darcy is nervous as fuck and I know this is hard for her. She's not used to talking to people about this kind of thing. We need to tread lightly here, so I catch Crash's eyes in the mirror and let him know we need to change the topic of conversation for now. Eventually, we'll be able to venture back to this conversation, but for now we need to let it rest. Darcy will end up overwhelmed and push us away when we try to bring the topic up again. Sometimes she shuts down completely when she gets nervous or scared about something. That's happening less and less though.

"You know there's no pressure for sex to happen, right?" I ask, leaning forward to rub the tension from her shoulders.

"I know. But, I don't want you guys waiting forever," she says, leaning into my touch.

"We'll wait as long as it takes you," Crash tells her, placing his hand on her thigh and rubbing small circles there.

Darcy is sitting there, trying to figure out who's touch to lean into. So, I make the decision easy for her and pull my hands off her shoulders. There's plenty of time to put my hands on her when we get home. She needs to learn the touch of both of us. Together and alone. Now that she's ours, we'll be touching her as much as we possibly can.

It doesn't take very long to get back to the house. We walk in to Darcy telling us that she's going to get ready for bed. I know that gives us about ten minutes to talk before we make our way in the room with her. It's time she gets used to sleeping in bed with both of us at once. There have been a few times we've slept in the bed with her, but we've kept our own rooms for the time being. Not anymore. Tonight, begins us sleeping in bed with her every single night for good.

I place a kiss on her head before Crash follows suit. We watch her walk away down the hallway. I'll never get tired of watching her ass as she walks away. The only thing that's better than that is when she's walking towards us. Eventually, she'll be comfortable enough to want to be around us more. Right now, she's still in the mind-set that she can't trust us. Not enough to open up the way she needs to.

"You know that we need to start sleepin' in bed with her every night?" I ask him.

"Yeah. I was thinkin' the same thing. That starts tonight."

"Couldn't agree more. What do you think she's goin' to say about it?" I ask.

"She might try to fight us, but we're goin' to win. Or, after talkin' to Skylar, she might be cool with us sleepin' in the same bed. I guess there's only one way to find out."

Crash and I make our way in the bedroom. Darcy is already in bed, the covers pulled up to her waist. She's wearing a small tank top, her hair up in a messy bun, glasses perched on her nose, and her e-reader in front of her. Darcy is trying to act like she's not paying attention to us walking around the room, getting undressed. I know better than that though. She keeps glancing at us and watching our movements.

We both strip down to our boxers. Usually, we go commando, but Darcy isn't ready for that just yet. So, we've opted for wearing boxers when it comes to being around her. Crash won't ever change the way he sleeps, so he sleeps naked no matter what. Eventually I'll go back to not wearing anything though. Right now, it's all about making her the most comfortable around us. Especially when we start going to the clubhouse more.

As we climb into bed, I know there's something that I want to ask our girl. It's something that I've been thinking about and I haven't figured out how to approach her about it. I guess there's no time like the present and I need to just come out with it and ask.

"Darcy, there's been somethin' that I've been wonderin'," I tell her, as she hands her e-reader over to Crash to put on the stand.

"What's that?" she asks, handing him her sexy as fuck glasses.

"I thought you weren't goin' to be in a relationship with anyone. Then you tell us that you're goin' to be with us. What changed your mind?"

"Um… after someone decided it was okay to destroy my sanctuary, I figured that we only get one life. I need to live my life to the fullest and not let my fear get in the way of that. I can't live in the past and think that you two are going to do what the few guys I've tried to be in a relationship with did to me. You have tried to prove yourselves to me and I've not taken the time to see that," she tells us, proving to us that she's put some serious thought about us. That she wants this to work as much as we do.

"I was just wonderin'. I don't want you to go into this without giving us some serious thought. This isn't a game for us, we're playin' for keeps," I tell her, knowing that Crash is feeling the same way.

"All I do is think about it," she answers honestly.

Crash and I look at her and I think our eyes about pop out of our heads. I know that I never thought that she would've thought about us like that. She was always pushing us away. Knowing that she's been thinking about this has my heart racing and a feeling I can't describe running through my body. I can see that Crash is feeling the same way and we're going to be stepping our game up to make sure that no one can tell her that we're not serious about being with her.

Crash

We wake up the next morning when Darcy's alarm goes off. I know she's got to get to the salon, especially since Riley starts today. So, I head to the kitchen at the ass crack of dawn to make coffee and start getting breakfast ready. Darcy usually only grabs something on her way out the door. This morning, I'm going to make her breakfast and see if that makes her day start better.

I hear movement coming from the bedroom and I'm sure that Trojan is helping her get in the shower. Part of me wants to be in there with her and the other part knows that she needs this just as much. We're both helping her out in ways she may not necessarily know she wants right now. She'll get it eventually and learn that we're going to be taking care of her for the rest of our lives. If that means making her breakfast and helping get her things ready for a quicker shower, then that's what we'll do. We'll do anything that we can do in order to help make her day easier.

I grab the bread, eggs, and the rest of the ingredients I need to make omelets. It's been a long time since I've cooked, but it comes right back to me. It's like riding a bike, you never forget how to cook. Maybe I need to do this more often for the three of us. Especially for Darcy.

"Mornin'," I tell her, as I scoop the omelets onto plates and set one in front of her.

I grab her toast and place it on the edge of her plate while Trojan grabs the orange juice out of the fridge and pours us all a glass. We each take a seat on either side of her and dig in. The moans and noises coming out of Darcy are sweet torture. I can't wait to see if she makes the same little mewls and moans when we're buried deep inside her, giving her all the pleasure she'll ever want. Looking over, I can see the same torture written plainly on Trojan's face. Darcy has no clue what she's doing to us. This is not some ploy on her part to entice us or play some game. She is simply enjoying the food in front of her.

"This is really good. Thank you, Crash," Darcy tells me around a mouthful of eggs.

"You're welcome," is my only response.

We finish eating in silence and Darcy goes to clean up, but Trojan stops her. He tells her to go finish getting ready and we'll take care of the kitchen. I rinse the plates off while he loads the dishwasher. It doesn't take us long to clean up the kitchen and when we go to sit down, Darcy is walking back down the hall towards us. She's wearing a tighter pair of jeans and a tank top under a button up shirt. She's left the top few buttons open and I see that she's getting braver in what she chooses to wear. She doesn't hide behind baggy clothes as much anymore.

"I'm ready to go. I want to get there early so I can get a few things ready before Riley shows up," Darcy tells us.

Personally, I think she just wants to get out of the house and away from us. Sometimes I can see the longing on her face, other times I can see the fear and panic rising up in her. Trojan can see the same things. That's why we're trying to take this at her pace and make sure that she is as comfortable as she can possibly be with us. Our relationship is going to go to a whole new level when we start bringing sex into the equation. Darcy knows this as much as we do. I think that's one of the main reasons she's so scared. She doesn't know what's going to happen once we take that leap. In her mind, as long as we're not having sex, she still gets to hold onto us. We won't leave her until we get what she thinks we want from her. We'll never have what we want from her though. Our time with Darcy won't end until we're buried in the ground and not able to take another breath.

"We're ready whenever you are babe," Trojan tells her. "You want to take the bikes or ride in the truck?"

"Can we take the truck please?" she asks, looking down. Something that we've noticed she does a lot of when she thinks we're going to be upset with her.

"Darcy, we love ridin' our bikes. It's part of the reason we joined the club. You get such a sense of freedom that it's like nothin' else in this world. But, we know that you aren't ready for all that and we're goin' to take this at your pace. Eventually, you'll start ridin' with us more and you'll grow to love it."

Darcy nods her head in acknowledgment and walks out the door. Something close to pain flashes briefly in her eyes before we can decipher what it is. Today she doesn't wait for one of us to walk in front of her. So, we both groan as we watch her ass sway to and fro as she makes her way out to the truck. Trojan discreetly adjusts himself before following her at a faster pace. He gets to her just as she goes to open the door. I watch on as he places his hand on the small of her back and opens the door for her. Before she can get up in the truck, I place my hands on her hips and lift her up inside.

As soon as we make sure she's settled in the truck, we each make our way to our respective doors. Trojan is going to drive again today while I ride in back. This gives me time to think as we make the short journey to the salon. We've been doing the unit thing, but I'm wondering if it's time to start taking Darcy out one-on-one. that way she can see that we're putting in the time with her and that we want to spend time with her. It's not just about getting her in bed.

I'm the first one out of the truck as we pull up to the salon. I see Gage and Riley making their way towards us. She's riding on his bike and I'm shocked. Bailey is the only other female to grace my President's bike. He reserves that seat for someone that's going to be his old lady. Granted, Bailey never made it that far, but he was ready to take that step with her.

I glance over at the front of the salon as I go to open the door for Darcy. Before she can turn to get out, I see the front windows plastered with something. Telling Darcy to stay where she is for a minute, I step closer and take a look at what it is. Trojan beats me to it though and I can feel the rage he's barely containing simmering from three feet away.

Plastered all over the window is one picture repeatedly. It's of Darcy, standing in her living room, stripping out of her clothes. She's standing in nothing more than a cami and a skimpy pair of panties. Darcy is relaxed and carefree in the moment that's captured. It's a look that we want to put on her face every single day, a look that no one deserves to see but us. Stepping closer, I see writing on the door. The words are written in red paint that I'm guessing is supposed to represent blood.

"You're mine bitch! I'll beat the dirty scum off of you when I finally make my move. I'm coming!"

Trojan and I were so busy trying to read the door and start pulling down the pictures that we didn't notice much else. Gage is here, and we know that he'll keep an eye on our girl. Unfortunately, he can't catch her fast enough to stop her from seeing the pictures or the words on the door. All we hear is the shocked gasp coming from behind us. I turn to see Darcy crumple to the ground. Trojan catches her just before she hits the sidewalk and hurts herself.

"Why? What have I done to deserve this?" she screams out. Her screams are agonizing and full of pain.

"We got you," Trojan murmurs softly into her soft hair. "We're not goin' to let anythin' happen to you baby."

"You can't promise that! Whoever this is, is always going to find me. They've destroyed my sanctuary and now they're coming after my business. No one can be in every place I am to guarantee nothing like this happens again. You two could get busy and take your eyes off me for a second and they could swoop in and take me away."

"We're not gonna let that happen baby," I tell her. "We'll make sure you're always with one of us. Please don't let this get to you and scare you to the point of runnin'. Because I promise you one thing, we will always find you and bring you back home."

My words are not an idle threat. It's a promise that I fully intend to keep. I'm going to do whatever I have to in order to make sure that Darcy doesn't pull a runner. She needs to learn to depend on us and let us take away her fears. Darcy is an independent woman and she needs to see that we don't want to stifle that, we want to nurture her and watch her finish growing into the amazing woman that we're already seeing.

We've finally gotten the mess cleaned up at the salon. Riley took Darcy inside and has her showing her where everything is. I know she's trying to distract her while we get everything cleaned up. I'm thankful that she's here and trying to keep her mind anywhere else but on what's going on outside. Gage called Shadow and Wayne, our prospects, in so there was someone to stand outside and keep guard at all times. I'm sure that one of them will be here all-night long.

Darcy and Riley have been in the back room pretty much since we got here. I'm not sure if they didn't have any appointments today, or if people just aren't coming in right now. All I know is that if this douche canoe messes with our girl's business, that just adds another reason to the growing list of reasons to tear this motherfucker up. She has worked her ass off to not only start her salon, but to grow her client list, and put out a solid reputation as one of the most professional, charismatic stylists there is around Dander Falls.

"Crash, I think I'm ready to head home," Darcy tells me, walking back up front. "People are cancelling appointments and I'm exhausted. Riley and I'll come back tomorrow and see if things are better."

The look of pure defeat is etched on our girl's face. This asshole is trying to take everything from her. I look to Gage and Trojan, they can see that we need to do something about this sooner rather than later.

"Come by the clubhouse first," Gage tells us. "We're goin' to have emergency church and then you can go home sweetheart."

Darcy nods her head and wraps her arms around herself. Riley is standing just behind her and I can feel the genuine sympathy and outrage pouring from her on her new friend's behalf. I am slowly warming up to her since she seems to be genuinely concerned for Darcy. Even though she kind of screwed Keegan over in the beginning, Riley seems to be proving herself to me more and more.

Chapter Four

Darcy

IT'S BEEN A FEW DAYS SINCE THE pictures were plastered all over the front of my salon. I'm not sure what they're emergency church was about, but I can guess it had something to do with me. business is slowly starting to pick back up again and I'm getting scared that this is going to ruin me. I've had this salon in Dander Falls for years now and I've never once had a problem. I offer multiple services and I was thinking about adding on to it since the storefront next door is for sale. Now, I'm rethinking that since I can't guarantee that my clients are going to remain loyal with a psychopath gunning for me.

Crash and Trojan have had my back and been by my side since they found out what was going on. Honestly, without them here, I don't know that I would still be sane. Riley has been a major help too. All three seem to know when I need a few minutes to decompress alone and when I need them to hold my hand. I'm learning who my loyal customers are though. Several ladies have been in, that haven't changed their appointments, and told me that no one is going to scare them away from coming to get their hair and nails done by me.

"Riley, can you take the next appointment please?" I ask, wanting to sit down for a few minutes because I feel a headache coming on.

"Yeah. I'll finish throwing the towels in the washer and get everything set up."

I sit down between Crash and Trojan on one of the couches in front of the salon just as Sandy comes strutting in through the door. She looks at me and turns her nose up in the air seeing me sitting between my men. With just a look at her, you know she's judging us, and she wants to make a comment. For her sake, I hope she keeps her mouth shut. These two men are strung tight right now and one wrong move is going to unleash their rage. I can feel it simmering just below the surface, they don't even have to say a word about it.

    Instead of sitting down and having a conversation like Sandy usually does, she chooses to stand on the other side of the entrance and keep her back to us. Today, I really don't care. Riley finally finishes the towels and calls Sandy back to her station. She walks the long way around as if the three of us are going to give her some disease or something. What the fuck is her problem? This is getting to be ridiculous. I can live my life any way that I want to, and I am choosing to be happy with two men instead of one. It may not seem like we're progressing, but slowly I am learning to hand my trust over to them.

Riley

    As soon as Sandy sits down in the chair, so I can wash her hair, I know that this is going to be a long appointment. Darcy is becoming a close friend and someone that I will defend no matter what. I poked my head out from the back when I hear the bell chime over the door and saw the judgement and overall bitchiness radiating from her. I'm really trying to keep my mouth shut and this appointment as pleasant as possible. And, it's working really good until the she-devil opens her mouth as we're making our way to my station. Sandy just blew that shit out of the water.

    "I can't believe that the little fat ass tramp is fucking two men! And she's got someone putting pictures up all over town that are made to be kept private," Sandy says, acting as if whoever is putting the pictures up is Darcy's fault.

    I keep my mouth shut and may have pulled a little bit harder than necessary on the comb as I brush her hair out. Sandy lets out a screech that makes me think of someone running their fingernails down a chalkboard. Darcy looks over and I shoot her a sweet, apologetic smile. I can see the laughter that wants to break loose from Crash and Trojan, but they hold it in remarkably well.

"What's next for the slut?" Sandy continues on. "A train from the 'gang' that these men surrounding the salon belong to?"

"That's it!" I yell, grabbing a pair of scissors and a huge chunk of her hair.

"Um…Riley, why don't you go in back and get the color ready for Mrs. Sampson?" Darcy asks, coming over to my station.

"Okay," I tell her sweetly, walking away from the bitch currently sitting in my chair.

The nice thing about Darcy is that she has everything labeled and all of her clients that come in on a regular basis charted out. All I have to do is find Mrs. Sampson's name and pick what I need to mix her color up. Otherwise, I wouldn't be able to do anything until she walked through the door. Since she should be here in a few minutes, I'll get everything ready to go and meet Darcy back out on the floor. Hopefully that bitch isn't here when I go back out there.

Trojan

I was sitting close enough that I could hear the venom that bitch was spewing about Darcy to Riley. Just as I went to defend my woman, Riley stepped in and I swear she would've made the bitch bald if she wasn't asked to go in back. What really shocked me was the way that Darcy handled the situation though. She didn't let this bitch get to her. Instead, she was calm and collected the whole time she was in her face.

"You're lucky that I'm feeling generous today and made Riley leave just now," she begins, getting right in her client's face and putting her hands on her hips. "If you want to be judgmental and a bitch, that's your choice in life. However, when you start slandering my name and making customers stop coming here, I will throw all the shit that you've ever said and gossiped about for every person in this town to know. How's slumming with the gardener working out for you? He still hot shit in bed? I'm sure your husband would love to know about him. Now, I suggest you walk out of here, after leaving a generous tip to Riley and paying for your wash. If I hear one more word leave your mouth, those two men over there will make sure that your life is hell. See, that's what happens when you have men that care about you and want to protect you. Not a pussy that lets you walk all over him and get away with whatever you want to do. Take your fat, judgmental ass out of here because you aren't the hot shit you think you are!"

The woman's face has turned a few shades whiter than her fake tan and she stumbles from the chair once Darcy steps to the side. I know that there's more she wants to say to our woman, but she makes the wise decision to keep her mouth shut. I'd really hate to have to show her how far we'd go to protect our firecracker. No, we wouldn't lay a hand on her. But, she doesn't know that and sometimes all you have to do is put a little fear into someone to make them back the fuck off.

An elderly woman is coming through the door just as Sandy is trying to make her exit. Instead of moving out of the way, the older lady stands there looking confused. However, I can see the mischief in her eyes and know that she's going to give her a hard time.

"Sandy, are you leaving so soon?" she asks sweetly.

"Um, yes. I'm done here for the day," Sandy replies.

"What a shame! I was hoping to hear more lies and bullshit from you. I wonder what your friends would think about all the shit you spew. Especially about them when they aren't surrounding you to do your bidding, so you don't have to get your hands dirty."

Crash and I can't help the laughter that comes bursting out of us. this sweet lady just put a vindictive bitch in her place. She kept the smile on her face and her tone sweet and innocent as she did it. If Ma were still alive, this lady would give her a run for her money! I might have to adopt her into the club so that we get a piece of Ma every now and then. And to keep an eye on her. Especially after witnessing Darcy's eyes soften towards her.

Sandy slams the rest of the way through the door once Mrs. Sampson moves. At least I'm guessing that's who she is. Crash goes to get up and follow her from the salon, but the lady tells him to take a seat. She has some questions for us apparently and we're not to go anywhere until she tells us we can. Yeah, she needs to be adopted by the club.

"Young men, I've been hearing some things around town and I need to know your honest answers to the questions that I'm about to ask you," she tells us, sitting down in the chair to have her hair washed. "I will know if you're lying to me too, so don't even think about it."

"What have you heard Mrs. Sampson?" Darcy asks, motioning for us to follow her closer to the wash sinks.

"I heard that these two are courting you and trying to keep you safe. That you're trying to make a go of it with both of them," she answers.

"That's true ma'am," Crash speaks up.

"Don't go calling me ma'am now. My name is Wilma, use it!"

"I'll remember that, Wilma," Crash replies, looking like a skulking, scolded child.

"What are your intentions with my favorite girl here?" she asks, motioning her hand in the general direction of where she thinks Darcy is standing.

"We want to teach her that she's ours to protect and cherish. We'll make sure she's safe and loved. And we want to gain her trust and teach her that not everyone is out to hurt her," I answer, looking at Darcy instead of the woman questioning us.

"And what about when you get to the point one of you wants to marry her? What happens then?"

"She marries one of us and commits herself to the other one. The decision is hers and we'll let her make the decision when that time comes," I answer.

"And if you hurt her, you know that I'm going to come after you. Right?" she asks, letting her voice turn dark so we know she means business.

Wilma tips her head back and let's Riley get to work on rinsing her hair. I truly believe that if we do anything to hurt Darcy or not protect her, she will come after us and make us hurt. What she doesn't understand is that if something were to happen to our girl, we would hurt more than anyone else could ever make us. Darcy has become someone that's more important to us than anything else. The only other thing that will ever come before her is our club. If I could change that, I would.

Darcy leads us back to the front while she goes and starts cleaning up her station for the next client to come in. while I'd rather be out looking for the person that's going after Darcy, I know that Gage has guys on it. Tech is running every program he can think of to try to find this person. And he's got guys around the clock monitoring the cameras on her house. So far, everything has been a dead end, and no one has shown back up there. Apparently, they know that she's not staying there and have decided not to waste their time going there. For now, anyway.

Chapter Five

Crash

IT'S BEEN A FEW DAYS SINCE THE SCENE at the salon. Trojan told me that he wanted to adopt Wilma. I can see his point, but no one will ever take the place of Ma. Wilma is an extremely close second to her, but she'll never take her place. He knows this and explained that he wasn't trying to replace Ma, he just misses the hell she would give any of us when she thought we needed it. That is completely understandable. I think we all miss that from her. We just miss her in general.

Darcy is continuing to come around more and more with placing her trust in our hands. She hasn't really opened up to us yet, but I know it's not going to be much longer before she does. Gage knows more than we do at this point and he's not saying a single word. While I'm grateful that he's keeping his word to her, and teaching her that she can trust us all, I want to know the full story of what's been going on.

"Crash, can you help me for a minute?" Darcy asks, walking out to the living room in nothing but a towel.

I swear my eyes are about to bug out of my head and there's only one thing running through my mind right now. Hell, I'm surprised I can put one foot in front of the other since all the blood flowing through my body has currently moved to the southern region. Darcy leads me into the bedroom that we've all been sharing, and I see that she's trying to reach one of the bags on the top shelf of the closet. I'm not sure why she threw it up there, but I'll help her out. This is the only way that my mind is going to be cleared of the vision she's currently showing me. Who am I kidding? Nothing is going to wipe the image of Darcy in nothing but a towel from my mind. Ever.

She has never walked around the house in anything other than clothes. This just shows that she's becoming more comfortable around us. we still haven't seen her naked, but this is damn close. Too bad Trojan isn't here to see this right now. As soon as the thought enters my head, he walks into the room. He's also taken a shower and I know that there's no way in hell he got to take one with her. I would know if he did and that might be something that we need to think about in the near future. If we can get her comfortable enough to take a shower with at least one of us, then maybe she'll let us know she's getting closer to being ready for us to take her.

"Why is this bag up here?" I ask, easily grabbing it and handing it to her.

"It's the clothes that Trojan grabbed that are a little bit smaller than what I usually wear. He grabbed them, so I might as well wear them," she tells me, like it's the most practical answer in the world.

"Oh. Well, I'll leave you to get dressed then," I tell her, walking towards Trojan.

"Who said you had to leave?" she asks, turning to look at both of us.

"You're really tryin' to kill us, aren't you?" Trojan asks her, starting to back up.

"No. But, I'm tired of going to bed wanting and making you guys wait for what's going to end up happening eventually."

Trojan and I look at one another and we're both wearing the same dumbfounded look. We didn't expect this to happen today. I'm definitely not going to turn our girl down, and we'll stop if it gets to be too much for her. But, I'm curious as to what changed her mind.

"I'm definitely not tryin' to get you to change your mind, babe, but I thought you wanted to wait?" I ask, starting to move closer as if I'm stalking prey.

"I did want to wait. I think that you guys are proving this isn't going to be a one and done. You've all but moved me into your home, you're making sure this madman doesn't get me, and I've been putting you guys off long enough," she tells us, letting us each know that she's been giving this a lot of thought.

I move in behind her and push in as close as I can get. Her neck is exposed, and I use that to my advantage and start kissing below her ear. Hearing movement, I know that Trojan is moving towards the front of our girl. He's going to make sure that she's primed and ready for us to take her. Tonight, we're not going to take her ass, we'll work her up to that. However, we're both going to get, and give, as much pleasure as we possibly can.

Trojan and I have had several conversations about this, and we decided that I would be the first one to take Darcy's pussy. He will be the first one to take her ass when we get her there. And he'll be the first one to fill her mouth with his cock. We just have to remember to take this as slow as possible with her. The last thing we want to do is scare her or hurt her any more than we have to.

"We don't want to hurt you," Trojan tells her, leaning down to take her mouth.

"It's going to hurt no matter what," she replies, just before Trojan invades her mouth.

I watch as he kisses her breathless. Slowly, I run my hands up to the top of the towel and begin to remove it from her body. I'm going to take my time and savor the moment we both get to lay eyes on our girl naked. Trojan leans back a little bit from her so that I can fully remove the towel, he doesn't break contact with her though. We don't want her to go inside her own head and start over thinking what we're doing to her.

Nudging Trojan out of the way, I get my turn. I lean in and gently kiss Darcy. She's going to set the pace of what happens here. She gently nips my bottom lip, letting me know that she wants more and isn't sure how to go about asking for it. I deepen the kiss and let my tongue duel with hers. Darcy is still guiding the kiss, but we're leading her closer and closer to the bed. Trojan is guiding us so that neither one of us trip up on our way to where we really want to be.

Darcy

I have been thinking about nothing else but Crash and Trojan finally taking me. They're trying to go at my pace and I love them for that. I'm over waiting though. Every single day I watch them with barely any clothes on. Crash usually has none on when we go to bed, and they have been slowly torturing me. I know I've done the same thing to them and I haven't even tried to. My only thought has been being comfortable when I'm relaxing and going to bed.

The two men consume me as they start to make me relax in their individual embraces. My main concern is that they're going to expect me to let them take my ass tonight. I know I won't be able to do that right now. It's going to be hard enough to give up my virginity to them. Just as I go to stop them and tell them my concerns, Trojan stops me.

"I know you say you're sure, just please know that we'll stop no matter what if you say the word. And we're not even goin' to attempt to do anythin' with your ass right now," Trojan tells me, and I feel my entire body relax even further.

Laying back on the bed, I make myself comfortable. Crash is the first one to climb up my body. He kisses and licks his way from my ankles, up my legs, and completely bypassing my pussy altogether. I try to get my legs as close together as possible to relieve some of the building pressure and tension. His massive body prevents me from getting any sort of friction I need though. Crash starts paying attention to my tits, moving from one to the other while gently biting and sucking them into his mouth.

Trojan moves closer to my head and I see that he's already naked. I'm not sure when either of them took any of their clothes off, but they're both naked. As Crash works my body over, driving me insane, I try to get my first glimpse of Trojan completely naked. His body is amazing. He's got muscles and ridges from head to toe. My eyes drift towards the part of his body I most want to see, and I can't believe that they think that thing is going to fit anywhere in my body.

"Firecracker, we'll both fit no matter where we fill your body," Crash tells me, sensing my hesitation. "Relax and let us give you pleasure."

"And in here, when we're like this, Crash and I aren't called that. We want you to call us our given names. I'm Dominic and Crash's name is Brent," Trojan tells me, inching closer to me.

Laying back against the pillow Trojan placed under my head, he angles his body closer to me and leans down to once again leave me breathless with a kiss. These men know how to kiss, and I wonder what else they know how to do as good as that. Crash makes his way back down my body, leaving a wet trail from my breasts down towards my aching pussy. An overwhelming sense of embarrassment washes over me and I try to close my legs. He pries them back apart and places gentle kisses on each one of my thighs, while Trojan moves from kissing me to moving his way down to that spot just below my ear.

My upper body arches off the bed on its own in an attempt to get closer to Trojan. Crash is using one hand to hold my hips in place where he wants them as he moves his mouth closer to where I truly want him. His first taste of me has my back arching even further off the bed and my eyes closing. As Crash slowly inserts a finger into my tight pussy, he moves his mouth to my throbbing clit. It doesn't take long before I feel my release crashing over me like a wave breaking on a reef.

"Brent!" I moan out, not wanting this feeling to ever end.

I feel moisture at my lips before I can even begin to come back down to earth. Opening my eyes, I see Trojan's cock at my mouth. I've never given anyone a blow job before, but my mouth opens, and I lick the head. His groan gives me the motivation I need to open even wider and begin to make my way down his silky hard shaft. I slowly move my head up and down a few times while using my tongue to swirl around his cock. Trojan continues to moan, and I look up to see his head thrown back with his eyes closed. There's a look of pure ecstasy on his face and I'm the one that put it there. This knowledge pushes me to do my absolute best to keep it on his face.

I'm so tuned into giving Trojan the most pleasure that I can that I don't feel Crash lining himself up to enter me. the only clue I have is the cock being pulled out of my mouth just as Crash breaches the proof of my virginity. My entire body tenses up and I feel tears running down my face. There's definitely pain, but it's not anything I can't handle. Looking up, I see the sweat starting to shine on Crash's body. He's holding himself so rigid and still to ensure that nothing happens before I'm ready.

"I'm ready for you to move," I tell him, placing my hand on his chest where his heart rests as the pain begins to subside. Making sure I look at him is the only way I can think of to let him know that even though it hurt, I trust him to make me feel good now. These men are rapidly earning my full trust.

Trojan puts his cock back at my lips and I immediately open up to take him back where I want him. Crash starts to slowly move in and out of me. The more he moves, the more pleasure begins to start building within my body again. So many sensations are running through my body that I don't know where to focus. I begin to falter giving Trojan a blow job and he places his hands on either side of my head to hold it still. Looking up at him, I use my eyes to let him know that I trust him completely. For a few seconds, he doesn't move.

"That means more than you know baby," Trojan tells me, his voice raspy and lower than I've ever heard it before. He's completely in the throes of passion and letting me know how much my trust in him means.

"So fuckin' tight, babe," Crash ground out, starting to add a swivel to his hips that rubs against my clit every time he moves back in my body.

Slowly I begin to raise my hips and meet him thrust for thrust. There's absolutely no pain left and I'm beginning to chase my release as I try to ensure that these two men find theirs as well. It doesn't take any of us very long to find our mutual release. Even though neither men wanted to hurt me, their movements become erratic. Trojan is pushing farther into my mouth, but paying close enough attention that he doesn't gag me or make me take more of him than I can. Crash was trying to be gentle and I know that there's no way he's giving me everything that he normally would. I can't wait until I get both of these men at their best!

My men follow me closely over the edge, each one growling out my name. Trojan tried to pull out of my mouth, but I wanted to taste him. So, I sucked on his cock just a little bit harder to let him know that I wanted to swallow everything he had to give me. In case Crash had any ideas about not giving me what I wanted, I wrapped my legs around him tight enough that he couldn't pull away before he found his release.

They keep me wrapped in their arms as we all come down from an earth shattering release. Trojan runs his hands up and down my back while Crash is placing gentle kisses on my face as I catch my breath. My men seem to be able to catch theirs remarkably quick. Just as I get my breath back and some feeling back into my legs, the guys get up and head to the bathroom. I'm not sure what they're doing, but I'm ready to fall asleep.

"You can go to sleep in a little bit, baby," Crash tells me, stretching his hands out to help me out of bed.

"Where are you taking me?" I ask, feeling sated and sore in all the right places.

"You need to get cleaned up and soak in a warm bath. Tomorrow you're goin' to be feelin' really sore and we want to make it a little better for you," he tells me, walking me into the bathroom.

Trojan is sitting in the tub already and Crash helps me slowly sink into his waiting embrace and the hot water still filling the tub. They have the water just on the warmer side of what I normally have, and it feels amazing. Crash leaves the bathroom and I can hear muffled movements coming from the bedroom. Before I can think about it a second longer, Trojan is rubbing a loofah up my arms and dripping the water down my body. At the same time, he's placing gentle kisses across the back of my neck. I wonder if he knows what he's truly doing to me right now.

After about a half hour in the tub, and the water cooling down, Trojan and Crash help me out and dry me off. They walk me back into the bedroom and help me get comfortable back in bed. The first thing I notice is that the sheets and blankets have been changed. Must be what I heard earlier. All I want to do is crawl under the blankets and sleep for a few hours.

"Darcy, let's get some sleep and then we'll get our day goin'," Trojan tells me, climbing in bed beside me.

"What are we doing today?" I ask, thoroughly confused.

"We're goin' to move our things into this room and make it official. Then we need to head to the clubhouse," Crash answers, climbing in on the other side of me and pulling the blankets up.

"Night guys," I tell them over a yawn.

Each man kisses me before I burrow down under the blankets as much as I can. It doesn't take me very long before I feel my eyelids getting heavy and sleep pulling me under. This is where I'm meant to be, safe in the arms of these two men.

Trojan

Waking up with Darcy snuggled in our arms is one of the best feelings in the world. My main concern is how she's feeling right now. I don't want her sore to the point that she has a hard time doing anything today. The salon is closed, it usually is on Sunday's unless someone schedules an appointment with her. Or Riley now. Today, she is ours for the day and we're going to spend the entire day worshipping her and putting our room together. Other than an hour or so when we have church.

Since I'm the first one up, I go in and make breakfast for the three of us. We never let Darcy cook breakfast. She works hard and helps us make every other meal here with us. So, if we can make it a little bit easy on her in the morning, we do it. Plus, it gives her a little bit of extra time in the morning to get ready. Now, I'm sure we'll find ways to fill her extra time while she's in the shower. We have a lot of things to show her when it comes to all the places and ways we can have fun with her.

After breakfast, it didn't take us very long to get our stuff moved into the room we've been sharing with Darcy. We need to plan another shopping trip, so we can get her some more clothes and things that she's going to need here. Maybe we can do that in a few days and bring Riley and Gage with us too. It can be a day for the girls while we suck it up and let them have some fun. Plus, Riley will get to get out and see more of Dander Falls. I'll mention it after church and see what they think of the idea.

I think it's time for lunch. Why don't we go out today?" Crash asks, sitting down at the island and downing a glass of water. We've been going nonstop since after breakfast.

"That's a good idea," Darcy responds, filling her own glass of water and pulling up a seat next to my brother.

"You sure you're up for that after everythin' we've done today?" I ask, concern lacing my voice.

"Yeah. It's been helping to keep moving," she tells us, stretching her arms above her head and moaning at the release of her muscles.

Darcy finishes her water in one swallow and sets her glass down before standing and walking to the bathroom. She tells us she's going to freshen up a little bit before we head out. Crash and I walk in the room after her and change our shirts. I'm just putting my cut back on when she walks out of the bathroom. She's changed her clothes and thrown her hair up in a messy bun. As usual, there's barely any makeup covering her face and she looks so pure and innocent.

"I'm ready when you are," she tells us, leaving the room and us to follow behind her.

We head out to the truck and I know that we need to approach the topic of her riding the bikes more. She'll have to when we go to the clubhouse in a little bit. It's just a matter of who she's going to be riding with this time. We'll take turns with her, but I know I want to feel her arms wrapped around me while we're on my girl.

Taking the truck, we head to the diner the club owns. We know there we can control who enter and that we're going to have backup if whoever is after Darcy shows up. Since we don't have a clue who we're looking for, it's hard to take her out in public right now. Usually, there's at least a few brothers there eating at any given time.

Walking in, we choose a table in the back. Crash and I sit with our backs to the wall behind us. Darcy faces us and grabs the menu placed in front of her by Sarah. The waitresses here know better than to flirt with us or try to get in our beds, so we don't have to worry about that happening and pissing our girl off.

"You know what you want?" I ask her, after giving her a few minutes to look over the menu.

"Yep. I want a BLT with fries and a chocolate milkshake," she answers, setting her menu in front of her on the table to indicate she's ready to order.

Sarah doesn't waste time coming back over to take our order. Darcy orders hers and we tell her that we'll have the usual. The time it takes to prepare our food is spent laughing and talking. We're keeping Darcy's mind off of all the bullshit that she has going on around her. She's asking us questions about random things and it's relaxing. Too bad we didn't know there was a shitstorm about to hit and shatter our girl even more.

Chapter Six
Darcy

AFTER AN AMAZING LUNCH OUT, WE went back to the house to pick the bikes up, so the guys could get to the clubhouse for church. I'm sure they were worried about whether or not I'd want to ride with one of them, but I love to ride. Before my dad passed away, he had a bike and would take me on long rides when my mom got too out of control. She had a slight problem with drinking and drugs. He would keep me out of harm's way when she was on a tear. I loved him more and more each time he came to my rescue.

My mom wasn't a bad person. She just wanted me to look a certain way, dress a certain way, and act a certain way. When she was sober, she would be the best mom around. It was only when she was drinking that she would rip my already fragile confidence to shreds and beat me down. I've always been a bit on the curvy side. So, growing up, if I wasn't getting picked on at school, I was getting picked on by the one person that should've always loved me and had my back no matter what I looked like. Hell, when one of the guys at school played a prank on me and acted like he wanted to be my boyfriend, she laughed when she found out what happened. It was my dad that consoled and comforted me. When my dad wasn't around to protect me, she would beat me when I wouldn't do what she wanted as fast as she wanted it done.

Dad would still be here if it wasn't for my mom. She left the house one night drunk off her ass. My dad loved her with his entire heart and couldn't let her hurt herself or worse, someone else. We both knew she wouldn't survive it if she hurt someone because she chose to drive drunk. The night was storming, and the roads were almost to the point of flooding in certain parts. While my mom managed to survive the minor wreck she was in, my dad couldn't survive his. He lost control of the car and was sent spinning into trees before flying over a slight incline. The cops told me he didn't feel a thing, and everything happened quick.

Shortly after that, my mom lost custody of me and I went to live with one of my dad's sisters, Connie. She wasn't able to have children of her own, causing her husband to leave her. I became the little girl she always wanted as her own. Connie never requested that I call her mom, she was still my aunt. However, she did become my confident, my source of protection, and our relationship blossomed. It didn't take much to convince my mom to sign over rights to her, so she could legally adopt me. We celebrated for days when that happened.

My attention is drawn back to the men in front of me when Trojan puts a helmet on my head. He does the strap, so he knows it's tight and won't move around on my head. Looking between the two men, Trojan makes my decision for me by grabbing my hand and leading me over to his bike. I take a minute to fully appreciate the machine before climbing on behind him.

"Been on a bike before?" he asks me, turning around to look at me.

"I used to ride all the time with my dad when I was little," I reply, wrapping my arms around his middle and appreciating his rock-hard body.

I've only been on the bikes with these two once before and I was in no shape to appreciate the ride or show them that I knew how to ride with someone. Hell, I barely remember anything that happened that night after witnessing my sanctuary after it was destroyed. Now, they'll know that I know how to ride and that I absolutely love it. I just figured they thought it was safer to put me in the truck when we left the house. Now, I think a little bit of it has to do with them being unsure if I would want to be on the bikes. Honestly, I might love it more than them.

It doesn't take us long to make our way to the clubhouse. My nerves are ratcheting up and I am feeling out of place. The only women that are usually here are the club girls and I don't want to tangle with them right now. They are very territorial when it comes to the men of the club. I've seen more than one old lady get into it with the club girls from Clifton Falls. Some of them are downright vicious when they realize that a man is off the market. And I've taken two of them, so I know that I'm going to be getting my fair share of attitude, dirty looks, and whatever else they decide to throw my way.

Walking into the clubhouse, I visibly relax when I see Riley sitting at the bar next to Gage. I wasn't expecting her to be here, but I'm glad that I'll have someone to talk to while the men are doing their thing. Practically running towards her, I let out a squeal to show how happy I am right now. Riley and Gage both turn around to see what's going on. She gets off the stool as I wrap my arms around her. Crash and Trojan aren't far behind me, and they take in the scene before looking at one another. I wonder if they had something to do with this?

"What are you doing here?" I ask, finally taking a seat at the bar with her.

"Gage and I were going to go to lunch and he has to have his meeting before we can go. How are you doing?" she asks, turning her full attention towards me.

"I'm doing good. We moved all our stuff into one bedroom today. I really don't have that much, but the guys do. Then we went to lunch. I've enjoyed this day off," I tell her, trying to convey that I have more to tell her than what I'm currently saying.

"You want a drink baby?" Trojan asks me, grabbing his beer off the bar top and looking at me.

"Yeah. I don't know that you have what I usually drink though," I say, beginning to think of something else I can drink here.

"Shadow, grab our girl one of the wine coolers," Crash tells the man behind the bar, coming up to stand behind me.

"You got them for me?" I ask, shocked that they would pay that much attention to what I drink and have it here waiting for me.

"Of course we did. We know that's what you usually drink when you don't want to get wasted and we want you sober for later," Trojan tells me, leaning in for a breathtaking kiss.

Crash gives me the same treatment before they turn to follow Gage through a set of doors. Right before they enter, Gage lets out a whistle to gain everyone else's attention and slowly all the men grab their drinks before following the other three into their meeting. I'm not sure what exactly they do behind closed doors, but I suppose if it were my business, I'd be told. So, I put them out of my mind for a few minutes and turn my attention to Riley.

"Now, what did you want to tell me that you couldn't with them out here?" she immediately asks, grabbing her drink and taking a sip.

"Well," I begin, my face turning beet red.

"You finally gave it up to them?" she asks, excitement taking her over.

"I did. But I don't think you realize exactly just what I gave up," I tell her, pulling her in closer to me so no one else can overhear our conversation. "I was a virgin until last night."

Riley has no clue what to say right now. I'm sure that was the last thing that she expected me to say. Recovering quickly, she pulls me in for a hug and asks me how I'm doing. I'm actually doing wonderful. I know that if I had given it up to anyone other than my two men, it wouldn't have been as good for me. Hell, it wouldn't have meant anything to the person that I gave it up to. With Crash and Trojan, I know that it means something major to them. And they've done nothing but take care of me since it happened.

Now that my secret is out to Riley, we sit back and laugh and talk. I really want to ask her what's going on with Gage, but I don't. When she's ready to talk to me about it, she will. If he hurts her, he'll have to deal with me and Wilma though. Speaking of which, I know she's coming in tomorrow. It started out when I moved into my house. Wilma is one of my neighbors and the first to come welcome me to town.

We're just getting another drink when a few of the club girls show their faces in the common room. They strut right up to us and act like we're new meat in the house. One of them steps up and asks us what the hell we're doing at the bar and not cleaning anything.

"Excuse me!" I say, turning my full attention to this bitch. "You must not know who I am and who she's here with."

"I don't give a fuck who you think you're with. Club girls are here to clean and take care of the men's needs. Since they're in church, I suggest you start cleaning," she tells me, putting her hands on her hips and attempting a look that she must think is intimidating.

"Why don't you get your fat, lazy asses to cleaning," I begin. "And you can ask Crash and Trojan who I am when they get done. I'm sure they'll set you straight."

"You honestly expect me to believe that you're with the two of them?" she asks, looking me up and down like I'm a piece of garbage on the bottom of her stripper heal.

"I am with them. And she's here with Gage," I tell them, finally turning my attention away from the little squad of bitchy club girls.

Before she can utter another word, Crash and Trojan run out of the room and head straight for me. They practically knock this head bitch out of their way as they try to get to me.

I'm not sure what's going on now, but it can't be good. What the fuck else am I going to have to deal with now?

Crash

We're sitting in church going over all of the business from the last week. Nothing has really changed other than our business with Darcy. She's now officially ours and all of the guys know it. Yeah, she agreed a while ago, but we gave her the chance to back out before we announced it in church. Now, it's been announced and we're not giving her a chance to back out on us. Hell, she lost that right when she gave up the one thing that meant more to her than most anything else in the world.

I tune back in when I hear Gage bring her name up. He's asking Tech if anything has been happening in the last week at her house. Trojan and I know that nothing has set any alarms off since Tech linked our phones to the security system. Just as he goes to let us know one way or another, we both get alerts on our phone. Tech pulls the computer up to the big screen and we watch in stunned silence as Darcy's house goes up in flames. This isn't just from a fire, there was just an explosion at her house.

"What the fuck!" I yell out, standing up and sending my chair flying backwards.

Tech is already on the phone and from his end of the conversation, I'm guessing that it's with the fire department. Gage is also on the phone as are a few of the other brothers. I'm not sure who the hell they're all on the phone with at this point in time. Trojan and I don't wait for anyone else, we run out of the room and make our way to Darcy. If anyone is going to tell her what just happened, it's going to be us.

Running out to Darcy, I don't even pay attention to the fact that the club girls have surrounded her and Riley. I make a mental note to ask her about it later when we don't have devastating news to share with her. Trojan and I each stand by her side and wrap our arms around her. She can tell that there's something going on and she looks afraid to ask us what it is. This is going to be hard as fuck!

"Baby, we got somethin' to tell you," I begin, not wanting to share this news with her.

"What now?" I ask, despair already lacing my voice. My imagination is running wild with all the possibilities of what's happened now.

"I think we should sit down somewhere quiet and talk," Trojan tells her, trying to lead her over to a table in the corner that's quiet and away from the rest of the room.

"No. Just tell me please," she says, standing up straighter and bracing herself against whatever bad news we're about to give her.

"When we were in church, Tech pulled up the feed for your house. Before it was fully up we got an alert on our phones. Darcy, someone blew your house up. I'm pretty sure that it's whoever has been doin' everythin' else," I tell her, both of us catching her as she starts to fall to the ground.

Riley and Gage are surrounding us as we comfort our girl. She's crying uncontrollably, and I don't know what we're going to do this time. There really isn't any coming back from this. Now, she has lost somewhere she called home and everything that was left in it. Thankfully Shadow and the two other prospects went and collected everything they thought she could save. Darcy hasn't had a chance to be told this yet though. I guess we'll tell her once the shock and grief at losing the rest of her things has gone away.

"I need to go there," she tells us after a few minutes. Darcy has screamed and cried, lost her shit over the bombshell we just literally dropped on her.

"I don't know that it's a good idea, sweetheart," Gage tells her, coming closer to us and trying to reason with her.

"I really *need* to be there. They need to know that I'm not going to let them get away with this. I'll file whatever I have to file, even though I know the cops are going to do shit. Please, take me there?" she asks, turning her tear stained face towards the two of us and pleading with her red-rimmed eyes.

Trojan and I look at one another and make a silent decision to take our girl where she needs to be. If that's going to her house to see the destruction, then we'll take her against our better judgment. We'll make sure that we're by her side the entire time and offer her whatever support she needs. Riley speaks up, telling us that she's going with us. She'll drive her car so that Darcy doesn't have to try to hold on to one of us on the bikes.

"Why don't we all go in one of the SUVs? Whoever else wants to follow can do so on their bikes," Gage says, heading off to grab the keys from Shadow.

This is why I love my club. These guys don't have to be there for us right now, yet looking around, every single man here is getting ready to ride. Shadow hands the keys over to our President and talks quietly to him. He's probably asking what he needs to do while we're gone. I'm sure that we should bring Darcy in for a soft lockdown, but I'm not sure if she's going to agree with it. Maybe we can get a few extra guys out to the house for protection.

Trojan

Pulling up to our girl's house, the destruction is absolutely incredible to witness. There are firetrucks and police cars littering the narrow road surrounding the area her house once stood. I knew we shouldn't have brought her here. Darcy gasps and covers her face with her hands. Gage and Riley are up front, and Darcy is sitting between the two of us in the back seat. We each wrap our arms around her and try to offer her a level of comfort. This is going to fucking suck!

Gage pulls up as close as he can before the cops start telling us to leave the area. Darcy jumps over me and gets out the door before any of us can stop her. She's telling the cops that this is her house and she needs to be here, she needs to know what's going on. So, they allow us to stay. Including all of our brothers that are now surrounding the SUV in a show of protection.

Looking over to the side, I see Wilma standing there. She's watching the blaze and the men trying to put it out before it spreads to other homes nearby. As soon as she notices us, the older woman heads our way. Making a beeline straight for Darcy, she doesn't stop until her arms are wrapped around our girl. They're whispering and both of them are crying. The entire scene before me fills me with a rage I've never felt before. It's crazy how protective I now feel over Wilma along with Darcy. But, she's important to our girl so she's important to us.

It seems like we've been standing here for hours and hours. Darcy isn't ready to leave yet so we're not going anywhere. Instead, we'll stay for as long as she needs to and then take her home to care for her and get the smell of smoke off her body and out of her hair. Finally, the flames are out and we're ready to have the conversation with the fire chief and a few police officers.

"It seems that one of your gas lines was cut that go to your stove. Whoever did this, made sure that your lines were turned on but not to lite the burners. They knew what they were doing," the fire chief tells us, wiping the sweat off his blackened face. He's definitely been fighting a battle all night long. "We'll go back in after we've had a few hours of sleep and see what else we can find out."

"Thank you, sir," Darcy says, her voice is almost a whisper.

"Let's get you back to the house," I say, wrapping a blanket from the back of the SUV around Darcy and pulling her close to my body. "We'll take a shower and relax. Today is going to be a very long day babe."

"Okay," she says, defeat and sadness lacing her already weak voice.

This shit is getting to our girl and killing the fire inside her. Every single time we start to get it out of her again, this fuckwad comes out and robs her of everything. She's not going to be able to take much more. Especially if anything else happens to the salon. It will rip every single thing we've worked so hard to bring back out in her to shreds and take away her spirit. We're not going to allow that to happen.

Riley hands over the keys to her car and tells me that she'll have Gage drop her off to pick it up later on today at some point. I'm thankful because I was really beginning to wonder how we were going to get her back to the house. The last thing I hear before we leave is Gage telling another prospect and Steel to head on over to the Salon. Darcy won't be able to handle something happening to that on top of losing her home. Sure, there wasn't much left inside but it was still hers. Now, nothing is standing where it once stood.

Pulling up to the house, Darcy waits until Crash and I get out of the car before she finally moves. She hasn't said a single word since she said thank you to the fire chief. I'm getting worried about her and I can tell that my brother is too. It's only a matter of time before she snaps, and I just hope that we're around when she does. If not, I'm honestly not sure what she's going to do.

"Let's get in the shower and wash up so we can go to bed," I tell her, all my previous thoughts about taking her mind off of everything with sex flying right out of the window.

Darcy nods her head and still says nothing to us. Instead we just follow her shaken and silent body into the house. Her head is practically hanging down and her shoulders are slumped forward. If she was shrinking into herself anymore, Darcy would be curled up into a ball. She needs some help to break out of this, help from someone to get her to snap out of the shock she's going into.

"You wanna head to the hospital and get looked over?" Crash asks her, letting his worry and concern shine through.

"No. I just wanna take a shower and head to bed," she whispers, going back to giving us the silent treatment.

We stand in the living room and watch her head into our shared room before we grab two beers from the fridge. As soon as we sit down in the kitchen, we take a minute to gather our thoughts before having the conversation that we both know we need to have. Between the two of us we'll be able to figure out what we need to do in order to help Darcy.

"You know that we need to do somethin' here, right?" I ask, my voice full of concern.

"I know. Hell, we both know that we need to help her snap out of this shit. I'm just not sure how we're going to make that happen. Too much has happened, and I don't know what we can do," Crash responds, letting his head sink down in concentration.

"There's only one way I know to snap her out of this shit. You wanna do it, or do you want me to?" I ask, letting my idea sink into his head while he processes it.

"Why don't we both do it. That way she knows we're both here for her and that we're both willin' to do what we can to help her take her mind off of everythin' that has happened. And I know by now she's thinkin' of what else can possibly go wrong," he tells me, standing up and starting to take his clothes off.

I follow his lead and start stripping on my way to the bathroom where our girl is in the shower all alone right now. As soon as we go through the bathroom door, we're immediately hit with the sound of Darcy crying. She's sitting on the floor of the shower and her arms are wrapped around herself. I can already tell that she's trying to stay quiet so that we didn't hear her if we came into the bedroom.

I'm the first one in the shower and I wrap my arms around her and pull her up off the floor. She immediately wraps her arms around my middle and holds me tight. I rest my chin on the top of her head after placing a gentle kiss in her hair. Crash steps in behind her and wraps his arms around her from behind. He gives her the same treatment as me and I can feel her body riddled with her shaking.

"Baby, we got you," I whisper into her hair. "You let go and we'll be here to catch you. Every. Single. Time."

We didn't get in here to have sex with our girl. Our goal is to get her to crack, let everything she's feeling out so she's not trying to hide it from us. If that means we're here while she cries, screams, and yells at the top of her lungs then that's what we're going to do. Crash sits down on the bench while I back Darcy up to him. He pulls her down on his lap and then cradles her while I grab her body wash and sponge. As he's holding her, I begin to wash her body. Yeah, I should be washing her hair first, but she's got her head buried in Crash's neck, so I can't get to it right now. Besides, he'll be able to wash her hair while I hold her.

I take my time to soap up every inch of Darcy's body. Not one single time during washing her does she move an inch away from Crash. He lifts her up while I wash her back and then pulls her away from him as much as she allows him to so that I can take care of the front of the body. As soon as I'm done, I grab the shower head so that I can rinse her off. Crash stands up with her and waits until I can sit down before placing her motionless body in my arms.

Cradling her head in the crook of my arm, I let her head fall back so that my brother can get her hair wet before massaging her the shampoo into her hair. I quietly murmur to her while she lets him do what he's got to do. As soon as he washes and conditions her hair, I pull her closer to my body. Looking over her head, I let Crash know that now is the time we need to put our plan in motion.

"You know that we're goin' to catch whoever did this, don't you, firecracker?" I ask, pulling her away from my body and taking a little bit of her security away.

"I know. But what else is going to happen before you guys catch this person? How much more can I lose?" she asks, trying to bury herself back in my body.

"We're goin' to do everythin' in our power to make sure that nothin' else happens," Crash tells her, pulling her attention away from me so she can't get back her security.

This is hurting me to know that we're taking away even a little bit of the security she feels when she's with us. I don't want her to back peddle and think that we're not going to be here for her. The only thing that we're trying to accomplish is getting her to let her pain and anger out. She can't hold it all in and not expect us to try to do anything about it. Crash and I need to try to do this for her.

"You can't promise that nothing else is going to happen! I don't know how much more I can take either. Now, when I need you two the most, you're pulling this shit," she yells out, tears streaming down her face and the pain finally starting to come out.

"We're doin' this because we need you to get this shit out," I begin telling her, still not pulling her back into my body. "You bein' quiet and stayin' in your own head isn't goin' to help anythin'."

"I know. And, I want to let it out, to lean on the two of you. I just feel like I'm already bringing a bunch of shit to you two. Plus, who would want to hear the shit running through my head right now?" she asks, fully sinking back into my embrace as Crash kneels down in front of her.

"We want to hear every single thing about you. If it's you goin' crazy because of someone attackin' you and goin' after everythin' you cherish then we want to hear it. You have a bad, or good, day at the salon, tell us all about it. It runs through your head, we want to know. We want you to let us all the way in and not hold anythin' back because you think we don't want to hear about it," Crash tells her, running his hand down the side of her face and holding her.

"And you're not bringin' anythin' to our door. We knew when we met you that you were the one that was made for us. You make this trio whole and no matter what you are goin' through, we'll fix it. Together. Now, we're goin' to wash up while you soak up the hot water," I tell her, setting down on the seat and washing up as quickly as I possibly can.

"I'll try to talk to you two more about things. And, I won't hold anything in. From now on, if I'm not talking to you two I'll talk to Riley. The main things going through my head right now are that I don't know what else is going to happen, what this stupid motherfucker is going to go after next. The only thing I have left is the salon."

"We know. And that's why Gage has more men posted on the salon so that no one is goin' to have a chance to do anythin' more to it," Crash tells her, soaping up his body.

As soon as the two of us are done, we dry off before turning around to face our girl. Darcy is staring at the two of us like we're her next meal. I'm definitely not going to deny Darcy anything and from the look on Crash's face, he's not going to either. Bedtime just got a little more interesting. We're not going to go to sleep, we're going to make sure that our girl is thoroughly satisfied and left sated before she closes her eyes.

Crash grabs her hand and pulls her up into his body. He wraps his arms around her as I grab a towel and begin to dry her off starting at her feet and working my way up to her pussy. I want nothing more than to take a taste of my girl right now. So, I lean in and let my tongue swipe through her slick folds from the back to her clit. I feel her legs threatening to give out as I continue my ministrations while Crash is doing whatever he's doing to her up above me.

It doesn't take very long for Darcy to crash over the edge of bliss and I lick up every single drop of her sweet essence. I continue to dry her body off as I stand up and Crash steps back after breaking the kiss he was giving her. Once her body is completely dry, we lead her into the bedroom and help her get into bed. Each of us take one side of her and let our hands run over her body. Darcy is writhing on the bed as we pay attention to her amazing body. She's still trying to hide from us, but we're not letting her. We're going to treasure every single inch of her body for the rest of the night.

Chapter Seven

Darcy

I'M SITTING AT THE KITCHEN TABLE, paperwork from the insurance company spread out in front of me. There's a shit ton of things that I need to fill out and get turned back in as soon as possible to see if they're going to cover the damages. At this point, I'm not even sure that I care whether or not they're going to pay for my house being blown up. It's not like I'd be going back to it. The only thing that I'd use it for is one of the houses for the domestic violence program that the club as a whole is doing. If I can contribute in that way, I'd do it in a heartbeat.

It's been relatively quiet in the past few weeks since this asswipe burned my house to the ground. The men have been watching me like hawks still and have taken every single opportunity to show me how much they love me. Hell, if they had their way, I'm sure they'd keep me in bed and naked constantly. You won't hear me complain though. If there was one thing that I would complain about, it would be being so damn tired because I'm getting woken up in the middle of the night and I'm worn out in the best of ways.

Crash and Trojan are teaching me every way possible to have sex. Hell, there's things that I didn't think were possible at all, but they've proven me wrong. So far, I think almost the entire house has been christened by us. I may have to say that the shower has been extremely fun lately. These days, at least one of them always seems to join me. They claim it's to help me reach the spots that I can't on my own. I'm sure it's just another excuse to see me naked and have their way with me though. It's a good thing they had a huge shower built in our bedroom.

"What's got you so deep in thought?" Trojan asks, coming up behind me and planting a kiss on my neck.

"I was just thinking about the last few weeks and how much you guys have been showing me," I answer honestly.

"Oh yeah? Well, we need to talk about somethin'," Trojan tells me, getting serious and sitting down at the table next to me.

"What's that?" I ask, putting the paperwork in a stack in front of me and giving my man my full attention.

"We have to go to the party at the clubhouse tonight. I know that you're probably not up for it, but we've got to put in an appearance. It's been a while since we've been to one," he tells me, moving closer and closer to me. "Crash and I really want you to go with us though. Hell, I think that some of the guys from Clifton Falls and the Phantom Bastards are comin' to it."

"Okay. It's time for me to get out of the house and start bein' around the clubhouse with you guys," I tell him, knowing that I need to be their woman and get over my irrational fear of going to the clubhouse with them.

"Alright. I need to go out for a while. Crash is in the bedroom if you need anythin'."

I give Trojan a kiss before he leaves, pour myself another cup of coffee, and grab a donut out of the box. Sitting back down, I stare at the last few pages I need to fill out. Most of this is mumbo jumbo to me, but I need to push through this and get it done. This is where I am when Crash comes out of the bedroom and kisses me as he sits down at the table with me. Grabbing a stack of the papers I've already filled out, he looks over what I've done already.

"How much more do you gotta do?" he asks, placing the papers back where I had them.

"Just a few more papers. And I have to make a copy of the fire chief's report so that I still have one and the insurance company has one too," I tell him, looking back at the paper in front of me. "There's a lot of the same questions. I'm sure it's going to be okay though. I have an idea I wanted to run by the two of you, but you're never here at the same time."

"What's up firecracker?" he asks, getting up to start fixing lunch.

"Well, I was thinkin' that if I'm goin' to stay here, then I want to do somethin' a little different with the money from the insurance company," I tell him, wanting to know that they want me to stay here permanently before I go much further.

"You know that you're not leavin' here now," he tells me, sitting back down to hear what I have to say.

"Well, in that case, I want to build a house where mine stood. Instead of me living in it, I want the club to have it, so you guys can use it for the domestic violence program that you're trying to start up," I say, my confidence completely leaving me.

"That's an amazin' idea!" he says, pulling his phone out of his pocket and typing out a message to someone. "I'm lettin' Gage know now so that he can figure it out before we have church."

I nod and smile at him before turning my attention back to the papers. Crash gets up and goes back to fixing lunch while I finish this up. Hopefully it doesn't take me too much longer. It seems to go by a little bit quicker with him keeping up his banter and making me laugh. This is what I need right now. By the time I'm done with the last paper, Crash is setting a plate with grilled cheese sandwich and a cup of tomato soup in front of me.

The rest of the day has been spent trying to get ready for tonight's party. I'm not sure what exactly I'm supposed to wear or even do tonight. About the only thing I'm going a hundred percent sure about is that my actions are going to reflect on Crash and Trojan. So, I need to keep my clumsy moves to a minimum if I'm not going to embarrass them. Fuck! This is not going to go very good.

I'm jumping in the shower to start getting ready when I hear knocking on the door. The guys are out in the living room, so they can answer it. As I shut the bathroom door, I hear someone coming in the bedroom and I figure it's just one of the guys. Hopefully they don't decide to make an appearance in the shower with me. I'm nervous enough as it is and while that will take my mind off of everything for a little while, it's not going to change anything in regard to tonight.

There's another knock on the door. That's not one of my men. They'd just walk right on in and join me. I have no clue who they would let in the bedroom knowing that I was going to be getting in the shower. If I know anything about my men, it's that they're very protective and won't allow anyone to see me. a few different scenarios run through my mind until I decide that I'm being a dumbass and open the door just a crack to see if I can tell who's in our room.

"It's about time Darcy!" I hear coming from Skylar.

Opening the door just a little bit farther, I see all the girls from Clifton Falls and Riley in different spots in the room. Mainly they're looking around and seeing the changes from when I moved in until now. Instead of just a few things in here belonging to me, all of Crash and Trojan's things now litter the surfaces of dressers, the stands, and in the closet.

"Um, what exactly are you doing here?" I ask, making sure the towel is wrapped around me tight and that everything is covered.

"We knew you were going to be nervous about tonight. So, we figured that we'd come rescue you. We'll tell you what's going to go on and what you're probably going to be seeing tonight," Skylar informs me, standing up and coming closer to me. "Now, you get in the shower and we'll pick out something for you to wear and shit like that."

As quickly as I can, I shower and dry off before walking back out into the bedroom. Yeah, I wouldn't normally go out in nothing more than a towel, but it's just a bunch of girls in the room. It's not like they haven't seen the good before. We all have the same things. Just different sizes and shit. Plus, I know these girls won't judge me for the way that I look. They are the sisters of my heart, ones I never had but always wanted. Even if I never would've wished them to be in the fucked-up situation I was in growing up.

"Come here babe," Bailey tells me, patting the bottom of the bed.

Looking at the dresser placed directly at the bottom of the bed, I see four different outfits picked out. Two of these outfits are dresses, one is a short skirt I've never seen before paired with a tank top, and the last is a pair of jeans with a different colored tank top and a light sweater. About the only thing I recognize out of all these clothes are the pair of jeans. I have no clue where the rest of this came from and I'm not going to ask any questions. Sometimes it's just easier that way.

"Which one do you think you like the best?" Skylar asks, looking each outfit over with a critical eye.

Standing up, I look at all four outfits and think about which one my men would like the best. Usually, I wouldn't give a fuck what anyone else thinks about what I'm wearing. Tonight, I feel like this is way too important not to pay close attention to what I look like. More than likely I'm going to do something embarrassing, so I guess I better look as good as possible. Choosing the skirt and tank top, I pick the sweater up too and make my way into the bathroom to get dressed.

As soon as I'm dressed, I walk back out of the bathroom and receive all sorts of catcalls and whistles from the girls. I do a little spin to show them what I completely look like. Bailey sits me down on the bed once again so that they can do my makeup. I'm going to do my hair as soon as they're done with my face. So, I sit still and let Melody do her best to me. The only time I move is when I'm handed a shot. It's not enough that we're going to be drinking at the party tonight. Everyone decided that we needed to get started now. Hopefully it helps cut down on my nerves and puts me at ease, so I can have a good time. Otherwise, I may end making the night worse because I'll be so concerned with my actions that I won't have a good time.

"Alright babe, your makeup is done. You get your hair done so we can go out and show your men exactly how gorgeous you are. I know you try to hide it, but there's no reason for you to hide your amazing figure under frumpy clothes," Melody tells me, trying to boost my confidence.

"I have to agree with her," Skylar says, sitting down next to me. "Trust me, I was the same way and now, I wear clothes that actually fit me and don't hide the curves that I've been blessed with. They show that I'm not a stick and that I live my life the way that I want to. Crash and Trojan want you for who you are and aren't going to leave you for some sickly thin bitch."

The rest of the girls nod and comment their agreement. They're words and encouragement mean the world to me because that's what I've done most of my life. I know that I have more curves than what society may see as appropriate, but I actually like the way I look. Growing up, I was taught to hide my body because if I didn't, I would get picked on more than when I wear the baggy pants and shirts. Crash and Trojan have already started putting extra clothes in the closet for me. Ones that actually fit and accentuate my curves in a sexy and understated way. I'll have to start wearing them out more and stop hiding.

Walking back in the bathroom, I take a minute to decide what I want to do with my hair as I look at my makeup. Melody did an amazing job and accentuated my eyes with smokey eye shadow and mascara. The rest of my face looks like nothing is even on it. Finally pulling my attention off my face, I focus on what I need to be doing now. My hair is longer than what I've had in a long time and I can do almost anything I want to it. Usually, I'm just at home or work so I style it in easy ponytails or just leave it down. Maybe throw a headband on to keep it out of my face when I'm at work. Tonight, I want it to be something special.

I take a bobby pin and pull just the front part of my hair back. Once it's secure, I spray it with some hairspray before grabbing my curling iron. The rest I'll leave down and curl, so it flows down my back. My hairspray is just used to hold the curl and not make it so you can't touch my hair without having a fear of it breaking off at a single touch. Curling my hair is going to take the longest, but I love the way it looks when I finish it. Hopefully the guys will too.

As I'm working on my hair, Riley brings me another shot and I take a second to drink it down as I'm done with one section and moving on to another one to curl. Instead of heading back out with the rest of the girls, she stays in with me and finishes the back of my hair for me. I always hate curling that part so I'm glad that she did it for me.

"You're going to the party tonight, aren't you?" I ask, making sure that she'll be there with us all tonight.

"Yeah. Gage asked me to come the other night," she answers, not looking me in the eye as she does.

"Even though I want to ask what's going on between the two of you, I won't. Just know that yes, I'm dying to know, and I'll be there for you no matter what," I tell her, not putting any pressure on her to fill me in on what's up between the two of them.

"He's just helping me get used to a new town. There's some things that no one knows and he's trying to help me out. Darcy, Gage is so sweet, and he said that he won't leave my side. I think that he wants more than a friendship, but I'm not sure if I can give that to him. Not right now," she says, a sadness and pain creeping up into her eyes. Filling them and taking away the sparkle that was just shining bright.

"I'm so sorry honey. I didn't mean to upset you," I tell her frantically, wanting to figure out how to take this look out of her eyes and off her face.

"Don't worry about it sweetie. It's not your fault and you didn't make me upset. One day I'll explain everything, just not tonight. Tonight, is all about you and getting you through your first party."

I nod my head in acknowledgment. My throat is clogged with unshed tears knowing this good friend is going through something she's choosing to hide. I'm not sure why she is, and I'm not sure we'll ever know. What I do know is that I'll do whatever it takes to be there for her and help her do whatever I can. Taking a minute, I pull out some of the tighter curls and make sure my hair is the way I want it before I turn to her and let her know that I'm ready to head to the clubhouse. Well, as ready as I'll ever be.

"Let's go show your men what a fucking beautiful, and sexy as sin, woman you are," Riley tells me, getting a laugh to break free.

Trojan

Crash and I are sitting in the living room while the old ladies from Clifton Falls help Darcy get ready to go tonight. We knew she was nervous as fuck and we wanted to make sure she knew that she wasn't going to be alone. Yeah, we'll be stuck to her like glue, but she needs to know that her girls are here for her too. So, we made some calls and got them to come down early. The guys stayed for a few minutes before heading to the clubhouse. Cage and Tank wanted to talk to Gage alone and I'm sure that we'll find out what's going on when we need to know.

It seems like we've been waiting forever for the girls to make our girl look even better than she does on a daily basis. Just as I go to suggest that we go and see what the hold-up is, I hear the bedroom door open up and we both stand simultaneously. The sight that greets us has our eyes almost popping out of our heads and our jaws dropping to the floor. Darcy always looks great if you ask us. It doesn't matter if she's wearing sweats with her hair thrown up in a bun thingy and her glasses, or just getting out of work. Tonight, she looks absolutely stunning. Fuck, I don't think there's words to describe the way she looks. She's wearing a short skirt that's sexy as hell, but not too short so everyone else around us will see what belongs to us. A tank top with a sweater thing is paired with the skirt while her hair flows down her back in ringlets. What really blows my mind though is the stripper heels that adorn her tiny feet. The entire ensemble makes Darcy look so stunning that I almost don't want to take her out in public.

"You look absolutely amazing!" Crash tells her, finding his voice before I can find mine.

A deep blush starts to creep up Darcy's face at the compliment and the way that we're looking at her right now. She may not be a virgin anymore, but she sure as fuck is still innocent as hell. She's way too innocent and good for us. We're both selfish fuckers though and we're not going to let some boring asshole with a nine to five take her away from us. Instead, we're going to keep her all to ourselves and dirty her in the best way possible.

"Are you tryin' to kill us?" I ask, finally getting my mouth and brain to start working again. "You look so good that everyone is goin' to want to be with you baby."

"Th-thank y-you," she murmurs as we make our way to her.

Crash and I each take our turn kissing her to the point of stealing her breath away. In all honesty, she steals ours as much as she says we steal hers. Personally, all I need to do is get a glimpse of her and I lose my breath. Darcy is so sexy, and she has no clue the way she looks to us. It doesn't matter what she's doing, all I have to do is see her and I lose all rational thought. Including how to act most times.

"Are you two done molesting your girl so that we can head out?" Bailey asks, never holding anything back for anyone.

"It's a good thing we love you like a little pain in the ass sister," Crash tells her, pulling her into a hug.

"I know. You don't scare me though big guy. I've got a secret weapon against you now. I'll have to tell Darcy all about withholding the goods from you when you want to misbehave and show your caveman tendencies," Bailey threatens, letting us know she means every single word she just said by a single look on her face.

"Don't forget we know how to get Grim to punish you too, little sis," I tell her, pulling her into my own hug in greeting.

As soon as they knocked on our door, they breezed through the house and straight into Darcy. There was no 'hello' or anything to us. All that mattered was our girl. It just goes to show that these women care about her and they all stick together no matter what. They've all gone to their first party at one point or another. This is no different than they've done for any of the other women.

"Enough talking. Let's get on the road before Cage or Joker call me again. They're getting pissy because I'm not there yet," Skylar says, cutting through everyone and heading straight for the door.

We all follow her out to the SUV and our bikes. We're going to follow them to the clubhouse while all the women ride together. Even though we want her with us and on one of our bikes, tonight is major for her and she needs to be comfortable and looking as sexy as sin like she does right now. We'll ride in front and back of them the short trip to the clubhouse and then she's ours for the rest of the night.

Once we pull up to the clubhouse, I notice that Bailey parks as close to the doors as she possibly can. It helps that Gage made sure that a spot was saved so the girls didn't have to walk across a crowded parking lot. Shadow is standing there so I'm sure that he was supposed to make sure no one parked there until we showed up. Crash and I meet the girls at the door and we all walk in together. The common room is already packed, the music is blaring, the drinks are flowing, and the club girls are already almost naked. Darcy hasn't been here for this kind of display before. Hell, I don't even think she's been around when it's happened at Clifton Falls. That's really the only clubhouse that she's been around. Until now that is.

Crash and I wrap our arms around her and we can feel her trying to get closer to both of us. We really need to get a rag made for her. Most of the guys know that she's ours and has been for a long time now. Darcy was the last one to get on board. However, there are always a few hang arounds here and I'm not going to have them trying to go after someone that doesn't belong to them. Our girl will try to be polite and have a conversation with these men when in reality, all they want is to get in her pants. I don't want to have to fight off a bunch of guys, so we really need to get her rag ordered now.

Looking at my brother, I can see the same thoughts swirling through his eyes. I'm going to have to talk to Gage and see who we're going to go through now. Ma always handled the rags for the girls. Now, I don't know if that's one of the things that Bailey took over for her or if we're going through someone else entirely. If we get a few minutes, I'll ask him and see what he says. Since Bailey is here already, I'll talk to her if she did in fact take it over. I'm sure she already has a clue that it's coming.

"Um, is it usually like this?" Darcy asks, her shyness coming out full force even though she knows most of the guys here. I think this has more to do with the club girls and hang arounds that she's never seen before.

"Yeah. At least on party night it is. This is actually pretty tame for now firecracker," Crash tells her. "In a little while, you'll see people havin' sex in the open, girls walkin' around naked, and a whole list of other things goin' on. We'll be by your side the entire time."

"Didn't the girls talk to you about this?" I ask, pretty sure that Bailey said they were going to give her the talk.

"They did. I guess I didn't really believe them though. I thought they were exaggerating to try to scare me or something," she tells us, putting her head down at her admission.

"They wouldn't do that. Whatever they told you, I'm sure wasn't as bad as it can get," I tell her, knowing that some of the girls tend to sugarcoat things sometimes.

"For now, we're goin' to relax and have a few drinks. If it gets to be too much, we'll go hang out in the room with you," Crash says, wanting her to know that she does have an out.

Darcy nods her head before she follows Riley and the rest of the girls over to a few tables in the corner. It's semi-quiet and I know that they'll be left alone for the most part. She'll be able to have a few drinks and loosen up before the party really starts to get out of control. Crash and I park our asses at the bar so we're not too far from our girl. Shadow grabs us our beers before taking a pitcher of some sort of concoction over to the girls. I'm not sure what the hell it is but they sure are excited about it.

We turn around as the main door bangs open and in walk the Phantom Bastards. I had a feeling they were going to make an appearance tonight, I just didn't know it would be so soon. They've heard what's going on with our girl, and they're going to help in any way they can. Before the end of the night, I'm sure that we're going to have to talk about what's been going on. Hell, it would be nice if we knew what the hell was going on. I watch as the guys flow through the door in a steady stream, crossing my fingers that Wood didn't make the trip. Unfortunately, Wood is in fact here. He comes strutting in last, stopping as soon as he gets in the door and looking around. Making his way over to us, I can only imagine what he has to say.

"Guys," he says, sitting down and ordering a beer. "Heard Darcy finally put you out of your misery and agreed to be your old lady."

"Yep. Now, we just have to figure out who's after her and then we'll be able to get on with our life with her," Crash tells him, drinking a sip of his beer and motioning for another one.

"If you need any help, just let me know," Wood tells us, standing up and going to join another group of guys.

The rest of the Phantom Bastard men and the guys from Clifton Falls are circling around, talking with all of us. I can't bring myself to stand up and mingle with other brothers. Everything going on with Darcy is weighing on my mind. There's no way I can fix this right now. Hell, there's no way that I can even truly promise her that we'll make sure nothing happens to her or the salon again. Not until we find out who's after her anyway. Crash hasn't left the bar either, so I'm sure that he's feeling the same way right now.

"Look at her," he suddenly tells me, his focus completely on Darcy sitting in the booth with the rest of the girls. "Our girl is havin' a good time. Hell, I'm sure that she's relaxin' really good right about now."

"It definitely looks like she isn't worried about anythin' right now. I wish we could find this fuckin' cocksucker and make sure nothin' else happens to her or the salon. We've made promises to her that we may not be able to keep. I don't like that, Crash," I tell him, knowing that he's going to feel the same way when he realizes what has me feeling bad.

"I get where you're comin' from, and I don't like it any better than you do. What are we supposed to do though? I don't know how we're supposed to get this twatwaffle to come out so we can catch him," he replies, letting me know that he's been having the same thoughts as me. Like me, he hasn't come up with any answers though.

"I say we table this discussion for the night and have fun with our girl at her first party. She's relaxin' now and the club girls are goin' to be gettin' here in a few minutes. I bet the old ladies stay here tonight so that Darcy doesn't have to be alone right now. They're goin' to want to make sure nothin' happens to her," I tell him, standing up to head over to our girl.

Before we get too close to her, she practically jumps over the table. I'm thinking that she's on her way over to us, but she completely bypasses us. Turning my head, I watch her head down the hallway towards the bathroom. Immediately, laughter erupts from me and I realize that Bailey told Shadow how to make the drinks and they're just starting to hit the girls. All of them, if them practically running over one another to get to the bathroom is anything to go by.

Crash and I sit down with Cage and Joker. They're laughing at the girls like we are. Hell, I think all of the men are doing the same thing we are right now. Picking up my beer, I drink some more while I wait for my girl to come back out.

Now, maybe we can talk to these two about the whole dating thing with Darcy. I know she's still concerned about spending enough time and attention with both of us.

"I think we need to talk," I blurt out, not wanting to delay this conversation any longer than we already have.

"What's up?" Joker asks, taking in my serious tone and giving me his full attention.

"We need to know how we make Darcy believe that she's spendin' enough time and attention to both of us. I'm at a loss right now," I tell him, looking at Crash to make sure he's paying attention too.

"It's never too early to start takin' her out on individual dates," Cage tells us, setting his beer down and leaning forward. "Don't let her know where you're goin' or what you're doin'. Plan the whole thing out and make each one special and different. It's not a competition, it's about showin' your girl love and attention. Plus, she gets one-on-one time with you both. It's goin' to be somethin' she craves if she's anythin' like Skylar."

"Don't let her plan any of them?" I ask, dumbfounded.

"Nope," Joker answers. "We each plan the entire date from beginnin' to end. The only other thing we tell her is a vague description of what she needs to dress like."

Crash and I take this information in and process it for a few minutes. This isn't going to be hard to do. It will be one of the easiest things Crash and I have ever done in regard to our girl. Speaking of which, she's still not back here. Looking around, I see all the girls making their way back out to the common room. Darcy still isn't out here though. Where the fuck is she?

Standing up, I start to make my way down the hallway she disappeared down a while ago. Crash is following me as we head towards the bathroom. It may be the women's bathroom, but I can guarantee that we're still going to go in there if that's where Darcy is. If there's something wrong with her, then we'll be by her side no matter what.

The closer we get to the bathroom, the louder the sound of laughter and pain is. Now, we're all but running to get to our girl. I can't tell if she's the one laughing, or the one in pain. Whoever is in pain, is groaning and almost screaming out. As we round the corner, the scene before me has me cringing and wanting to burst out in laughter right along with our girl. Crash does start laughing his ass off. The fucker almost has tears running down his face from laughing so hard right now.

Darcy is flat on her ass, laughing so hard she's holding her stomach and trying to hold it in. Wood is sprawled on the floor in front of her. One hand is holding his junk and the other one is holding his foot. I'm not sure exactly what's wrong with him, but Darcy needs to get off the nasty ass floor. So, I walk over to her and pick her up, never letting go of her.

"Wood, I'm so, so sorry," she's telling him over and over again. More laughter is bubbling at the surface and she's doing all she can to hold it in.

"What happened here?" Crash asks, finally pulling himself together. "Or do we not want to know because he'll be in more pain than his current state?"

"It's totally my fault. I was coming out of the bathroom as Wood was walking down the hallway. We crashed into one another and when I landed on him, my knee went right into his um…" she begins, a blush creeping up her face.

"His cock?" Crash asks, trying to get the whole story out of her.

"Yeah. I think I stepped on his foot and that's why he's holding it, but I'm not sure. I'm sorry guys," she finishes, apologizing to us so that we don't get upset with her.

"We should've know," I grumble out, but trying to keep my tone light so she doesn't think I'm pissed off at her. It's just another one of the situations these two find themselves in constantly. "Let's get you back out to the common room. Crash, you want to help him back out there?"

"Fuck no!" he says, pissed that Darcy and him had yet another incident. "One of the club girls can offer him assistance."

The three of us make our way out to the common room, with Darcy walking in between us. Crash pulls Red aside and tells her to go see if she can help Wood. If he's busy with a club girl, we don't have to worry about him and Darcy anymore for the rest of the night. Boy Scout stands up and follows her in the hallway. Yep, knew he'd be following her back there. I sit down at a table with Slim, Grim, Cage, and Joker. Darcy is pulled down in my lap as the club girls start circulating the room, trying to find a single brother to land for the night. Sally keeps looking our way and I let her know with my eyes that it's not happening.

"Do I even wanna know what happened this time?" Slim asks, a smile breaking out on his face.

"I hit Wood in the junk with my knee," Darcy blurts out. "I didn't mean to. We just ran into one another in the hallway."

"Is he okay?" Slim asks, looking at us for his answer.

"He will be. Red and Boy Scout are tendin' to him right now," Crash responds, letting us all know that he's not happy about the situation.

Crash

The party is in full swing. Darcy, Trojan, and I have moved with most everyone else outside. Darcy is dancing with her girls, Wood is sitting with ice still on his cock, and Trojan and I are keeping a close eye on our girl. I love watching her dance and move to the music. She's carefree and doesn't worry about who's watching her, Darcy is the sexiest when she is dancing without a care in the world.

Before we can really get into watching our girl Sally makes her way over to us. No matter how much protesting or anything else we do, she won't take the hint and leave us alone. I go to stand up to make sure she takes the hint this time, but someone beats me to it. All of a sudden Sally goes flying backwards and lands on her ass. Standing behind her I see Darcy, hands on her hips, a scowl on her face.

"Is this what you want? Some skank to get a quick fuck from?" she asks, the scowl turning into rage on her face.

"Fuck no!" I bellow out, trying to move towards her.

"Then what the fuck is going on here?" she asks, tears starting to pool in her eyes.

"We were tryin' to get her to back away and leave us alone. You got over here before she could truly take the hint," Trojan tells her, circling around her so we can both get to her.

"Well, if we're going to do this, then I'm the only one riding your cocks. There will be no club girls, girls you meet wherever, or anything else! It's me only or nothing at all!" she tells us, the fight leaving her.

Before we can reply to our girl, Sally decides she's going to have some input in our lives. "I don't know who the fuck you think you are heifer, but you will *never* keep the attention of these two men. They'll be back in bed with me between them in a matter of days. Fuck, I give it to the end of the night."

Darcy absolutely loses her shit. She punches Sally in the face and follows her down to the ground. I want to drag her off of the nasty bitch, but at the same time, it's hot as fuck to see her beating the shit out of her. Hell, she's sexy as fuck claiming the two of us. Whether she knows it or not, Darcy just laid claim to Trojan and me in front of all three clubs. The rest of the girls are standing back with awe and respect shining through. Finally, I realize that we need to stop Darcy before she gets hurt.

Trojan grabs our girl and pulls her kicking and screaming away from Sally. Steel grabs her so she can't be a complete bitch and attack our girl while she's in the arms of one of us. I stand in front of her so that she can't even see the bitch and place my hand on her cheek, forcing her attention to me. We need to get her calmed down, so we can get her back into party mode. I only know of one way to do that and I'm not going to use sex right now. We're going to let her have some time with her girls before we ravage her.

"She means absolutely nothin' to us. We want you and only you. Before you made your way over to us, we were in the process of pushin' her off of us," I tell her, not letting her look away from me. "Now, while it was hot as fuck to see you go ape shit on that skank, I want you to relax and have a good time. That's why we're here tonight."

"I just didn't like seeing her all over you. Wondering if you were going to choose her over me," she says, relaxing in Trojan's embrace and leaning into my hand. "I'm going to go around the corner for a minute and compose myself. I'll be back in a few minutes."

"We'll go with you," Trojan tells her, moving to step beside her and go with her.

"No!" she all but screams out, looking at both of us and trying to make us understand. "I'll be fine and be back in just a few minutes."

"I'll go with her," Riley tells us, wandering over to stand by her friend's side. "I won't let anything happen to her."

Trojan and I look at her before nodding our heads. After what I've seen the last few days or so, I know Riley will put herself in the way if anyone attempts to get to our girl. I'm not sure where the fuck Sally is now, but I hope I don't see her for the rest of the night. If I do, I won't be held responsible for my actions. And, I can guarantee that Trojan is going to feel the same way. Without a doubt, he'll step up and make sure that not only no one gets to our girl, but that these skanks around the club leave us alone.

Darcy has been back at the party for a while now. Things are really getting crazy as everyone tries to find their pussy for the night. We brought extra girls in for the single guys, but I still think there isn't going to be enough for everyone. We'll cross that bridge when we get there I guess.

Our girl is definitely feeling carefree and relaxed with the amount of alcohol she's had tonight. And I'm watching her as she watches everything that's going on around her while she dances. There's a few particular sexual acts she's watching. Even though she's trying not to pay attention. Her gaze constantly flicks back to Wood and Boy Scout sharing a girl over in the corner and then there's a few nomads sharing a girl in another spot by the fence. These two groups of threesomes are doing things that we haven't tried with her yet.

Over the last few days, we've been getting her ready to take both of us together. At first, Darcy was extremely embarrassed and shy about using a butt plug to get ready. Or have us pay any attention to her 'forbidden zone' as she calls it. We've talked about it and she's willing to try to take Trojan in her ass. I know she's going to be nervous as hell, but maybe tonight is the night we need to try it.

Looking over at my brother, and best friend, I nod my head toward our girl. He's already been watching her and paying attention to where her gaze has been travelling. Standing up, we finish the rest of our beer and make our way over to her. Music is still blaring into the night, people are dancing, couples are in all different stages of sexual activity, and we need to dance with our girl. It's one of the things that we haven't had a chance to do yet. Seeing how open she is when she lets go and follows the beat of the music is one of the sexiest things we've ever seen about her. These are the moments we love seeing her in. Especially with trouble around the corner.

Trojan and I surround her, and we begin to move to the beat of *Paradise City* by *Guns 'N Roses*. I don't care if the song is fast, slow, or one you can't possibly dance to. We're going to stay here with our girl, working her up until she's all but begging us to take her. Running my hands down her sides, I lean in close and kiss her neck.

"We've seen you watchin' what's goin' on around you. You like what you see firecracker?" I ask, kissing, licking, and biting her neck. Darcy is trembling in our arms and I relish the response we can bring from her.

"I'm just trying to figure out what I have to look forward to trying," she tells us, leaning in to my touch while pushing her ass closer to my brother.

"Anytime you're ready to try it out, just say the word and we'll go to our room," Trojan tells her, pushing her hair to the side so he can kiss on her neck while grinding into her ass.

Darcy is really trying to pay attention to what's going on around her and ignore the response that we're drawing out. She wants to keep dancing, but I can tell that she's starting to go crazy with the way we're making her feel. It's not going to be long before we head to our room for the rest of the night.

"What's the matter baby?" Trojan asks her, watching her as she looks at Wood and Boy Scout with the club girl. "You want to try that out?"

"I don't know if I can," she answers, staring in their direction.

I'm not happy that she's watching Wood of all people, but she's seeing another way that we can have some fun and make sure Darcy gets all the pleasure she'll ever want. I lean to the side to make sure that I don't get in her line of sight and continue to rub my hands up and down her. On my way back up her delectable body, I make sure to pay attention to her tits. They're one of my favorite assets of hers.

"We'll never let you fall. Crash and I are down to try anythin' you want to. And we'll teach you a few things along the way," Trojan tells her, continuing to kiss the back of her neck and right under her ear.

"Let's get out of here," I say, pulling away from our girl and starting to make my way through the crowd.

Trojan and I never let go of her hands as we weave our way past our brothers, hang arounds, and family. I'm not going to stop for anything. Well, apparently, we're going to stop for Gage as I see him step out with Riley tucked in his side. We let the girls talk for a few minutes while Gage lets us know what's going on. Hopefully nothing more has happened to the salon.

"Need to talk to Darcy in the morning. We need to know everythin'. It's not goin' to be easy on her so you're goin' to have to tell her about it tonight. Especially since I want all the patched members there," Gage tells us, leaving me more confused about the whole situation.

"What's changed?" Trojan asks, his protective streak coming out in full force.

"Nothin'. And I want to keep it that way. The more we know about her past and the situation as a whole, the easier it might be to find the asshole attackin' your girl," Gage responds, trying to calm us down before our girl make her way back over to us.

"Alright, we'll talk to her. I'll message you when we get up in the mornin'," I tell him, turning towards my girl after giving my President a man hug, complete with slaps on the back.

It took forever to get Darcy away from the rest of the old ladies. I swear they did that shit on purpose but it's okay. We made sure to keep our girl nice and ready for the plans we have with her tonight. Trojan and I are definitely going to be taking her together. We've been going slow and at her pace, but she's ready for us to be one. The only thing holding her back is her fear of the unknown. But, we've been earning her trust and she's been giving more and more of it to us. So, tonight is the perfect night to introduce to her something new.

"You ready baby?" I ask, when we finally get into our room at the clubhouse.

"I guess so," she responds nervously, shifting from one foot to the other and wringing her hands together.

Taking her hands in mine, I pull her to the bed and sit with her before anything else happens. She's had too much time to think about tonight and she's gone in her own head now. We need to get her out of it and relaxed again before anything else happens. Trojan and I have gotten pretty good at learning the signs of her overthinking and letting her nerves get the best of her. If she doesn't want to do what we have planned tonight, then we won't do it. I'm not going to let the reason be her fear though.

"You know by now that we're not goin' to force you to do anythin' that you don't want to do. We want to pleasure you this way and show how much we care about you as one. If you don't like it, then we stop and do somethin' else. Don't let your fear and nerves get the best of you. Please, baby, what's goin' on in that beautiful head of yours right now?" I ask, wanting, no needing, to hear the words from her.

"I know I talked about this with Skylar, and you guys. It's just different when it comes down to actually following through with the act itself. I'm not going to back out of doing this with you two. I want this to happen," she tells us, looking between the two of us so that we can see the truth written all over her face.

Looking at Trojan, I silently let him know that we're going to have to help her get relaxed again. We know just how to get her back in the mood and her mind off of everything going on right now. Once we're relaxing afterwards, we'll talk to her about what Gage needs to have happen tomorrow.

I lay Darcy back and we stretch out beside her. This can take all night long, we have nowhere to go. Hell, there's nowhere I'd rather be than right her in this bed with my best friend and our girl. Tonight, Darcy takes the initiative and turns to me leaning in for a kiss. I'm not going to say that she's never initiated contact with us the last few weeks, but it's rare for her. She's still trying to find herself when it comes to sex, so she's unsure of what she can and can't do with us. No matter how many times we've told her that she can touch us and do whatever she wants to us whenever she wants. Even when we've had sex, she's still so unsure of herself and what she should be doing.

For the next few minutes, we run our hands up and down Darcy's body. At the same time, we slowly remove the clothes from her body. She doesn't even realize that we're stripping her body from everything that's blocking our view of her gorgeous body. Before she comes back down from the bliss we have surrounding her from our kisses alone, she's completely naked and we're half naked.

"Baby, you ready for us both to take you?" Trojan asks her, sliding down her body and burying his face between her soft and creamy thighs.

Darcy nods her head as I begin to pay attention to her lush tits. I pull one nipple in my mouth and begin to suck and bite down on it. To take the sting away, I lick it before moving back over to the other one. The entire time Trojan is finally tasting her, I switch from her tits to her neck, finally making my way back to her mouth to kiss her senseless.

I'm swallowing her moans as her body shakes and writhes under our touch. She's close to reaching her release and I can't wait until she breaks apart so that we can switch up what we're doing. Her hand starts running down my chest and I can feel my muscles rippling under her silken hands, her nails just brushing over my skin causing me to tremor and feel like no one else has ever made me before.

Trojan taps my leg to let me know to roll to my back. I see him slipping from between her legs, so I roll to my back, pulling Darcy with me. Once she's laying fully on my body, I kiss her as I feel my brother running his hands down her back. From his movements I can tell that he's kissing his way down her body. Reaching my hand between our bodies, I line my hard cock with Darcy's entrance before slowly sinking inside her. He leaves the bed for a second to get what he needs for our girl.

Before long I hear the familiar crinkle of a condom wrapper as he crawls back up the bed. Knowing that he's about to enter our girl's ass for the first time, I stop her from moving up and down on my aching cock and hold her still. To keep her mind off of what's going on, I kiss her while moving my hands up from her hips to start playing with her amazing tits.

I know exactly when Trojan starts playing with her ass. Based on the noises I hear and his movements, I can tell that he's playing with her ass and making sure that she's lubed up really good for him. Darcy's entire body tenses up as I look over her shoulder to see him lining himself up with her forbidden zone. Quietly talking to her while Trojan uses one hand to smooth up and down her back, we get our girl to relax while he breeches her ass. We both hold still and let her adjust to us both filling her for a few minutes. We'll take all the time she needs.

"C-can y-y-you move now?" she almost pleads, looking directly in my eyes.

Nodding to Trojan, he pulls out while I remain still. Taking a few minutes to find our rhythm, we move slowly in and out of Darcy. She remains still between us as we move back and forth. The only thing I'm hearing from our girl is the little moans and mewls coming from her. She's now writhing and moving the faster that Trojan and I move. Especially once he starts adding a twist to his hips.

I reach down with one hand and I start to play with her clit. With the two of us in our girl, I know it's not going to take long for her to find her release. While I'm playing with her clit, and we're moving in and out of her, I reach my mouth up to take a nipple in my mouth. Sucking and biting it, playing her body to get the most pleasure from her.

"I can feel that you're close," Trojan grunts out, slamming into her. "Give it to us."

Darcy throws her head back when I pinch her clit again. Between Trojan's words and me, she's not going to last much longer at all. I start twisting my hips at I move my hips up and it sends our girl over the edge. She screams out our names as her release crashes over her in waves. My brother follows her over the edge and after a few more thrusts, I follow him.

The three of us are panting and sweating as we lay together in a heap of arms and legs. Trojan is the first one to move and I feel Darcy's body relax once he's fully out of her. Knowing that he's going to get her a washcloth to clean up, I run my hands up and down her body to get her breathing back under control and slide out of her. He returns after a few minutes and starts cleaning her up.

Once again, I didn't wear a condom. Unless we're taking her ass, we haven't used any protection. Darcy hasn't brought it up, but I think we need to. I honestly don't care if she gets pregnant, and I know Trojan feels the same way. She may have other ideas about it, but until we talk, then I don't know how she feels about it. Trojan and I will have to sit her down later today and talk about it with her.

"I'm going to take a shower and then head to bed," Darcy tells us, standing up and heading for the bathroom after stretching.

"We need to talk," I say, looking at Trojan. "Neither one of us use anythin' when we're with her. I don't know if she's on anythin' or how she feels about the possibility of gettin' pregnant."

"I know we don't care if she gets pregnant, you know that. We should check with her about it though," he replies, sitting down on the bed after pulling on a pair of boxers.

While we wait for her to get out of the bathroom, the two of us come up with how we're going to bring the topic up to her. Tonight, is definitely not the night for that discussion, but tomorrow when we get back home, we'll sit her down and talk to her about it.

Chapter Eight

Darcy

ONCE I WOKE UP THE MORNING AFTER my first party at the clubhouse, I had minimum time to get ready before I had to meet with Gage and the rest of the men of the Wild Kings. Including the guys from Clifton Falls and the Phantom Bastards. Now, everyone knows what's been going on with me. Crash and Trojan know and they're the last two I wanted to know.

Walking into the game room, Crash and Trojan lead me to the three chairs sitting in front of everyone else. They each take a seat on either side of me while everyone else sits down and gets ready to have their impromptu meeting. The entire time, I sat there wringing my hands and looking at my feet. Until the men grabbed my hands and held them until I was allowed to leave the room and go spend time with my girls.

"Darcy, you know why you're here. Right?" Gage asks me, sitting directly in front of me with Grim and Slim, letting his authority shine through with the tone of his voice.

Nodding my head, I look up at the three men sitting front and center. There's no way that I can calm my racing heart or my nerves, so I have to fake being confident about what I'm about to tell them. Hell, I'm exposing myself in front of all these men and letting them know things about me that no one else knows. Including my aunt. But, the faster I can get this out, the faster I can get out of this room. Away from the men that have come to mean so much to me in the few months that I've been in close contact with them, that I've been there's.

"I'm going to start at the very beginning, so it's going to take some time. Please, don't interrupt me while I get this all out," I say, picking a point in the back of the room to stare at while I go back in time and let them in on my life. "Growing up, the only person in my life that gave a damn about me was my dad. He used to take me for long rides on his bike to get me away from my mom. She was a drug addict and there were times she was down, and we would just spend the day riding. In hindsight, I think that he was trying to make sure she didn't do anything to me. There were a few times that she did beat me when he wasn't home. Anyway, he got killed one night when he went chasing after her. She was drunk and left the house. It was the worst day in my life.

"Anyway, with my dad not around to protect me, my mom went off the rails. She was even worse than before drinking and ingesting anything she could get her hands on. One day, a 'friend' of hers was at the house and she offered me to him. Just so she could get a fix. I ran out of the house as fast as I could and didn't look back. For days I slept on the street until one of my teachers stepped in and realized what was happening. The authorities came in and placed me with my aunt, Carol. She was my dad's sister and I loved her almost as much as my dad. Carol became my reason for living, doing good in school, and opening my salon."

"Everything was fine until I met a man named Glen. At first, he was everything I thought I wanted in a man. He was a gentleman, complimented me, and we had fun. He made it seem easy to fall in love with someone and I thought I was finally getting the fairytale. Instead, things changed about a year into our relationship. He became demanding, controlling, made sure I lost all my friends, and started beating on me. I left as soon as I could and didn't look back. This is what brought me to Dander Falls. No one knew me here and I thought I would be safe."

Taking a break, I sit there and get lost in the memories of my past. Trojan leans into me and places a soft kiss on my cheek. Crash squeezes my hand and wraps his arm around my shoulders. They're both showing me their silent support while I struggle to get through my past and what's been going on the past year. Nodding to my men, I begin to go on.

"About a year ago, I started receiving little notes and packages. They came on my car, at the salon, and then to my house. In the beginning, they seemed harmless and I figured someone was admiring me from afar. After a few months or so, everything started getting worse. The notes became more detailed about what this person wanted to do to me, I started getting lingerie, and then everything at my house," I tell them, finally finishing without going into too much detail.

"Well, Gage has been pretty cryptic about what happened at your house, Darcy. I think Slim and I would like to know what happened," Grim tells me, speaking with anger and pain filling his voice.

"I came home from work one day and someone had trashed my entire house. They took all of my panties and most of my toiletries. Then, there were the pictures plastered to the windows of my salon. Finally, my house was blown up," I tell them, looking between Grim and Slim.

"Nothin' else has happened?" Slim asks, rubbing his chin in thought. "I'm surprised he, or she, stopped after somethin' so big."

"There have been a few notes, but I don't know what they say," I let him know. "And it's been a few days since they sent anything."

"Alright, you go on out with your girls, Darcy," Crash tells me, leaning in to kiss me on the mouth before turning me to Trojan. "We'll be out in a little bit."

I nod and head out the door, wondering what they're going to be saying about me and the situation I find myself in. All the old ladies and Riley are sitting at a table in the corner. Based on the looks I'm getting from them, I know the inquisition out here is about to start now. So, I'll tell them everything that I just told the guys. I'm not going to leave my girls in the dark when I just spewed my guts to their men. If I wait until another day, there's no way I'll be able to tell them everything I just revealed in that room.

Bailey is the first to speak after I finish telling them all what's been going on. "I can't believe that you hid this from everyone! We could've done something to help you. Told one of our guys to help you out. Hell, we would've taken you in with us for a while."

"That's the thing, I didn't want help. At first it wasn't anything to bad. Now, I can't say the same thing. That's why I called Gage and asked for his help. Crash and Trojan just came along for the ride," I tell them, wanting and needing them to understand what's been going on and why I made the decisions I made.

"I get it," Skylar tells me, patience and understanding filling her voice. "You wanted to handle things on your own and not let anyone else in. We've all been there a time or two. At least you knew when you needed to make the necessary call and you didn't hold back."

The girls all nod their heads in agreement. I'm glad that everyone in my life now knows my secret and what's been happening to me. Now, we can all move on and hopefully find this fucker soon. Then, we can all rest and the guys and I can fall into a routine that works for us without having to look over our shoulders constantly.

The last few weeks have been absolutely crazy. Between Crash and Trojan, the salon, and hanging out with Riley, I have been going nonstop. On top of everything else, whoever is sending me packages has stepped up their game. More and more packages arrive daily to the salon along with notes. I really don't see anything that comes because my men seem to be intercepting them before they get to me. While I'm thankful that I don't have to see anything, I kind of want to know what the notes say. Shouldn't I know if I'm being threatened?

On top of all of that, the guys got me a burner phone for emergencies. Somehow, this person has gotten the number and I now get calls on a regular basis from a blocked number. Whenever I answer, no one answers. All I hear is heavy breathing and a silent background, so I can't even tell where this person is calling me from. There's no signs of anything I can let the guys know about. Well, if they knew I was getting the calls to begin with. I haven't mentioned it at all. Thankfully, I'm the one that answers the phone whenever they call the salon too.

"What's goin' on with you, firecracker?" Crash asks me, pulling me out of my head as we sit out back enjoying the sun and peace.

"What do you mean?" I ask, trying to fake innocence.

"What's up with the calls goin' to the burner? Tech has been watchin' the phone and mentioned that you've been gettin' a bunch of calls from a blocked number. Who is it?" he asks, trying not to get pissed off.

"I don't know who it is. No one is ever there when I answer," I begin. "They've been callin' the salon too."

"Why the fuck haven't you mentioned it before now?" Trojan asks, coming out the sliding door and handing us drinks before sitting down on the other side of me. "You didn't think we'd want to know this shit?"

"I know you wanted to know. I didn't really want to say anythin' until I had more information about it," I answer, throwing a little sass in my tone.

"What were you hopin' to gain as far as information goes?" Crash asks, giving me his full attention.

"I was trying to see if there was any noise in the background or anything so that I could gain an idea of where this person is when they call me," I answer, smugly while trying not to gloat at the same time.

"Let me guess, you didn't hear a fuckin' thing," Crash growls out, finally letting his anger snap. "I'm tryin' real hard not to yell at you right now, but I know that you're puttin' yourself in danger right now. You don't even realize it, do you?"

"How do you figure that I'm putting myself in danger. It's the burner phone you guys gave me. I thought you couldn't track it?" I question, taking a minute to think about my actions regarding the phone calls.

"If this person can get your number, you don't think they can figure out where you're goin'? Where you're at durin' the day?" Trojan roars, practically scaring the shit out of me with the tone and loudness of his voice.

"I wasn't thinking about that. I just wanted to prove that I can help you guys. And that this person isn't going to scare me away from anyone or anything that I have in my life," I tell my amazingly overprotective men. "I'm sorry I didn't think about the danger I was putting myself in." I continue, tears starting to slowly roll down my face.

Crash and Trojan look at one another. I can see the regret and pain flash across their faces at how harsh they're being with me. This only leads to more tears running down my face. I don't want them to be upset or regret how they're acting with me. In reality, I know that they're trying to protect me, and I've been keeping things from them about what's going on. This is only going to hinder them in their attempt to figure out who is after me.

"I'm sorry guys, I was just trying to take care of this myself. I'm so used to worrying about myself lately, that I forget I have you two now," I tell them, standing up to go in the house and get a few minutes by myself.

"Don't you cry firecracker. We didn't mean to take this shit out on you. We're just worried for your safety," Crash tells me. "After all this time, we finally got you to be ours. Trojan and I don't want to lose you. Or have anythin' happen to you."

"Exactly. We know that you're independent, strong, and you want to take care of this yourself. Unfortunately, you're stuck with us now and we want to make sure that it lasts a lifetime. Just know that when we get upset, when we yell, and when we get pissed as fuck, it's never aimed at you. We're just tryin' to hold it together right now. Everythin' will calm down once we have this twatwaffle and there's not a threat against you anymore," Trojan says, leaning in close to me and planting a breathtaking kiss on my open mouth. Crash follows suit and I'm left wanting while they go in to make dinner for us.

Trojan

I can't believe that our girl has kept the fact that she's been getting random phones calls on the burner and to the salon without saying a word about them. There's no way that this asshole should've had a way to get the number. Not even everyone in the club has it. The girls in Clifton Falls don't know it. As a matter of fact, the only ones that know the number are Crash, Gage, Tech, and myself. The only reason that Tech has it, is so he can do what he has to if we ever need to trace the number or view the activity on it. Now, we have a new problem that we have to deal with; finding out how the number of a burner phone got in the hands of a fucking psychopath.

"We're goin' to get you a different phone, firecracker," I tell her, making sure she knows that we have to step up the game and put more men on her. We also have to make sure that you keep the phone off until you absolutely need it. I'm not sure how that's goin' to work, but we'll figure it out."

"I'm goin' to call Gage and let him know what's goin' on. I'll let you know what he says," Crash tells us, kissing Darcy again before heading into the house.

"I think I'm going to go clean something," she tells us, walking past Crash and into the house.

Crash looks at me and sits his ass back down in the chair since our girl isn't out here anymore. Placing the call, I watch him as he explains what's been going on with Darcy and the phone calls. Before I can hear what Gage has to say, a nose turns makes me turn my head towards the door. Darcy is standing there; her face pale and a look of pure fear shines bright on her face.

"What's the matter?" I ask, standing up quickly and putting my hand at the back of my pants where my gun rests. We've all started carrying since this shit has been going on with her.

"I-I-I didn't expect to see a room filled with guns. There's so many in there," she says, heading back inside and towards the room we share.

"Fuck!" Crash mutters, thinking this was the last thing that she was going to find. He must have forgotten to lock the door when he grabbed his gun this morning.

Following her into the room, I see her sitting on the edge of the bed, starting at absolutely nothing. She's in shock with the shit she's seen. I have to make her understand what the guns are all there for. Most of them are Crash's for when the military calls him to do a job for them. It's nothing more than that. Well, along with a few of our personal guns we both have.

"Baby, I get that seein' that room is a complete surprise. You need to understand what's in that room though," I begin, kneeling down in front of her so she can see my eyes. "Most of the guns in that room are for Crash when he gets called out. He chooses them based on the job they call about."

She sits there and takes a few minutes to process what I've just told her. I know it's a lot to take in for her. Maybe there's something else we can do about it. Something to make her feel more comfortable around guns. I'll run my idea by Crash and see what he says. I think it's going to be the only thing that's going to help her out.

"Instead of cleanin', why don't you go relax in a hot bath? It will help you relax. I'm goin' to go talk to Crash and we'll be in shortly," I tell her, standing up to lead her into the bathroom.

As she strips down, I run the bath to the temperature that I know she loves. Adding bubble bath, I let the tub fill as she steps in and sinks down into the hot water. For a minute, all I do is stand there and stare at the woman that is capturing my heart more and more every day we spend together. Before I strip down and join her, I leave the room. So, we can easily hear her, I make sure the bedroom door is open and the bathroom door is left open a crack. I'm sure that Crash is already inside waiting for me to return.

Walking into the kitchen, I grab a beer and make my way back into the living room to talk with Crash. Just as I sit down, he shoves his phone back in his pocket. I can see the anger still radiating off him in waves. There's also concern for Darcy. I'm sure he feels horrible that she saw the one room we never wanted her to see. At least for now.

"She okay?" he asks, not letting go of his concern for our girl.

"Yeah. I got her in a bath relaxin'. We need to talk about that. I have an idea and I think we need to push this," I begin, letting the idea sink further into my head about how to help her. "I think we need to take her to the range and show her how to shoot. Maybe then she won't be afraid to go near the room we've taken over for guns."

Crash mulls over the idea for a few minutes. I can see the wheels spinning in his mind about my idea. He's the perfect one to teach her everything she needs to know about using a gun. From tearing it down and cleaning it to actually shooting one. I'll be there every step of the way, but it will be better coming from him. Hell, maybe we should include Riley in this so she's comfortable around it all too.

After a few minutes, Crash looks at me and I can see that he's going to go for the idea. There's a light in his eyes and it's a way that he can open up a little and share something of himself with our girl. Part of me doesn't want it to come to this, but I think it will be good for everyone involved.

"I'm down. Do you think she's actually goin' to go for it though?" he asks, hesitation firmly set on his face at the prospect that she won't want to do this.

"We might have to talk to her more than once about it, but I think she'll see reason. Let's let her relax for a little bit and then we'll talk to her about it. Why don't I call Gage and see if we can get Riley on board with this? Maybe then it will be easier to talk Darcy into doing it," I tell him, seeing the hope flair once more.

Pulling out my phone, I place a call to our President and let him in on my idea. At first, he's hesitant, but the idea quickly grows on him. We have the perfect area already set up behind the clubhouse, so no one will ever know what's going on. Gage tells me that he'll talk to Riley about it and get her on board so that we can do this for them. There's no way that we can be with them constantly, not even the prospects can be with them all the time. This way, we'll know that they have the tools to try to protect themselves if the occasion ever arises.

Telling Crash Gage's response, I slide my phone back in my pocket and sit back and enjoy the rest of my beer. This way we can give her time to unwind after the shock of seeing a ton of guns in one room. I'm sure that she's never seen as many as we have in the house. And, that's not the only room we have them in. There's guns in almost every room of the house. She doesn't need to know that at this point in time. Eventually, we'll tell her.

We're sitting down for dinner, after preparing a meal at home and I look at Crash. The time for the conversation about teaching her to shoot has come. He nods his head, so I can take the lead on this one. Setting my beer down, I clear my throat and put all of my focus on her.

"Darcy, we need to talk to you about somethin'," I start out, making sure I have her full attention. "We want to take you and Riley to the range we have behind the clubhouse. Crash will teach you everythin' you need to know about guns."

Darcy sits in stunned silence and I can see the shock of the idea slowly start to fade. There's something else brightening her eyes and I'm not quite sure what it is. Hopefully, we won't have to fight her on this.

"Okay," she says, completely unsure of what she's about to get into, but willing to take a chance anyway.

"Thank you, firecracker," Crash tells her, leaning forward to kiss her temple showing his appreciation.

Finishing our meal, Darcy and I cleanup while Crash goes in to take a phone call. I'm sure that he's getting ready to head back out on a job. The only time he ever hides is club business or a call from the military. If it were club business, he'd stay outside while we were in the kitchen. Since he's gone in a different room entirely, I'm going to guess that he'll be heading back out of town to do a job. This sucks, but it's who he is and what he does.

Crash

We no sooner finish dinner and my phone rings. Looking at the blocked number, I know already who is calling. My old boss always calls from a blocked number when he needs me to go do a job. While the timing isn't ideal, I know that I have no choice in the matter. Even though I'm not truly with the military anymore, I'll always go when my old commander calls me. He saved me in more ways than one and I'll be forever grateful to him.

"Jim, always good to hear from you," I answer the phone, walking into my gun room.

"No, it's not," he replies, laughter filling the phone on his end.

"What can I do for you?" I ask, wanting to get the job description so I can find out when I'm leaving as soon as possible.

"We need your help. Got a guy we've been tracking for months now. He always manages to escape at the last second," he tells me, his tone going serious. "There's reason to believe that he's working with a militant group and we need to get him as soon as possible to find out what he knows."

"When do I leave?" I ask, needing to know.

"At first light. Need you to meet me at the office so I can give you more information. Not doing it over the phone," he tells me, knowing that we never discuss anything over the phone.

"I'll see you in a few hours," I tell him, hanging up and deciding what I need to do right now.

For now, the only thing I can think about is spending time with Darcy. Hopefully Trojan won't mind if I spend some one-on-one time with her before I leave. Whenever I go on a mission for Jim, I always act like I'm not going to make it back. This is something that I need to talk to Trojan about before I leave too. He needs to know what I have planned and that he's going to need to be there for our girl.

Walking back out in the kitchen, I see them laughing and doing the dishes. Trojan senses me and turns to face me. He can tell based on the look on my face that I'm going to be leaving. So, he kisses our girl on the head and disappears. Based on hearing his bike rev outside, he's going to give us some private time. Right now, I need to lose myself in our girl. Forget everything for a while before she goes to bed, and I walk away from her for a little while. This time, I have something to come back for, but walking away in the first place is going to be hard as fuck.

"I need to talk to you baby," I tell her, grabbing her hand and leading her into the living room.

After getting comfortable on the couch, Darcy turns to me and waits for me to tell her what's going on. This is a lot harder than I thought it would be. She wasn't ours when I had to leave for this shit before. Now, I don't know that I'm going to be focusing on my mission when I know that someone's after her. Fuck, I don't want her worrying about me either.

"I got a call and I need to head out for a while. I'm not sure how long I'll be gone for either," I tell her, trying to focus on her and not hide because I don't want to do this anymore. There's too much to live for here now.

"Where are you going?" she asks, her voice laced with worry already.

"That's the thing, I can't tell you. I'm not doin' anythin' wrong, it's for the military. That's all I can really say. Just know that as soon as I can, I'll be back her with you," I say, grabbing her hand and holding it tightly in mine.

"Will you be safe?" she asks, my safety her number one concern. "Hell, will you be able to call us at all?"

"I don't know if I'll be able to call this time. Sometimes I can and sometimes I can't. It just depends on the job and where I am," I answer her honestly.

"Okay. Well, there's nothing I can do. So, I'll miss you, but there's nothing I can do about it. What about your work for the club?" she asks, wanting to know as much information as she can.

"They'll cover it. This isn't the first time, but it might be the last one," I reply, thinking of the long-term plans we want to make with Darcy.

"Why? Just because I'm in the picture now doesn't mean you have to change your life. If you want to keep working for the military, then do it. I don't want either one of you to give up anything for me," she tells me, leaning in and resting her head on my shoulder.

I wrap my arms around her and pull her even closer to me. There's nowhere else I'd rather be right now. I'm upset that Trojan isn't here with us, but I'm thankful he's giving us this time together. It's something I need before leaving for however long. Hopefully it's not as long as in the past. More than once, I've been gone for over a month. I don't want that to happen this time. So, hopefully I can find the guy and get back home.

Standing up, I lead her into the bedroom. Yeah, there's been a time or two we've taken Darcy in the living room, along with other rooms in the house. Tonight, I want it to be somewhat special. Not just for her, but for me too. I need to take this memory with me. Hell, there's been a ton of memories we've been making, but I need more. There's never a guarantee with anything and I'm going to be alone on this mission.

Once we get in the bedroom, I turn and face my girl. Slowly, I start to strip her. There's no need to rush. If Trojan gets home, he can join in. For now, I want to take my time and devour her body. So, I take one piece of clothing off at a time and kiss my way to the next item for removal. Darcy is standing there making noises and opening up her body to me. I love the fact that she is trusting us and comfortable enough to open herself completely to us. She's changed so much since we've made her ours.

As soon as she's bared to me, I stand back up and start to remove my own clothes. It doesn't take me as long, especially with her helping. The only time she stops is when she wants to rub her hands across my body. I freeze when she leans forward and licks a path from my chest to my aching and hard cock. Sinking to her knees, she licks the precum leaking steadily from me before taking as much of me into her warm, wet mouth.

I sink my fingers into her hair after pulling out the hair tie holding it away from her face. I'm not going to use her hair to control her movements or pace, I just want to feel her silky strands wrapped around my hands. This show is all hers to control. Growing even bolder, Darcy uses one of her hands to gently roll my balls as she sucks and licks my cock. My eyes roll to the back of my head at the feelings she's making me feel. I've never felt anything like I do when we're with Darcy. Honestly, this is the first time that it hasn't been both of us with her.

Knowing that I'm not going to last long if she keeps going, I pull her off of me and stand her up. Leading her to the bed, I lay her down and climb between her creamy thighs. I spread them with my shoulders and lift one over my shoulders to lay across my back. Taking my first lick, I swipe my tongue from her opening to her clit. Darcy's back arches off the bed and I continue to take my fill of her sweet pussy. I'll remember the taste that is all her while I'm gone.

Adding in my fingers, I suck her clit into my mouth and bite down on it before laving it with my tongue. My fingers continue to thrust in and out of her willing body as I kiss and lick every inch of her I can reach, continuously going back to work her clit. When I know she's close to going over the edge, I pull back. Doing this several times, I know I'm driving her crazy. She's not going to cum on anything other than my cock though.

Finally sliding up her body, I wrap my arms around her and roll her over so that she's on top of me. Her taking the lead and taking what she wants is something that we're trying to work on. She needs to learn that she can initiate anything at any given time with us. We're not going to be the only ones to start something and she's going to be the one riding my cock tonight. Everything is at her pace and what she wants to do.

"You take the lead baby," I tell her. "And don't forget what I want you callin' out when you cum all over my cock."

"Brent," she says breathlessly, rubbing herself up and down my cock without putting it inside her.

Finally, she pushes her body off of mine just enough to slide my cock inside her drenched pussy. Sliding down, I hold my breath as she takes her time filling herself up with me. Once she's fully on me, Darcy sits still and doesn't move for a minute. I'm not sure if she's getting used to me, or thinking that Trojan is going to be joining in. Maybe she's just used to waiting for one of us to lean over her.

"I don't want to move," she finally tells me, with tears shimmering in her eyes. "If I do, then this gets over with sooner or later and you leave."

"Baby, I'll be back, and we'll have all the time in the world to do this as much as you want," I tell her, grabbing on to her hips to encourage her to move.

"Promise me?" she asks, starting to raise herself off me.

Nodding my head is all I can manage right now. The feeling of her wrapped around me is almost my undoing. It's never been like this with anyone. Maybe it feels this way with her because I love her and she's the one I was always meant to be with. Trojan and I are meant to be with her for whatever time we have left on this earth.

Darcy riding my cock is the sexiest thing I've ever seen. She's letting loose and not caring about what we think she looks like. So, I reach up and pull one of her nipples into my mouth. Sucking on the swollen tip, her movements become just a little bit faster and harder. She's chasing her release and bringing me closer to finding mine at the same time.

"I'm so close," she murmurs, letting herself go and adding a twist to her hips every time she slides down me.

"Get it baby," I tell her, feeling that all familiar tingle in the base of my spine starting.

Grabbing her hips, I help her movements go harder. Darcy puts her hands on my chest to hold herself up away from my body as she throws her head back. I can feel the strands of her hair brush against my thighs with her movements. Reaching between us, I rub circles around her clit, making sure to add a little bit more pressure each time she bottoms out.

"Brent!" she yells out, clamping down on me as waves of her release wash over her and tighten her body up.

Within three more thrusts into her body, I feel my release begin and call out her name. I pull her hair and bring her head down so that I can kiss her through my release. Stilling within her body, I let it flow from me and begin to rub my hands up and down her back. Darcy collapses on me and tries to get her breathing back under control.

"Let's go take a shower," I tell her, once she's calmed down and can breathe normally again.

I groan as she slowly slides off me. she climbs off the bed and I watch her ass sway from side to side as she makes her way into the bathroom. Following her into the next room, she gets the water how hot she wants it and lets is warm up before stepping in and under the spray. It cascades down her body and I can't help but want to follow the path of every drop down her delectable body.

Instead of standing here and watching her, I climb in the shower and take the bottle of shampoo from her hands. I massage it into her hair and then grab the shower head, so I can rinse it out of her hair. Repeating the same process with the conditioner, I grab the body wash, so I can run my hands all over her body. As soon as I'm done, I go to grab my shampoo and she takes the bottle from me.

"I want to take care of you," she tells me and motions me to sit on the bench seat, so she can easily reach my head.

I relish the feeling of her hands massaging my head and making sure my hair is washed. Standing up, I stand under the shower head to rinse the soap from my hair. As I'm doing that, she grabs the body wash I use and begins to wash my body. Darcy's hands on my body feels better than almost anything I've ever felt before. The only thing better is when I'm deep in her tight pussy.

Once we're done washing up, I stand behind her under the hot spray for a few minutes, just holding her body to mine. There's nothing sexual in the way that I'm holding her right now. With me leaving, I need to hold her close and get all the time with her that I can until she falls asleep in my arms. This is what I love most about our time together. Especially when Trojan is with us and we have her body between ours.

"Let's go to bed," I tell her, shutting the water off and grabbing a towel to dry her off.

Darcy lets me take care of her and then gives me the same treatment. I lead her into the bed and we fix the blankets before I help her climb in. Once I know she's settled in, I walk through the house naked to lock the place up tight. Trojan is sitting in the living room watching some show until I walk in. He shuts the television off and helps me check everything before we make our way into our girl.

She's in the middle of the bed and her eyelids are fluttering shut. I know that she's trying to stay awake as long as she can, but she's not winning the battle. We climb in beside her and wrap her in our arms. Just as she closes her eyes and lets out a sigh of contentment, I whisper to her.

"I love you. I'll be back as soon as I can," I tell her, knowing that I have to be up in a few hours to pack my bags and head out. There's no way that I'll be able to leave if she wakes up.

Settling down next to her, I wrap my body around her and feel Trojan do the same on his side. I look over her body at him and communicate that he needs to be on his game and take care of our girl while I'm not around. He nods at me and his gaze assures me that he'll do what he needs to do to protect her. I've already talked to Gage about adding someone on her with my brother.

My eyes soon close and I dream of the life that I want to come back to. I want to move things along faster with our girl. We need to do something special for her and make sure that everyone knows that she's ours. I'll place the call as soon as I land to get her rag made. I want it here when I get back, so we can give it to her.

Chapter Nine

Trojan

CRASH HAS BEEN GONE FOR A FEW days now. Darcy isn't taking it well, and I'm starting to lose my mind as to how to get her out of the funk that she seems to have fallen into. She goes to work, comes home, and tries to put up a good front for me. We talk and laugh, but her heart isn't in it. She's missing him and worried that something is going to happen to him. Plus, she's been even more tired than usual and goes to bed almost as soon as we walk through the door. Tonight, I'm going to make it all about us though.

I'm cooking her dinner and setting a romantic table, complete with candles. Riley helped me find some candle holders that will work outside and are beautiful, her words, not mine. Then I'm going to spend the night ravishing her body. Crash got his one-on-one time with her, and tonight is mine. I'm going to make the most of it.

Don't get me wrong, Darcy doesn't care about one of us more than the other. I'm just the one here while he's on a mission. It's not wrong for her to miss him, I'd be worried if she didn't care anything about him not being around here on a daily basis. She's proving to me just how much she does love us, even if she can't say the words yet. We've both told her as she was falling asleep on a few different occasions. The only reason we're not ready to tell her when she's coherent is because we don't want to scare her away from us.

"You ready to head out?" I ask Darcy as she walks from the bathroom while I've been sitting on the bed playing around on my phone.

"Yeah. Wilma will be at the salon a little after nine. Riley is going to be a little late today, so I need to be there for her color and cut," she answers, picking up her bag and moving to walk past me.

I grab her around the waste and pull her into me. Right now, I need to feel her in my arms and let her know that I'm here for her. If she wants to yell, scream, cry, or just talk about missing Crash, she needs to know she's not alone. Burying my face in her neck, I breathe in her scent. It's like a calming balm to my soul. She makes us want to be better men for her, for our future, and for anyone that comes along to join our family. That doesn't mean we're going to quit the club and what we have to do as part of that. What it means is that we want to belong to her, not worry about loose pussy throwing themselves at us. They don't mean shit to us and we don't even look at them. Haven't for a long time since we first met her.

"He's goin' to be fine baby. Crash will be back before you know it. He'll be fine, he always is. If there's one thing he knows, it how to do his job and this time will be no different." I tell her, meaning every word of it. "Besides, he has somethin' worth comin' home for now. Let's use this time to spend together and not worry about anythin' else."

"How do you know that he's going to be okay? This isn't some game he's playing!" she snaps at me, her carefully controlled composure finally slipping and letting her get all of her fears out. "I wasted so much time denying what we all wanted, and we'll never get that time back."

Darcy is now crying on my shoulder and I can't help but wrap my arms even tighter around her. She needs to get this shit out and I'm more than happy to take all the pain from her. I'm here to make sure that she doesn't go in her own head with anything and that she talks to me, us when Crash is home, about whatever is going through her pretty head. She doesn't need anything else to weigh her down. Tears don't need to leave her beautiful eyes unless they're tears of happiness.

My hope is that as soon as we figure out who is after her that she doesn't ever have another care in the world to darken her days. She needs to be filled with light and true happiness. If we can make sure that happens every single day, we'll both die happy men. It's been said before by other brothers that their girl is the light to their darkness, they brighten their world and make them whole. I never truly understood it until we met Darcy. Now, I see what they mean, and I know that we're going to do everything in our power to make sure she stays that way.

Heading out to my bike that's parked in the garage, I climb on before Darcy throws her bag over her shoulder and climbs on behind me. Once I know that she's got her helmet on and her arms are wrapped around me, I start my other girl up and we make our way into town. The drive is short, too short for my liking. I'd ride all day long with her body wrapped around mine. In fact, Crash and I were talking about taking her away on a trip. It will be just the three of us and we'll find somewhere secluded. I think I know the perfect spot and I'm going to make sure we make this trip a reality when my brother gets home.

Pulling up to the salon, nothing looks out of place. Well, other than the vase filled with flowers sitting in front of the door. Darcy's body tightens, and I know that she's thinking the same thing I am; that they're from her stalker. Tech is doing everything in his power to find out who this is and how they're getting all the information they are about her phone number and where she is on a daily basis. Yeah, the hours of the salon are posted by the door, but I'm sure that he knows wherever she is when she's not here too.

"Stay by the bike. Shadow, make sure you stay with her and don't let anyone else near her," I ground out, letting my unhappiness and uneasiness with this situation run rampant.

Walking up to the door, I take my time in case there's anything else going on that I don't see right this second. We honestly have no clue what this sick fuck is going to do. Before I touch anything around the flowers, I take a look all around the area. Slowly bending down, I see that there's a card on the flowers and I carefully pluck it from the holder before taking my knife from my pocket.

Opening the small envelope, I peel the card out of it and read what it says. My blood is boiling, and I want to shred everything around me. I won't though because it's her salon and I won't destroy what she's worked so hard to build. So, I reign that shit in and bite my tongue. Turning around, I see Darcy with concern written all over her face and I want to reassure her, but the words on the card are making it hard for me to do that. I have to get this over to Tech and have him hack into the florist's computer system to see if we can find anything out about who ordered the flowers.

"What's it say?" Darcy asks, striding over to me with more bravado then she truly feels. There's a slight tremble to her lips and I can see her hands shaking, letting me know that she's freaked the fuck out right now.

"You don't want to know baby," I tell her, trying to slide the card in the back pocket of my jeans. I don't need to read the card again, the words are already burned into my brain. "I'm goin' to get this over to Tech later on to see what he can find out."

Darcy stands there with one hand on her hip and the other hand stretched out towards me. There's no way in hell that she's going to give up until she knows what the card says. So, without truly wanting to, I pull it out of my pocket and hand it to her. While she's pulling it out of the envelope, I wrap my arms around her and make sure that I'm there for her. As soon as the words reach her, I know. Her skin instantly pales and the shaking and trembling from moments before becomes a million times worse. I'm truly terrified that she's going to pass out from the look of her alone, not to mention all the other signs she's giving off right this second.

The card reads:

I told you that you were mine. You don't want to listen, but you'll have no choice in the matter soon. It's only a matter of time before you're where you belong. Not being the slut that you seem to have become.

Taking the card back from her, I hand everything to Shadow. My main focus has to be on Darcy right now.

"Get this to Gage. Now!" I growl out, needing him to know that he needs to get on this now. "Tell him to call me as soon as he has it in his hands."

Shadow scurries to his bike after grabbing everything from me. Peeling out, he makes his way to the clubhouse as fast as he can. This is why he makes a great prospect and he'll be a great brother when he gets patched in. I'm sure that will be soon, there's no reason why it shouldn't happen very soon.

"Baby, I need you to look at me," I tell Darcy, pulling back as much as she'll let me. "Nothin' is goin' to happen to you. Now, before Wilma gets here and flips her shit, let's get inside and get done what you need to. I'll help you any way I can."

Darcy nods her head, takes a minute to compose herself, and hands me the keys to unlock the door. As soon as we get in, she turns the lights on, sets her bag behind the counter, and sets about making sure everything is ready to go. I turn on the music then begin to do a quick sweep of the salon, and get rid of the flowers so there's not a reminder of them around her while she keeps herself busy and not thinking about what just happened. Eventually she's going to want to talk about it, and I'll be there for her. Until then, I'm going to let her stay occupied and keep a close eye on her.

As I'm making my way back to the front of the salon, I see Wilma make her way to Darcy's station. She's setting her stuff down as my girl makes her way out and tells her to take a seat at the sink. Wilma does as she's asked, and it doesn't seem like she's her usual self today either. I hope everything is okay with her. It's not like she would tell us if something were wrong. Much like all the other women in my life, Wilma wants to handle things alone and not ask for help. I'll keep an eye on her and make sure that nothing's going on with her that she needs help with.

I listen to the two women banter back and forth, amazed at how calm Darcy is right now. She's putting on an amazing front for one of her favorite people. The last thing she wants to do is make the woman sitting in her chair worry about her. My attention is pulled from the women as someone else enters the salon. It's a delivery guy and I stand up to take the package from his hands. Signing the clipboard, I nod my thanks and watch him head back out the door.

"You expectin' anythin' babe?" I ask, walking closer to Darcy holding the package in my hand.

"Nope. Unless Riley ordered something. You can open it if you want to," she tells me, barely looking in my direction. I'm sure it has more to do with the flowers that were left outside.

Going around the corner so that Darcy can't see what's inside the box if it's anything menacing, I grab the scissors from the desk and carefully open the box in front of me. once I have the sides open, I don't rip the paper out of the way, I peel it back one layer at a time until I see the contents. This has my stomach turning more than the flowers or anything else does. Inside the box, I see more pictures of Darcy, mainly at our home, a piece of lingerie I'd love to see her in if the circumstances were different, and something that looks like blood throughout the entire box. There's a note on top and I'm sure that I don't want to know what it says, but I'm going to have to regardless.

I walk over to the first station and grab a pair of gloves before returning to the counter. After putting them on, I pick the note up by the corner of it and open it, so I can read what's written this time. It has my blood boiling once again and I can see nothing but red. This motherfucker's time is limited and grows that way with every package, picture, note, and other bullshit he sends to our girl.

I told you I'm coming for you. You have taken things to a whole new level by continuously throwing away what I give you. Now, I'm coming for you and your men won't be able to stop me. They won't see me coming at all. Bitch, you're mine!

What the fuck does this scumbag think she was going to do? Keep everything he has sent her on a pedestal or something like that. I don't fucking think so. I'm going to have to call this shit in and make sure that there's extra guys here. There's also going to need to be extra guys at the house. Darcy won't ever be alone enough for this maniac to get his hands on her. I don't care if I have to go to the bathroom with her to make sure that he never gets his hands on her. Ever.

Looking over at Darcy and Wilma, I see them laughing and being carefree. Maybe Wilma was just tired or something when she came in. I'm not really sure, but I'm going to keep an eye on her. This is something I'm willing to do for Darcy because I know that Wilma is close to her heart and she wouldn't want anything to happen to her at all. Maybe I can get one of the other prospects on her to make sure nothing is going on. Shadow is definitely going to be on Darcy.

I take the package before my girl can see it and dispose of it. She's already had her nerves set on edge with the flowers, and I know this will send her right over that edge. Honestly, I'm glad that Crash isn't here right now because he wouldn't be able to contain his raw fury and aggression at not knowing how to get this person. He's probably hiding right in plain sight with none of us the wiser. That's usually what happens. It would just help if we had some sort of idea as to what direction to look in.

"Where did you go?" Darcy asks, as I make my way back in to find her standing at the register talking to Wilma.

"I had to take care of somethin'. Trust me, I didn't leave you alone, I was just outback," I answer, striding behind the counter and wrap my arms around her.

I need to have her in my embrace to ensure that she's not anywhere other than right here with me. At the blink of an eye, anything can happen, and the people you love the most can be taken from you. Ma is the perfect example of that happening. Not a single one of us had an inkling that anything remotely like that was going to happen. With her in my arms, she feels real, alive, safe, and I feel like I'm home. Darcy in my line of sight keeps me grounded.

"Everything okay, babe?" she asks, calling me babe for the first time. I'm floored and can't respond a few minutes.

"Yeah. I'm perfect." I reply, kissing the top of her head and going back to sit on the couch at the front of the salon so she can finish up with Wilma and take the walk-in.

Pulling out my phone, I text Gage and let him know of the newest threat against Darcy. And read the message that he sent as soon as Shadow delivered the card from earlier. He's got Tech doing his thing and is looking into the florist to see if he can pull the records to see when the flowers were bought. If he finds out that the person was a dumbass and used a credit card to pay, we can hopefully figure out who he is. Then, it's just a matter of getting our hands on him and torturing the fuck out of this douche canoe before finding him a new home. One that's six feet under.

Gage immediately responds and tells me that he's going to have someone come pick the newest package up immediately. I'm glad I put it in a bag before setting it behind the dumpster out back. The door, that you would miss since it's designed to look exactly like part of the wall of the building is locked and I've triple checked that shit. I pocket my phone and sit back to watch Darcy do her thing. Just before she's finished up with her current client, Riley comes breezing in the door winded and looking flustered.

"Is everything okay here?" she asks, sitting down next to me and whispering her question.

"Yeah, why?" I ask, not sure how much she knows and not wanting to give her any more information than she already has.

"I was in Gage's office talking to him about something personal when Shadow came running in," she tells me, getting up and heading toward the back to take care of her things.

"It's gettin' handled," I tell her retreating back.

Sitting back and relaxing as much as I can right now, I watch the girls and keep an eye on the traffic outside of the salon. It's just a matter of time before we leave for lunch and I plan on keeping her safe surrounded by a group of us. Before I can begin figuring out a plan, Gage plops his ass down next to me and looks at me for a few minutes. I know he can tell that I'm on edge and ready to jump at anything.

"You good?" he asks, giving me quiet reassurance that everything is being taken care of regarding this.

"As good as I can be. Especially with Crash bein' gone right now. It's like this guy knows that he's not here and is steppin' up his game or some shit," I answer, finally giving a voice to my fears without scaring Darcy in the process.

"I get the same feelin'. You looked deep in thought when I sat down, what's up?" he asks, moving a little bit closer so no one can overhear us.

"Well, Darcy is goin' to want to go to lunch and I don't want her out there without guys on her. I'm not goin' to be able to protect her on my own if we walk to the diner," I tell him, wanting to know what he thinks. "Granted, I can protect my girl, but there's too many unknowns out there."

"I'll still be here. And, I'll have Shadow and Steel go with us. We'll close the salon up for the hour and take both girls with us," he tells me, letting me know what's going to happen.

We're all on red alert now and he wants to protect Riley as much as I want to shelter Darcy from anything bad happening to her. Now that the lunch situation is taken care of, I let myself relax just a tiny bit, but keep my guard up. Riley, Darcy, and the client's in their chairs are talking and making the day go by faster for themselves. Gage and I spend the rest of the morning talking about business and how we're going to proceed when we finally catch the scum we're trying so hard to locate right now.

Darcy

My nerves are absolutely shot after seeing the card that was attached to the flowers this morning. I know that Trojan got another delivery from this insane person, but I'm not asking anything about it. Honestly, I don't want to know anything about it right now. Eventually I know that my curiosity will win out, but all I want to focus on is getting through the rest of the day. Everything about it seems off right now and I'm not sure why.

When Wilma came in this morning, she laughed and talked to me, but she didn't raise her normal amount of hell. On a weekly basis she gives the guys hell and today she didn't even ask why Crash wasn't here. We were both putting up fronts to make sure that the other one thought we were okay, but it couldn't be farther from the truth in either case. I'm not going to pry into her personal life though. I will, however, mention it to Trojan and see what he says.

Riley is in the middle of a perm and there's no one else in here right now. Knowing that I need a few minutes to myself, I make my way out back and through the door. No one will know that I'm out here since we don't even park out back.

We're always on the street. I did knock on the door to the bathroom and let my man know where I'd be. Gage had to step out for a few minutes and I don't know if a prospect or other member is out there.

Leaning against the wall, I take a few deep breaths of the fresh air. It does nothing to help the tension ease from my body, but it does give me a second of peace. I'm just sorry that I didn't know that I would come to regret my decision. Within a matter of seconds, I feel a hand cover my mouth at the same time a needle pinches the skin in my neck. My body starts to feel heavy and I can't seem to keep my eyes open as whatever was injected into me takes over my entire body from my head to my toes.

Just before I pass completely out, I can faintly hear a few things. The first one is Trojan screaming at the top of his lungs moments before a bullet whizzes past us. Then I hear that I'm going to pay for my man shooting whoever has me and the bullet grazing his arm. It was intentional to hit him there because I know my men are both excellent shots. I've been to the range with them and they don't miss their intended target. I'm thrown into some sort of vehicle as my eyes close.

Starting to stir, my head feels fuzzy and I'm disoriented. As I slowly sit up on the bed, I try to open my eyes enough to take in my surroundings. At this point, I'm not sure what the hell is going on, I don't remember anything, but once my eyes open enough to get a quick glance around, everything comes rushing back to me. The drugs being shot into my neck, being kidnapped, Trojan's pained screams filled with agony and defeat, him shooting whoever had me, and being told I was going to pay.

Almost immediately I become alert and take in my surroundings. Shock is the biggest feeling consuming me right now. Wherever I am is designed to look just like my bedroom before my house was blown up. Right down to the furniture and bedding. Everything is in the same place as where I had it in my old room. There's a few doors lining the walls and I can almost guarantee that I know what each one is without moving off the bed. The door directly across from the bed I'm currently occupying will be a closet. To the left of the dresser is another door that will lead to the hallway, and the door to the left of the bed will be a bathroom.

I stand on shaky legs and test my theory out. Opening the door, I believe is a closet proves my instincts to be right. Remembering that all of my panties were stolen, I take a chance and open the top drawer of the dresser and almost cry out seeing all my panties. Not knowing where this sick bastard is has me remaining silent and not falling in a heap on the floor. I would try opening the door, but there are a few things holding me back. The first one is being pretty sure that it's going to be locked. If it's not locked, I don't have the first clue as to who has me right now. So, I don't want to run into them any sooner than I absolutely have to. Maybe I'll check door number three before coming back to door number two. Walking over to what I assume is the bathroom, I fling the door open and peer around the doorway. Inside is the exact replica of my old bathroom, including my toiletries. Why I'm surprised I honestly don't know. Everything else in here is a version of my old life. The life I led before my men came into my life and swept me off my feet.

Thinking of Trojan going crazy and Crash not even being home stills my body and fills me with heartbreak and an overwhelming urge to do whatever I have to in order to get back to them. They are the ones that fill my life with meaning and give me a purpose for getting out of my shell and adapting to the new lifestyle that I'll be living. Trojan's scream is on a loop in my head and I know that he's going to be filled with rage and that he let me down by not protecting me. Well, I'm the one that chose to go outside alone instead of waiting two minutes for him to get done in the bathroom. Crash is going to be in the same exact boat when he finally finds out what happened to me. I don't want him to leave what he's doing just to come home, but if I know one thing about my man is that I am always going to be his number one priority. The same goes for Trojan. Let's just hope that I can find a way to survive until they find me.

These thoughts are what lead to my decision to try to open the door that I know will lead to a hallway. If this room is anything to go by, I wonder if this psycho fuck designed the entire house to mirror mine. I'm not sure who would do something like that, but this room fills me with dread and a desire to puke. Well, I'm not sure if that's the drugs wearing off, this room, or something else. I've been feeling like shit for the past two weeks. This morning and yesterday morning were the first time I actually threw up.

Anyway, back to the task at hand. Slowly inching my way over to the door, I have yet to try, I put my ear against it and listen for a few minutes. My heart is racing and beating so hard, I'm sure that whoever else is here will be able to hear it from wherever in the house they are. When I'm positive I don't hear anything, I raise my shaking hand and grab onto the handle. Turning it as slowly as I can, I meet resistance and know without a doubt that it's locked. Fuck!

With no other choice, and a huge feeling of being tired consuming me, I make my way back to the bed and lay down. I'm sure there are worse places I could be right now, but I'm still leery and going to try to stay awake for as long as I can. The last thing I need is to fall asleep and have the devil himself haunt me when I'm awake. That's what's been happening since this shit started. Now, it's reached the peak and I can only hope that I'm found before irreparable damage is done to me.

I'm not sure how long I've been in this room, but I must have fallen asleep at some point without meaning to. The bed being kicked is what eventually wakes me up. I almost jump up out of bed, but I suddenly remember that I'm not at home with my men, I'm in some unknown location with some unknown asswipe that wants to do who knows what to me. Looking up into the eyes that have haunted me for many years, I gasp and try to scramble away as fast as I can. How can this be?

"Gene! What the fuck are you doing?" I ask, the terror I'm feeling in this moment causes my voice to raise to the highest pitch ever. Goosebumps break out on my skin and I'm literally trembling from fear.

"Miss me sweetheart?" he asks, venom dripping from his voice.

Gene is my ex-boyfriend that tried to kill me. Taking in his appearance now, I can see that he's definitely taking something. Before he was built, had a good complexion and color, was put together, and clean. Now, he's nothing but skin and bones, his long hair is now oily and the odor emanating from him is the worst that I've ever smelled in my entire life.

"I would never miss you!" I scream at him, making myself as small as I possibly can in the corner farthest away from him on the bed.

"That's no way to talk to your future husband," he tells me, climbing on the bed toward me. "We *will* be married as soon as possible!"

"No, we won't. There's no way that I would ever marry you and I'd make that abundantly clear to whoever you tried to get to marry us," I tell him, vehemently.

"You'll whore yourself out to some biker scum, but you won't marry someone that you loved once upon a time? That just proves how much of a biker slut you are, and I should've taken what was mine when I had the chance," he tells me, ripping my hair and bringing my head closer to his.

"I'm not whoring myself out to anyone! And why do you want to marry me so bad anyway?" I ask, trying to keep him talking so that he'll forget whatever he has planned for me.

"I'll be taking your money from the salon that has become so profitable. That won't be your money anymore, it's all mine. See, I know how much you make and how much you have saved up. It's all going to be transferred to me," he spits out at me, practically in my face. "You're going to marry me, pop out a kid, and then I'm going to kill you."

Gene has a demonic look on his face and I know that arguing will only get me hurt, but there's no way that any of that pipe dream of his is going to happen. I'm going to fight for all I'm worth, so I can get back home to my men. We're building a life together and I've never told them that I love them. I really do, I just haven't given voice to my feelings with the fear running through my body at the thought they won't return the feelings.

"Yeah, um, that's not going to happen. My men will find me before anything can happen to me," I tell him, crossing my arms over my chest and plastering a smug smirk on my face.

Like I said, I know better than to poke the bear, but I can't help it. I want to piss Gene off, I want to make sure he's as pissed the fuck off as I currently am. Unfortunately for me, he likes to hit when he gets mad. So, it's really no surprise when he reaches out and punches me dead in my face. I'm not sure if he broke my nose, but I know I am not bleeding and the pain radiating through my head is absolutely horrible. At this point, I know there's no pleading with him to stop. He's reached a level of insane that he can't be talked to, it's like he's gone inside his own head and no one can reach him when he's in there.

Gene lands two more solid hits to my head before I can blink. The last one hits me directly in the temple and I'm out for the count.

Waking up once again, I go to sit up and I can't move. Panic immediately overtakes my body and I begin to struggle against the ropes that have me tied to the bed. My wrists and ankles are tied to the bed, looking down I see that I'm almost completely naked. The only thing covering me right now is my bra. Now, I'm past panic and I can feel myself starting to retreat into my head. Memories of my friends, family, and Crash and Trojan play on a constant loop. This is the only way that I'm going to be able to get through anything that this sick fuck does to me.

An overwhelming pain consumes me from between my thighs and I don't even want to begin to contemplate why. I want to break down and cry, scream, hit something, and kill this fucker. With the pain I'm feeling, I can only imagine that Gene took something that I wasn't willing to give him. And he chose to do it when I was knocked out because he knew I would always fight him. Before, there was always a reason as to why I didn't want him touching me. Now, he's chosen to take it from me without my consent. Crash and Trojan will never want anything to do with me now.

I close my eyes as wave of nausea overwhelms me. There's no way I can get up to make it to the toilet the only thing I can do it turn my head when I get sick. This is what my life is boiling down to. I'm going to die alone in this room with a bed covered in whatever happens. If I get sick, raped, have to go to the bathroom, it doesn't matter I guess. Gene is pulling me down to his level and I can't do anything about it.

"I see you're awake again," Gene says, walking into my room wearing nothing but boxers. "I knew you'd be a good fuck and I was right. I'll make sure you never remember the assholes taking advantage of you."

"It will never happen! You raped me, and I will never follow through with your plan. My men are looking for me as we speak!" I scream at him, not being able to hold back any longer.

"They'll never find you. No one even knows who was after you. You're mine just like I told you," Gene tells me, getting in my face once again. Unfortunately, he's found the spot that I got sick in. "You dumb bitch! How dare you!"

"What do you want me to do Gene? You have me tied to the fucking bed," I yell back.

Gene yells and screams but I can't understand a single word he's saying. The look in his eyes is one that tells me he's on something and he's gone way past his breaking point. I really don't want to provoke him right now, but another wave of nausea rolls through my body and I can't stop from being sick. He just happens to be on the side of the bed as I get sick. This makes him completely lose his shit and I'm the one suffering for it. Once again, I'm knocked the fuck out.

Chapter Ten
Crash

I HAVE BEEN CHASING THIS STUPID FUCK for days now. Every time I get right on his ass, he seems to slip right through my fingertips. Not today though. I know where he's going to be in about a half hour and I'm already sitting here waiting. The one ace I have up my sleeve is that no one ever knows what I look like. This is why Jim always calls me to help him on these missions.

The waiting is killing me, but I am down to less than five minutes before he gets here. I look up as another customer comes strolling into the bakery, and see my target. He's acting like he doesn't have a care in the world and that no one is on his ass right now. Too bad for him that I'm already here and he's about to go down.

There's only one other customer here and I know that it's a now or never situation. He will run if he gets outside and this area is known to him. I'd be out of the loop and not know where he would hide. So, I have no choice but to catch him in the building. Standing up, I make my way to the counter as if I'm going to place an order. In all reality, I'm getting my gun in one hand and my cuffs in the other. The guy, Craig, has one hand by his side which is going to be easy for me to wrap the cuff around one wrist while he still has no clue.

My plan goes off flawlessly as I get his free hand cuffed while he's still waiting. I place my gun to his head and tell him to give me his other hand. Knowing that he has no way out, he complies and lets me cuff him. Being the nice guy that I am, I let him have his coffee and bagel as we make my way to the car I rented for this trip. Placing him in the back seat, I make sure both the child safety locks are engaged so he can't escape at a stop light or some shit.

As soon as I sit in the car, I place the call to Jim and find out what he wants me to do with this guy. He tells me that he wants me to take him to the police station so that he can pick him up through the 'proper' channels. I'm not supposed to be here right now, so I'm going to do as he asks. Craig is asking what's going to happen to him and I let him know. More than likely he's going to be cut loose as soon as he gives up whatever information he knows. Jim never told me that this guy actually did anything wrong, he just has a possibility of knowing pivotal information that could stop things from happening on a grander scale. Letting him know this, he visibly relaxes. I can tell that he's not a hardened criminal, he just knows that he was being hunted and didn't know why. Now he does, and he can figure out what he's going to do to save himself.

Pulling up to the police station, my phone begins to ring. Looking down, I see Trojan calling me and I silence it before leading Craig inside the station. I'll call him back once I drop this guy off. As soon as he's not in my company, I am no longer working for Jim and can do whatever I want to. Right now, I'm still on radio silence to everyone but my boss.

After fifteen minutes inside, I can finally call Trojan back. He's been blowing my phone up the entire time and I'm getting a feeling deep in my gut that isn't making me comfortable. Something is going on and I know that I'm needed at home. Just as I go to call him back, Trojan is calling me yet again.

"What's up? Is Darcy okay?" I ask, knowing that she's the only reason he would be calling me like this. The feeling in my gut intensifies as he doesn't respond immediately.

"Well, I don't really know. I'm goin' to assume that she's not okay," he tells me, pausing again and letting my mind start racing with what's happened since I've been gone. "She was taken from the salon yesterday afternoon. I was in pissin' and Gage stepped out for a minute. Darcy told me she was goin' out for some air and I told her to wait. As soon as I got outside a man had her limp body and was draggin' her toward a fucked-up van."

"What the fuck!" I roar out. "You didn't fuckin' stop them? You let this motherfucker get his hands on our girl?" I question him, letting all the pain and rage fuel my anger. "I'm callin' Jim to get a flight home from here. I'll be there as soon as I can. Do you have any leads yet?"

"Tech is goin' over the footage from the camera now. He's been combin' it since last night when this happened. I'll have somethin' by the time you get here," he tells me, pain also filling his voice and letting me know that he's beating the shit out of himself right now for what's happened.

"I'll text you soon," I answer, hanging up and placing the call to Jim.

Jim found me a flight out almost immediately. I barely had time to get to the airport and on the plane. That still wasn't soon enough for me. My girl is out there alone with a psycho dipshit and we have no idea where she is. Trojan and Gage are picking me up from the airport and I was told that they found something. Now, I'm jumping to get out of this seat and into the SUV they'll undoubtedly be driving to get me.

As soon as the pilot tells us that we're free to leave our seats and make our way to the exit, I'm pushing myself through everyone in my haste to get out of here. I only had a carry on, so I don't have to wait for any luggage. There's no way in hell I'd make it long enough to stand there and wait. The only thing on my mind right now is finding Darcy and getting her back home where she belongs. Along with that are the thoughts that are consuming me about what's being done to her right now. Darcy is strong, but there are just some things that people can't come back from. A murderous rage consumes me, and I need an outlet before I do something I'll end up regretting.

"Crash, over here," I hear Gage call out to me as I make my way toward the front door.

Making my way to him, I see that Trojan is sitting right outside. He's practically parked on the curb in his haste to get here and pick me up. Looking at my brother as I climb in the front seat, I can tell that he's not had any sleep and that panic and worry are the main emotions running rampant through him. Placing my hand on his shoulder, I give him the reassurance that I have calmed down and realized that this is not on him. He did what he had to do and there was just a second that he didn't have his eye on her. We have other things going on and can't have someone on her constantly. It's not like he was out fucking around or something, he was going to the bathroom.

"What do we know?" I ask, not being able to sit quietly about this and wait for them to say something to me about it.

"It was her ex, the one she told us that almost killed her. Tech is runnin' everythin' he can find on the asshole, but nothin' yet. His name is Gene and he's been usin' every drug under the sun for years. Right now, we're runnin' leads as to where he would be hidin' with her," Trojan tells me, barely taking his eyes off the road. His jaw is clenched, and I know he's ready to lose his shit on someone. He needs to keep it locked down until we get our hands on this dirty fucker.

"He can't be that far if he's a user. No matter what, he's goin' to want to stay close to his dealers and not have to worry about findin' new ones so he doesn't have to go without his fix. Do we have any previous addresses on him yet?" I ask, new ideas running through my head. "And, that's goin' to make it more dangerous for our girl too. Who knows what he's actually takin'. We need to find them now!"

Gage and Trojan simply nod at my statement. We all know it's only a matter of time before he starts losing his shit on our girl. I'm praying that we get to them before that happens, but I don't think that it's going to be the case. Not when he's already put his hands on her before. With so many years of putting shit in his body, he's bound to be worse off now. Our poor girl has to be so scared and not sure if we're coming for her. I'm sure that she's going to be reverting back to not wanting to be with anyone and all the other bullshit he filled her head with before.

Pulling up to the clubhouse, I jump out before my brother even has the SUV in park. I make my way into Tech's room with a short knock on the door before I burst through. Red is on her knees in front of him giving him a blow job as he keeps his eyes moving over screen after screen in front of him. He's so focused that I don't know if he even realizes that she's down there right now. Before I can sit down next to him, she looks up at me and starts putting more effort into what she's doing. It's almost like she's trying to put a show on for me. I'm not buying it when I have a girl and she means the world to me. Fuck! I need her back in our arms.

"Anythin' yet, brother?" I ask, starting to look at the screens to figure out what he's looking at.

"Nope. All his arrest records have false addresses on them and the only house he was ever listed as living in is the one he shared with his parents until they died. The year that he met Darcy, he was on top of the world. Had a six figure a year job, was in the process of buyin' a house, and had more money saved than a lot of people would in less than a year. I'm not sure what changed just yet, but there's somethin' that we're not seein'," Tech tells me, grunting while he spills his release down Red's throat.

"You ready for a release, baby?" she asks, turning toward me and moving her hand up my thigh.

"Get the fuck off me!" I roar out at her. "I'm lookin' for my girl and I wouldn't touch you if I had to!!"

Red goes to say something else, but Gage puts a stop to that really quick. He tells her that she has two choices, stay here where she's not wanted and leave the clubhouse permanently. Or she can leave now, not offer herself to Trojan and myself again, and keep her home and job. The choice is completely hers and she doesn't hesitate to scramble from the room. She knows that Gage isn't fucking around, and he will ban her from here for good without batting an eye. There's always going to be more girls waiting to take her place and do the same thing she is right now. If they can't listen and leave the attached guys alone, then we don't need them around the clubhouse.

"Grim and Slim are bringin' their clubs in to help us with this shit. Slim already has Fox helpin' me while he's on the way here. I'm runnin' a few different things and he's runnin' a few different ones. We'll find her guys, I promise you that," Tech tells us, never once taking his eyes off the screens or his fingers off the keyboard in front of him.

"We have no leads or anythin' right now?" I ask, trying to pay attention to everything. Especially the footage from the salon when she was taken. Tech has it playing on a loop, so he can see if he missed anything.

"Not yet. I ran the plates and they're stolen. I didn't honestly expect anythin' less than that," he tells me.

"I'll be back. I'm goin' to go see if I can figure anythin' out from the salon or the boxes that we did manage to salvage from her house. They still in one of the rooms downstairs?" I ask Gage, heading out of Tech's room with my bag slung over my shoulder.

"Yep. Trojan is headin' down there too. Go grab a shower and meet him. No one else is goin' to touch her stuff but you two. If you want help takin' it home, let me know and we'll get it loaded up and over there," he tells me, sitting down next to Tech to offer any help he might need and waiting for the other clubs to get here.

Trojan and I are down in the basement, I didn't stop longer than it took for me to throw my bag in my room and lock the door back up. I'm ready to get down to business and go through our girls shit so we can try to find out if there's anything in there that might help with a location. We've made it through four boxes a piece when we hear feet pounding down the stairs and toward the room we're sitting in. We both look up to see Tech standing in the doorway, out of breath and bent over to catch it so we can hear what he has to stay.

Now, I'm not usually known for my patience. With something going on with Darcy, someone holding her against her will and doing who knows what to her, I'm about to snap at everyone around me. I feel like they're holding me back from finding her even though I know that's not truly the case. My brothers, the guys from Clifton Falls, and the Phantom Bastards all have our back and want to do anything in their power to help us find her and bring her home safe.

"F-Fox f-found her," Tech murmurs out, taking another second to finish catching his breath. "He found some sealed records from when his parents died. They left him a house, and no one knows about it because he changed his name. I'm not sure why and I don't give a fuck. We're waitin' on them to get here so we can make a plan of attack."

Trojan and I immediately stand up and forget about the boxes for the time being. We'll clean everything up and bring it to the house once we have our girl back in our arms where she belongs. For now, I'm going to clean up and wait for the rest of the guys to get here. My focus will be solely focused on her and what I want to do with this drug addicted scumbag.

Darcy

I can't even begin to tell you how long Gene has had me now. The only thing I know for sure is that I'm in constant pain, I keep losing consciousness, and I'm constantly feeling sick to my stomach. Honestly, I don't even want to think what's going on there. I would say I'm relieved when I black out from pain or whatever else, but I can't be. Not when I know what's happening to my body. I know that he's raped me multiple times and there's nothing I can do to stop him. I'm always knocked out or just tied to the bed. Gene loves to see my tears as he's doing his thing.

I'm let up once a day to go to the bathroom and that's it. The rest of the time, he makes me piss in the bed I'm laying in. He put a plastic sheet cover on it, so I don't 'ruin' the mattress. Hell, if I have to get sick, I have to stay in the bed and do it. I'm not aloud to take a shower or clean up at all. Even the one trip daily I make to the bathroom, I'm not allowed to clean up. This is disgusting, and I can't stand smelling the nastiness of myself. If I ever get out of this hell hole, I will *never* again take being able to wash myself for granted.

Take away the smell and how dirty I am, my hair is matted with disgusting things, sweat, and blood from the hits to the head. I'm pretty sure that I have a concussion that I can't seem to stay awake for. I'm honestly surprised I haven't gone to sleep and not woken up by now. Gene beats me daily and I've woken up more times than I can count with his hands wrapped tight around my neck. Today included.

"Come on, you dumb bitch! Wake the fuck up!" he screams and yells at me. His hands are wrapped around my neck and his sweat is dripping in my face.

Immediately, I begin to throw up. The smell of him and having his nasty sweat dripping on me is enough to fling me over the edge of sanity. Something inside me snaps and I know that I have to fight him tooth and nail to get away from him. There's no window I can escape through in the bathroom, so I need to come up with another plan. With my mind all muddled from the pain, the only thing I can think to do is fight. Sometimes he leaves the room with the main door slightly ajar when I'm in the bathroom. I'm not sure what he's doing, but that might be my only chance for escaping.

Once I'm done, Gene unties me, almost snaps my arm in half when he yanks it behind my back, and leads me into the bathroom. He's pretty much dragging me there and I can't even yelp out in pain because I've become numb to it all. For now, I'll let him do what he wants and then I'll make my move to get away from him. Even though I can barely move or walk with the sprains and possible broken bones.

"I have to make a phone call, don't fucking try anything stupid," he tells me, leaving the bathroom and me.

This is my chance, I take a minute in the bathroom before easing my way out of the bathroom and then the room. I can hear him talking to someone from the back of the house. That means my chance to get away is through the front door. As quickly as I can, I move toward the door without making a noise. I'm almost there when I feel my hair being grabbed and pulled back. My head snaps back and I can't help the yelp that erupts from me.

"Where the fuck do you think you're going?" he growls out, pulling me back against his body.

"I'm getting the fuck out of here and away from you!" I scream back, picking my foot up and jamming it back into his leg.

Gene lets go of me and I take this opportunity to turn quickly and kick him straight in the nuts. I'm not sure that it's hard enough to do any damage, but I know it's hard enough to let me have the chance to get away from him. I'm back at the door and about to throw it open when the door flies open, and my life is standing right in front of me.

"Crash! Trojan!" I exclaim, reaching out to them as I fall to the floor, blackness surrounding me.

Trojan

As soon as the rest of the guys get to the clubhouse, we're ready to go. Hell, we've been ready as soon as we found out that Fox knew where our girl was. It's been three days of pure fucking hell and I can't believe that in a matter of time she'll be home. Darcy needs to be okay so that we can prove to her that nothing like this will ever happen again. Not to her or anyone else she loves.

Fox explained everything as they got closer to us and Tech pulled up the maps so that we could see exactly what he was talking about. He circled a bunch of buildings on the maps and pinpointed a house nestled in the center of a bunch of warehouses. It wasn't there a year or two ago based on previous maps and other documents that Tech pulls up on the big screen. Looking at it carefully, I need to see a closer look at the house.

"Tech, blow that fuckin' picture of the house up," I tell him, standing up. Yeah, I'm being demanding as fuck right now, but this can't be happening.

"What's goin' on?" Crash asks me, standing up next to me to try to figure out what I'm flipping out about.

"Look at the fuckin' house! That cocksuckin' fuckin' little psycho bitch!" I yell out, now that I can plainly see the house and what this asshole has done.

Crash's entire body tenses up next to me. He finally sees what I'm seeing, and the rage is running rampant through his body. He's ready to go get our girl now! Usually, he doesn't go all ape shit, but I can tell that he's barely hanging on right now. Hell, I'm barely controlling the anger coursing through my veins. This is absolutely fucking disgusting.

"Okay, can you please fill the rest of us in on what's goin' on?" Gage asks, coming to stand next to us with his eyes squinted at the screen.

"That motherfucker built a house to completely resemble Darcy's house before he blew it the fuck up. The outside is the exact replica of hers so I'm sure that the inside is going to match too," Crash tells them, walking closer to the screen with his fists clenching and unclenching at his sides.

There's murmurs of anger and disgust throughout the main room of the clubhouse. Every guy in this room is ready to kill this stupid twatwaffle on our girl's behalf. I can't even begin to describe what I want to do to him. It's not going to be easy, it's going to be long, drawn out, and as painful as we can possibly make it. This is going beyond too far. I can't even begin to imagine what is going through Darcy's mind knowing that this house resembles her own. We need to get to her now.

Before I can do anything stupid, the main door opens and in walks the guys from the Phantom Bastards. There's back slapping and guys ordering a beer so that we can make a plan of attack to get her back in our arms where she belongs.

It doesn't take us long to come up with how we're getting in and getting Darcy out safe. Just as we're ready to head out, armed to the teeth since we don't know if anyone else is going to be in the house, Grim and the rest of the guys from Clifton Falls pull in. They turn their bikes around and sit until the rest of us start heading out of the gate. I'm sure that Gage is talking to them on his Bluetooth to let them know what's going on, but if not, we'll have to update them once we pull over about a mile or so from the house our girl is in.

The ride takes us about an hour before we pull over to get in our groups and head towards the house on foot. There's no reason to warn Gene of our arrival now so he does something else to hurt our girl. My adrenaline is pumping and I'm ready to go now. I have to tell myself continuously to stay here while Gage is talking to Grim and splitting his guys up among us. Crash, standing next to me, is bouncing on his feet so he doesn't take off on his own. I know that's what he's doing. Everyone else, is waiting to head out, checking their weapons, and focusing on what's about to happen.

"You two ready?" Gage asks, directing his attention to Crash and myself.

We both nod, not wanting to lose focus about what we have to do. Our task at hand is the most important one out of everyone as far as I'm concerned. Crash and I are to get in and find our girl, getting her out as quickly as possible. I can pretty much guarantee that we're going to need to get her some medical attention if this douchebag's rap sheet is anything to go by.

After what seems like forever, we head out and start making our way to the house sitting in the middle of about six warehouses. There's a ton of places for us to hide while we're making our way there. The closer we get to the house, the more the adrenaline starts flowing through my veins. Crash is continuously clenching and unclenching his fists and I know he's itching for a fight. The way that fight turns out depends on how bad Darcy is.

Stepping up on to the porch, I can hear the screams of our girl radiating through the inside of the house. Looking at my brother, I know that there's no waiting anymore. I step to the side of the door and try the handle. It turns without resistance and I know that Darcy is extremely close to the other side. Crash pushes the door open as she goes to pull it toward her.

"Crash! Trojan!" she screams out, immediately falling to the floor just inside the door.

We quickly rush to her side and take a second to look over the injuries that we can already see. My blood is boiling, and I can't wait to get my hands on this slimy motherfucking scumbag. There are bruises over almost every inch of her body, her arm is swollen, one of her legs is swollen and at an odd angle, and I can make out handprints surrounding her once flawless and swanlike neck. Crash lets out a growl and scream like nothing I've ever heard before. The pain is finally coming out in the one way it can at this point in time. When we can finally get our hands on this fucker, the rest will come out.

Crash and I carry our girl out and gently lay her on the ground after laying our tee shirts down. With every mark on her body, I don't want to take a chance and her get some sort of infection on top of it all. I immediately drop to my knees next to her and check her pulse after dropping my cut over her naked body. Yes, she was just awake, fighting for her life. However, we don't know what her injuries are and what she's been through the last three days. It may not seem like a lot of time, but with the psychopath Gene is, there's a lot that he can do to anyone he has in his clutches for that long. Hell, there's a lot he could do in the span of a few hours.

"Someone call an ambulance!" Crash yells out, to anyone standing near us.

"We've already done it, brother," Grim tells us, kneeling down next to him and going to reach out for her.

"Please! Don't touch her!" we both yell out. We just got her back, and no one is going to be putting their hands on our girl.

Grim holds his hands up and nods his head to let us know he understands where we're coming from. He was the same way when Bailey went through anything and we're going to be the same now. It's going to be tough as fuck for the paramedics to get close to her. If it weren't for them being the ones that need to help her right now, they wouldn't get anywhere near Darcy. Crash and I are just going to have to suck it up and let them in.

Finally, after what seems like a lifetime, we hear the first wails of the sirens approaching us. Shadow, Gage, and Wood have already loaded Gene up in the van and started back to the clubhouse. They'll make sure he's put downstairs and held until we can get there to deal with him. Crash and I will be the one to end Gene's stupid ass. Knowing how everyone feels about our girl, they'll all be taking shots at him. Probably more than a few before we get the chance to lay our hands on him.

Slim and Steel meet the paramedics and give them a story that Darcy was kidnapped, and we found her in the house. Alone. We don't know who took her, no one else was around when we got here, and the few of us remaining here are the only ones that ever stepped foot on this property. Everyone else will stick to the story. Darcy can let the cops know what she remembers when she wakes up and we'll go from there.

It takes Steel, Fox, Tech, and Grim to pull Crash and I away from Darcy so that she can be loaded up on a stretcher and put in the back of the ambulance. There's no way that both of us aren't riding in there with her and I'm sure that Slim already mentioned that because no one puts a fight up when we head toward the back of the ambulance. The only thing we're told is that one of us will have to ride up front. Knowing that Crash needs to be with her just the slightest bit more than I do since I was here when this all went down, I make my way up front and tell everyone to move their asses or I'm going to be driving the fucking thing myself.

"We'll meet you guys there," Grim calls out, pulling his phone from his pocket and placing a call to someone.

It doesn't take us very long to make it to the hospital Darcy will be staying at. Once we pull in, nurses and doctors open the back doors and pull the stretcher out. They rush her into the emergency room and one unlucky nurse, leads Crash and I to the waiting room. We begin to pace the length of the room, scaring the shit out of everyone else sitting there waiting to be seen or make their way back to their loved ones.

We're still pacing twenty minutes later when our brothers begin to make their way in to us. Other than finding out that Darcy was being taken for tests to see what all the damage is, we haven't heard a fucking word from anyone. I know I'm getting pissed the fuck off and Crash is even worse. Every time the door opens, we're turning toward it and starting to head that way. It's never for us though. This waiting shit is for the birds as far as I'm concerned.

"Family of Miss Quinn," a doctor calls out, standing on just this side of the door.

We all move toward him and it doesn't even phase the man that has us holding our breath. My heart is racing, and I feel like I can't breathe waiting to hear what's going on right now. He needs to hurry the fuck up before Crash lets loose too. He's pale and I can see the sweat beginning to form along his face and chest. He's holding so much in that he's about to erupt.

"Miss Quinn has several open cuts and wounds that we've stitched up after cleaning out. There's bruising surrounding her neck and we won't know the extent of the damage until she wakes up. The rest of her body is covered in bruises, especially her wrists and ankles. It looks like she was tied up to something. And, during an exam, we did discover tearing and bruising in her vaginal area. I'm going to say that she was raped multiple times. We're getting ready to take her back to surgery so that we can set her leg and arm. Her arm was broken in three spots while her leg is broken, and her ankle is sprained. There is going to be risk to the fetus, but at this point, she is my number one priority," he tells us, pausing only for a second before shocking the shit out of every one of us standing before him. "I'm sorry that I've had to tell you all of this. I hope you catch the bastard that hurt her this bad and make him suffer."

With that, the doctor turns on his heal and makes his way back to see other patients. A nurse comes out as we're standing there and lets us know that we can follow her to a separate waiting room until Darcy is out of surgery. Crash and I follow behind everyone, filled with pain, sorrow, and shock at learning that we're going to be adding to our family. Doing something I haven't done in an extremely long time, I send up a silent prayer that our girl and unborn child will make it through the damage that's been inflicted on them and the necessary surgery.

"You okay?" Crash asks, as we sit down in chairs away from the rest of our brothers. They're giving us some space so that we can digest the information that we've just been given.

"I don't know how Darcy is goin' to be when she wakes up from all this. No matter what we have to do, we'll do it. And I can't believe that we're goin' to be dad's soon. We need to figure out how we're goin' to tell her this news," I answer, not sure of what we're going to have to do in the coming weeks, months, and years to help our girl but knowing that I'm all in no matter what. "You?"

Crash takes his time responding. "I will be. How did this happen to our girl? And she still had the balls to fight and try to get away from that sick fuck? She's stronger than we know and with help, she will get through this. I'm not leavin' her side throughout it and I know you aren't either. I love the fuck out of her and it's the same for you. Let's cross one bridge at a time. We're goin' to have to scale back on touching her and makin' love to her."

"She's goin' to have to let us know when she's ready for anythin' again. I don't give a fuck how long that takes either," I tell him, meaning that down to my bones.

Crash nods his head in agreement and we settle back in for the long wait before we can lay eyes on Darcy again. Every once in a while, our brothers come over to check on us, and we make small talk with one another and them. Neither one of us have our mind on anything else but our world that's laying in that operating room being put back together.

Chapter Eleven
Darcy

THE ONLY THING I CAN FEEL is pain radiating throughout my entire body. My eyes won't open, and I don't want to feel anything anymore. Normally, the pain wouldn't bother me, but with the severity of it and knowing that more than likely Crash and Trojan will head for the hills as soon as they find out what's been done to me, wants me to let the blackness blanket me. I want to let it take me away and not face living life without the two men that have come to mean so much to me.

I'm not worried about the girls finding out and leaving my side. Most of them have been through their own torture and live with it on a daily basis. If anyone can help me through it, they will be the ones to stand by my side and hold me down when I need it. Crash and Trojan would do the same thing if they stick around, but even this might be too much for them to handle. I won't know until I wake up. The fog may just be too much for me right now.

"When the fuck is she gonna wake up?" I hear through the haze that's threatening to pull me back under.

"I don't know. She should be wakin' up soon. Her body needs to heal and it's goin' to wake up when it thinks she's healed enough," another voice I love hearing says, trying to calm the other one down. I can't really distinguish which one is which man, but I know it's them.

A hand grabs mine and I can feel a soft kiss placed on it before the splash of something wet. The wetness slips down the top of my hand and rolls around the side. I want to catch all of their tears and I must make a movement because I hear a noise start to beep faster. What the fuck is that? I think to myself.

"You hear that?" one of the voices asks, hope surfacing for the first time since I started hearing my men talking. "The heart monitor is goin' crazy."

"Can you hear me baby?" Crash, everything becoming clearer as I pull myself out of the darkness shrouding me and keeping me from the men I want to see. "Try to squeeze my hand if you can."

I put all of my concentration into trying to make my hand move. The way that the hand is gripping me harder proves to me that I did manage to make some sort of movement. Now, if I could only open my eyes and see their faces. That's going to be the thing that tells me all I need to know. When I can clearly see their faces, I'll know if there's disgust or revulsion flowing through them at what's been done to me. I'm done hiding from them and holding myself back. If this experience has taught me anything, it's that you never know how much time you truly have. I need to move forward making the most of the rest of my life. Hopefully it's with the men I love. Too bad the darkness is more than I can pull away from. It drags me back under and

I'm not sure how much time has passed since I was last semi-awake. This time, the darkness doesn't seem to have as much of a pull on me and I might be able to actually open my eyes this time. I can sense Crash and Trojan still in the room with me, but I don't hear them talking anymore as everything begins to come clear to me. Slowly, I try to open my eyes and manage to open them a little bit.

The room is shrouded in darkness with only a light coming from behind the bed I'm currently lying in. My eyes hurt a little and I'm glad that lights aren't on to blind me and force my eyes shut again. I look around and the sight that greets me is one that will forever be burned in my memory. Not in a good way either.

Crash is sitting on the right side of my bed. His head is laying next to my hand that's encased in a purple cast. I can see that he hasn't shaved in multiple days and the want to run my hand over the growth that now covers his face. There are worry lines covering his face even in sleep. Crash's clothes are wrinkled as if he's been wearing the same ones for days instead of changing daily.

Turning my head to the left, I see Trojan in the same condition as his brother. The only difference is the amount of growth gracing his handsome face. I can only imagine that he hasn't done much of anything since I was taken. There's always been a fire in these two when it comes to me, and I've seen them when it comes to them getting ready for 'missions' and helping the other clubs out with things. Now, their attention was focused on finding me and bringing me home, so I can't imagine how they were. The surprise is that Crash is here, I just hope that he finished his work before he got called away.

"Baby," I hear from Crash, his voice filled with sleep and surprise that I'm awake.

"What?" Trojan asks, his voice low and gravelly while raising his head to meet my eyes.

"W-w-water?" I ask, noticing the pain coming from my throat. I'm not sure if it's from not using my voice for so long, damage from Gene, or something from whatever they had to do during my stay here.

Crash and Trojan both jump up to get me some water. After reminding me to take small sips and not drink too much right this second, the straw is moved toward my mouth, so I can finally get some cool relief. As soon as I'm done drinking a little bit, I take a deep breath and gamble with taking a look at my men. There's relief, pain, regret, and another emotion I'm not quite sure about plastered on their faces. Trojan takes his seat back and holds my good hand in his. At the same time,

Crash checks to make sure that no one is going to be coming in the room. That's kind of weird.

"Baby, I know that you're just wakin' up, but we need to talk to you about somethin'," Crash tells me, sitting back down on his side of the bed.

My nerves go through the roof and my heart starts beating like crazy. I'm sure it's about to bust right out of my chest. This is it. This is the minute they tell me that my current predicament is too much for them to handle. They want someone with less strings and baggage to be with. I guess I should've braced myself more for what was about to come out of their mouths.

"I don't know how to tell you this, so I'm just goin' to act like we're rippin' a band-aid off," Trojan starts, a nervous look plastering his face and I know that I've never seen either one of these men nervous. They're always so sure of everything they're doing and what they're going after. "We found somethin' out when you got brought in two weeks ago. We've had time to adjust to the news, but you're goin' to need some time."

"What is it? Do I have some life-threatening illness or something?" I ask, all sorts of scenarios running through my head, almost overwhelming me with what could be going on.

"No," Crash tells me, gently touching my cheek and holding my face in his big, strong, warm hand. "We found out that you're pregnant."

This is the last thing that I expected to hear from these two. I know I haven't been feeling well for the last few weeks, but I figured it was due to the stress of not knowing what was going on with the person stalking me. When Gene had me, I chalked it up to being whatever Gene had injected into my body. Oh no! What if it has hurt our child? Tears immediately start running down my face as I think of everything I've been through.

"What's the matter firecracker?" Trojan ask me, leaning in closer and wiping some of my tears away. "What has tears runnin' like that?"

"You guys don't understand. He drugged me, raped me more than once, and beat me. What if he's done something to the baby? What if the drugs hurt the baby and now this baby is going to suffer because of it?" I ask, everything running out of my mouth faster than I can think almost. "And, I've had some drinks and shit since being pregnant. What if I've done something to the baby?"

"Slow down, baby," Crash tells me, placing a kiss on my temple and leaning back so he can look in my face while talking to me. "We'll get the doctor in here to talk to you and do whatever we have to in order to get you some reassurance. Okay?"

"Please?" I practically plead with him.

Laying my head back on the pillow, I think about the fact that there's a little baby growing in me right now. I've never really thought one way or another about having a baby because I didn't want to be with anyone. Crash and Trojan broke down every single wall I have ever built around my heart and have invaded it. They make me want things that I haven't wanted before, and I haven't dared to dream of anything more. Until now. No matter what their decision is, I'll have a little piece of them with me for a lifetime.

"What's goin' through your head right now," Trojan asks me after the technician from ultrasound leaves the room, taking the machine with her.

"I can't believe that a little piece of one of you is growing inside me, and has been for almost twelve weeks now.

No matter what you choose to do, I'm keeping this baby," I tell them, taking my eyes off of the picture I'm holding in my hands. I've never seen anything so precious in my life. The doctor explained to me that I probably missed the signs of being pregnant with all of the stress I've been under since someone was after me.

"What are you talkin' about?" Crash asks, making me look him dead in the face while he waits for my answer.

"I'm sure this is too much shit for you both to take on. Just me being raped more than once is a lot for a man to take on. I don't expect you two to be any different. Just know I'll take care of this baby while he or she is waiting to be born and I'll never keep either one of you from them once they're born," I tell him, tears starting to form in my eyes once again at the knowledge that I'll be a single mother.

"Let me tell you somethin'," Trojan says, interrupting my thoughts. "Neither one of us are goin' anywhere. You are still the feisty, strong, beautiful, and courageous woman that we fell in love with and have been chasing until you put us out of our misery. Now that you're ours, you're not goin' to get away from us. You've been through some terrible shit and I wish to anyone that will listen that you didn't have to suffer what you just did. However, that's not enough to scare us away from you either."

Crash has moved to stand next to his brother and is nodding in agreement at everything Trojan just told me. The only thing that I can hear is that they've both fallen in love with me. While I know that I love them, have been falling in love with them since they first started paying attention to me with all the little gestures they've made to ensure that I'm happy and safe. I never believed it would be easy for them to love me. Especially with the way I've spent most of our time together pushing them away. My mind is spinning with all of the information I've been given by the doctors and them. I just want to take a while and process everything.

"I love you both, you have to know that. Right now, I just need some time to process everything you and the doctor has told me. I'm going to get some rest so that I can get the fuck out of here," I tell them, leaning back against the pillows. The ultrasound picture is still clutched tight in my grasp, so I have a reminder that it's real.

The doctor filled me with all of his technical jargon as he explained my long list of injuries and healing time. I'll need to stay in the hospital a few more days, but then I can go home with the promise of taking care of me and the baby, keeping my appointments, and starting therapy when it's time. I'm more than happy to do all that if it means I can go home and get out of this environment. I've never liked hospitals and this time is no different.

Crash

I move my chair closer to Darcy's bed as I watch her try to get comfortable enough to get some more rest. She's been sleeping a lot, and I'm glad that she's resting to heal her body faster. If she were up, trying to do shit she shouldn't be, we'd be having a problem. Trojan and I aren't going to let her do anything she doesn't have to do. I foresee a ton of fights and arguments in our future when it comes to her doing things too soon. Wouldn't have it any other way though.

As I watch her, her words of loving us continue floating around my head. We've both been telling her as she falls asleep every night that we love her. I wasn't expecting to hear those sweet words leaving her mouth so soon. Maybe it has something to do with being kidnapped and everything she suffered through. I can see that there's a fire back in her eyes that hasn't been there since her house was blown up.

Even when the construction crew started to rebuild it for her, and her decision to use the house for the domestic violence program, the fire didn't shine bright. Now, I know that she's going to need to talk to someone about what happened to her and there's still a long road to travel before she heals fully, but her spirit is coming back, and I think she's going to be better than ever. Darcy is a strong woman and not many people get to see that side of her. She's full of sass and not afraid to back down against anyone. I can't even begin to tell you the amount of times she's put Trojan and myself in our place when she thinks we need to be knocked down a peg or two.

Darcy slept most of the afternoon away. I know that she was having dreams and nightmares. You can tell just by looking at her gorgeous face, even covered in fading bruises and scrapes, whether she's having a nightmare or dreaming of something good. When she's in nightmare mode, Trojan and I wrap our arms around her until she calms down. It kills me to know that she's probably dreaming of that fucking scumbag, but there's nothing we can do about it right now. The only thing we can do is let her know we're here for her and bring Karen in. Trojan and I have already talked about it and put a call in to Skylar about getting in touch with her.

The girls are chomping at the bit to come see Darcy. We've been holding them off since they got to Dander Falls, but it's not going to last much longer. Hell, someone told my mom what happened, and she even made the trip here. She wants to be here for me and meet the woman that finally captured my heart along with Trojan's. Trojan has always been like a second son to her and she is overprotective of him the same way she is of me. One look at us from her and her heart broke into a million pieces to see the desperation and pain etched on our faces.

"Baby, we haven't been lettin' the girls in to see you, and they're pissed as fuck about it. We knew you needed rest though. Before I let them in, there's someone else that I'd like you to meet first," I tell her, taking her good hand in mine. "My mom is here, and I want you to meet her. She looks at Trojan as a second son and we want her to be the first one in here. Is that okay with you?"

For a few seconds, Darcy just stares at me like I'm crazy. I can just imagine the thoughts running through her head right now. "Are you sure now is the time? I mean, look at me. I must look awful!"

"She's not goin' to care what you look like, firecracker," Trojan tells her, standing up and walking toward the door. "I'm goin' to get her and give you a few minutes to calm down. She's goin' to love you Darcy. Just like we do."

While he's gone, I plant a kiss on her lips, being careful not to cause any pain. Darcy wraps her good arm around me, now that they have most of the wires and iv's out of her. Just before Trojan and my mom walk through the door, I pull back and place my hand on her cheek. Leaning into my touch, I can't help but be filled with the satisfaction that we have our girl back, we're in love, and she's giving us a baby. Now, all we need to do is give her the rag that's sitting in the top of the closet at home, and put our rings on her finger. We have one being specially designed for her to represent both of us.

"Brent, why are you sending Dom out to get me when it should be you?" my mother scolds me a little coming in the room. "I wanted a few minutes to talk to you, and you send your brother out to me."

Darcy giggles a little bit at the scolding I'm getting and its music to my ears. My mom's attention is brought directly to her and I see the assessing gaze linger on our girl. Trojan is standing behind my mom, a smirk plastered to his face. Meanwhile, I stand up from my chair and make my way over to her. Pulling my mom into a hug, I murmur that I'm sorry and we'll talk in a little bit.

"Darcy, I'd like you to meet my mother, Grace. Mom, this is Darcy," I say introducing the two women in my life.

"You two go do your thing. I'm going to spend some time getting to know Darcy since you haven't attempted to get us together before now," my mom tells me, walking over to my vacant chair and taking a seat. "Gage wants to talk to you both anyway. We'll be fine."

Trojan and I make our way over to the hospital bed to kiss Darcy and tell her that we'll be right down the hall if she needs us. Then we give my mom a kiss on her head before making our way down to the waiting room the rest of the guys are sitting in. They've been here every day since Darcy was brought in. The only time they leave is when business needs tending to or to get showers, rest, and something to eat. Even then, at least three guys are here with us. The girls have been here almost as long as the men.

Riley is the main one to leave so that she can keep Darcy's salon up and running. Even though the rest of the girls don't have any experience with styling hair or manicures, they go to the salon to help out. They're doing everything from answering phones, scheduling appointments, washing and drying the towels, and all of the cleaning so that Riley can focus on working with the clients. This is what's amazing to see when the family pulls together like this.

"Guys, I know that Darcy is still your main focus, but any idea when you want to deal with Gene?" Gage asks me as we take a seat in the middle of everyone. "We're all having fun giving him a punch here and there, but I want this matter settled before too much longer."

Trojan and I look at one another. Darcy goes home tomorrow or the day after. Yes, she's been pleading with the doctor to let her leave here tomorrow. That's when we plan on taking care of this and ending that piece of shit once and for all.

"Our plan is to get Darcy settled in at home when she can leave, maybe tomorrow mornin', and have the girls sit with her. We'll come to the clubhouse, do what we have to do to this cum guzzling gutter slut, and then let her know when it's all over," I tell my brothers, looking around at all of them. "Does that work for everyone?"

"Sounds like a plan," Gage tells us, looking at everyone surrounding us in this moment. "How is she doin'?"

We let everyone know how she's doing, that her fire and spirit are starting to make an appearance once again. I'm nervous that she's alone with my mom right now, but that's to be expected. My mom can be brash and brutally honest sometimes. And, she never misses an opportunity to tell everyone any awkward moment I ever had growing up. Darcy is going to have a field day with this new information. Trojan isn't to be left out though because my mom has stories about him too. You'd think we've known one another since we were kids with the number of stories she has. I didn't meet him until my early twenties though, when I got out of the service. So, we've known one another going on almost ten years now.

For now, I take time to look around me, thankful for everything I have in my life. I'm surrounded by family, friends, and I have a woman that has graced me with her love and acceptance of who I truly am. I can't ask for anything more in life. Well, not once we know that our baby is fine, and that Darcy will be ours for the rest of our lives.

Trojan

The last few days have been rough. Darcy has been throwing a fit to get out of the fucking hospital. Her words, or variations of them every time a nurse or doctor came in her room. Today is finally the day that we get to take her home though. We're just waiting on the doctor to sign off on her paperwork so we can get going. If he doesn't get on it soon, Crash and I can't be held responsible for what our little firecracker does. She's going crazy.

"Trojan, please go see what the hold up is," she pleads with me while Crash is down getting the SUV parked out front along with Grace.

"Alright baby. Shadow is right outside the door. Yell if you need anythin' while I'm gone, yeah?" I tell her, heading for the door to prevent any injuries from happening if she doesn't get out of here in the next few minutes.

"I'm good. I just want to go home. I know I'm being a bitch and I really don't want to be, but I'm tired of feeling cooped up in here. And I know you two are going to be unbearable once we get home. I'm sorry," she tells me, hanging on to my hand while she apologizes.

"There's nothin' you gotta be sorry about," I tell her, leaning in for a kiss.

Crash and I, along with the rest of the women and men in our family, would be acting the same exact way right now. None of us like being here, and she's been here for a few weeks. Granted she was asleep for most of that time, but she's been up for days and ready to leave. And, she's right about how Crash and I will be once we get home. She's gonna get sick of us hovering over her and waiting on her.

Stepping out of the door to her room, I almost run right into a nurse making her way in. "You here to let my girl go?" I ask, needing to know if I have to go in search still or if this nurse is answering my girls wishes.

"Got her paperwork right here," she tells me, continuing on into her room after giving Shadow a look.

"Hey Renee!" I hear my girl call out, still sitting in the wheelchair I got her earlier.

"You're all ready to get out of here, aren't you?" she asks, as I make my way back in the door after watching Shadow follow Renee's movements with his eyes.

"Yep. I was ready when I woke up. Please tell me you're here to let me go," my girls says, a smile gracing her face and a lightness I haven't seen since she woke up.

"I am. All I need is a signature here and to give you the meds you'll need until yours are ready at the pharmacy," Renee answers, handing the paperwork to Darcy and her meds to me.

Renee goes over all the information that's needed as Darcy signs a ton of papers. I listen intently along with Crash who's made his way back in the room with us. Grace is fussing over Darcy in the chair. To say that they hit it off is an understatement. Grace has been here, in the room with our girl, every single day for at least a few hours. She spends time talking to her, laughing, telling more stories, and being a sounding board for Darcy about the baby and pregnancy. Just what we need for her.

Darcy pulls me from my thoughts by yelling at us to get a move on. Everything is good to go, and she can leave. She's not wasting any time getting the fuck out of here. Grace is pushing her so that Crash and I can carry everything that we haven't already taken home. The sight that greets us as we make our way to the entrance of the hospital has tears flowing freely down our girl's cheeks. Every single member of all three clubs are standing guard waiting for us. The women are standing front and center, smiles gracing their faces and unshed tears in their eyes at finally seeing our girl. A giant purple cast surrounds her arm and leg, the bruises and cuts are mainly gone, but you can still see them, and all the marks left behind by medical equipment that was attached to our girl.

We make our way to the SUV followed by everyone as they help us get Darcy in and settled. Half the guys are going to ride in front of us while the SUV the girls are riding in will be behind us followed by the remaining guys on their bikes. No one is going to have a chance to get to us. Darcy is still crying, and I can't help but feel grateful that our family is showing her their strength and support right now. She needs to see it.

Especially when her first appointment with Karen is tomorrow. Thankfully, she's coming to the house, so we don't have to take her out.

Darcy is settled on the couch at home. Getting her inside was easy, the fight about where she was going to relax was not. Crash and I wanted her in our bed, but she wasn't having any of it. She wanted to be in the living room so that she could talk with her girls at one time and not have to have them sitting on one another in the bedroom. Grace finally talked some sense into us and Darcy got her way. I see this happening a lot the next few months while she's recovering.

"Baby, we have to leave for a while, you gonna be good?" I ask her, bending down to kiss her and see that she doesn't need anything before we head out.

"I'm good," she replies, tilting her face up for a kiss and smiling against my lips. "I've got more than enough people here to help me if I need it. And I know Grace is staying here for now."

Yeah, Crash's mom is taking the spare room so that she's here for the rest of Darcy's pregnancy and to help out when we have to leave. She knows that today is a big day for us and we're going to be gone for most of the day taking care of business and getting revenge for our girl. Grace is going to keep her mind busy if the girls have to leave for any reason. Even though it's a day the salon should be open, we all decided that it should be closed today so everyone could spend the day with Darcy. Wilma will even be over in a little while. Grace is going to pick her up.

Crash comes over to kiss her goodbye after putting her bags in the room and grabbing our bag with extra clothes. We're going to need to take a shower when we're done this afternoon. No one outside of who is in the room with us, will know what we do. Coming home in clothes covered in blood isn't an option. They'll be burned along with anything else involved so no one will ever be able to pin this shit on us. Spending our life behind bars isn't part of the plan. Not when we have Darcy and a baby to look forward to spending every day with.

Finally making our way out of the house, the guys follow us to the clubhouse. With the number of bikes riding together, it sounds like thunder is rolling through the sleepy little town of Dander Falls. The ground is shaking with the vibrations from our bikes and everyone we see along the ten-minute ride stops to stare at us. Some people run in fear of us while others stand with awe on their faces. Women with children turn them away from us while single women stand there drooling and pulling their shirts down a little more in front to entice us. Not going to happen, including the single guys. We all have one thing on our minds and that's ending a life of someone deserving nothing but torture and pain.

We all park in our designated spots while the guys from Clifton Falls and the Phantom Bastards fill the rest of our side lot. Shadow didn't follow us to the house, he made his way here to get us drinks and set up the tools we'll need downstairs. Wayne and Mike have been tasked with staying at the house to keep an eye on things there. I'm sure that no one else will be coming after our girl, but we're not prepared to take any chances. Not when we just got her back.

Walking in the common room, I down two shots and grab a beer before heading down to Gene. Crash is hot on my heels and I know that we're going to go as hard as we can on him. As soon as we walk in the room, the smell of piss and shit assault us. He's been here for a while and not given any luxuries. Gene has been chained by his wrists and ankles, just like Darcy was based on the marks on her body. He's forced to stay upright, only being able to hang his pathetic head. Currently, he's only wearing a pair of stained boxers. I'm sure that no one wanted to touch him, but I already have an idea of chopping his balls off with a dull, rusty knife followed by the pathetic excuse for a pencil dick he has.

"Well, well, well, what do we have here?" I ask Crash, wanting to play with Gene for a little bit. It's no less than he deserves.

"I don't know about you, but I see someone about to lose his life after heavy amounts of pain are dished out," Crash responds, his voice low and menacing, as the rest of the guys all file into the small room holding Gene. "I know I'm goin' to make sure that he feels every single thing that our girl did while he tortured and abused the fuck out of her."

"I couldn't agree more. I'm sure we can do worse than what he's ever thought about doin' though. Don't you agree? I mean, we have all these men here that still want a piece of this asshat. Not to mention what we're goin' to do to him," I respond, letting my words hang in the air as he finally raises his head to look at the room filled with men.

Each one of us has a look of pure hatred and rage marring our faces. We don't take kindly to anyone laying their hands on a woman. Make it one of our women, and you're pretty much fucked beyond belief. Gene doesn't even have the decency to look nervous or that he feels any remorse. Based on the look on his face, as far as he's concerned, we're the ones in the wrong here. I don't fucking think so, but we'll let him believe that for a few more seconds. Let the torture fucking begin!

Walking over to the table that Shadow set everything up on, I take my time looking over the assortment of tools to choose from. To begin with, I choose a pair of pliers so that I can rip out every single fingernail and toenail from his disgusting body. His screams echo throughout the basement and I relish the sounds as I go excruciatingly slow. Once I'm done, I step back and let Crash have his turn. He immediately grabs the pliers and starts removing his teeth. Since Gene is an addict and uses everything under the sun, his teeth are brittle as fuck and it doesn't take my brother long to remove the few teeth remaining in his head.

While he was doing that, I picked one of Blade's dull and rusty knives he brings to this shit and make as many little cuts on his body as I can. I cover him from head to toe, front and back. By now, the weak little 'man' in front of us passes out. Shadow douses him with a bucket of freezing cold water and Gene comes sputtering back to life, shouting incoherently. I know that there's only a few more things that Crash and I personally want to do to this man, so we better let our brothers have their little bit of fun now.

We walk over to the wall and drink some *Jack Daniels* straight from the bottle. Crash grabs a smoke and lights his before handing one to me. Neither one of us smokes that often, but times like this we do. Standing against the wall, looking relaxed when we're anything but, we watch our brothers get their shots in. Tank is the last to go and I can see the rage pouring off of him in waves. This whole situation brought Maddie's to the forefront of his mind and that's not a good thing. Not for Gene at least. He takes several shots before landing the final show of disrespect, spitting in his face. The same thing every guy before him did.

"Now, all of that was nothin' more than a little taste of the hell you're about to get," I tell him, grabbing another dull and rusty knife off the table. "Time to see what you're really made of." I tell him, taunting him as I step closer.

"F-fuck y-y-you!" he groans out as loud as he can. "S-s-she's m-m-mine!"

This does nothing but send rage flowing through my veins and I can't stop the red haze from clouding my vision. Roughly ripping his boxers from his body, I take the knife and slash through his balls until they fall from his body. Handing the blade over to Crash, I let him take the disgusting little thing he calls a cock from his body. It takes several chops with the dull blade and his screams are piercing our eardrums. Gene finally pleads for it to be done, for us to kill him.

"Did Darcy scream and beg for mercy? Did you show her an ounce of sympathy or remorse for the hell you put her through?" I yell, getting in his face. "Did she cry out for us? I'm sure she did, yet you ignored her pleas and did whatever you wanted to. Fuck you, you sick fuckin' psycho!"

I reach out for the bottle of whiskey Crash and I were just drinking from as he makes more slices to the back of this asshole. Before I can pour the alcohol over his back, my brother takes salt and rubs it into the fresh wounds. Gene is trying not to beg and plead, but he can't help it anymore. The pain is getting to be too much. Frankly, I'm ready to be done with this shit, get cleaned up, and back home to Darcy.

"Anyone want to get in anymore shots before I pour this and light him up?" I ask, looking at each and every man in this room. Usually we don't allow prospects to get their hands dirty, but I'm willing to make an exception in this case. "If Gage, Grim, and Slim don't mind, I'm willin' to open this up to Shadow and the rest of the prospects standin' in this room right now."

The three Presidents look at one another and shrug their shoulders to say that this is our show and they're not going to stop anyone of the prospects that want to partake. Shadow immediately steps up and lands four quick blows to random parts of Gene. When he's done he spits in his face and tells him that was for Darcy. Pride shines through from every full patch member standing in the room. Boy Scout from the Phantom Bastards and Travis, a newer prospect, from Clifton Falls both step up and give Gene their best shots. Travis breaks his nose and I can hear the crunching of bones break as he lands two shots to his ribs. Pride is definitely one of the main feelings going through this room right now.

Finally, I pour a ton of whiskey down Gene's back and let it sink into the cuts and scrapes that have already been done to his body. He attempts to scream, but no sound comes out he's lost his voice from screaming so much the last few minutes. Even though it feels like hours have passed by. Crash takes his lighter and puts the flickering, dancing flame to Gene's back. The alcohol make it go up in flames rapidly, not giving anyone a chance to cover their nose against the stench of burning flesh and hair. Those are two or the worst smells I've ever had the displeasure of smelling. But, we all stand there and watch as the flames consume Gene. Once the screams are silenced by death, Gage nods to Shadow to put him out and get the mess cleaned up.

The rest of us make our way upstairs to get cleaned up and have a few drinks before we head home. Travis and Boy Scout stay with Shadow and help him out even though no one asked them too. These three are going to make amazing full patch members of their respective clubs. I wish all of our prospects were like these three, but not everyone is. That's why we ride some harder than we do others. But, we've all been through it, and countless others have tried without success.

Right now, Crash and I are going to hang out with our brothers before they all make their way back home. Plus, it gives Darcy time to hang out with her girls before they all leave. They might only be a phone call away, but it's not the same as having them here to talk to in person or do things with on a regular basis. So, we're going to take advantage of it and let our girl do the same thing.

Chapter Twelve
Trojan

THE PAST TWO MONTHS HAVE BEEN A whirlwind of activity. Between appointments with specialists, getting the cast off on Darcy's arm and starting therapy to strengthen it, and baby doctor appointments with Doctor Sanchez, we haven't had a break. Plus, we've had to work and done things regarding club business. Crash and I have been busier than ever. I wouldn't change one thing about it though.

Well, I would change the mood that Darcy's been in. She's pissed and frustrated that she can barely do anything. And that was before the cast on her arm came off. We're still riding her ass about doing too much, but Grace has kept all of us in check. Darcy just doesn't understand that we care about her safety and don't want her to hurt herself. She's been taking pretty good care of herself if Crash and I are honest about it.

Today is another big day for several reasons. First, we go get the cast on her leg off. Then we make our way over to Doctor Sanchez's office for Darcy's ultrasound and to possibly find out the sex of the baby. We've all talked about it and we want to know what we're having. Darcy is becoming withdrawn though and stays inside her head a lot about something. Karen has assured us it's not about what happened to her. She's taken what happened, dealt with it, and has become a different person. Darcy is in no way weak or letting this negatively impact her. Instead, it's forced her to live life to the fullest and realize how strong she truly is. So, Crash and I have been planning a special surprise for her.

"Baby, you need help gettin' washed up?" I ask her, walking into the bedroom and finding our girl standing at the closet to find something to wear.

"Yeah. Can you help me get one of the dresses from the back of the closet please?" she asks, looking at me with her eyes softening in love.

"What's goin' on with you baby?" I ask her, handing her the dress she picked out.

"What do you mean?" Darcy asks, sitting down on the bed and setting her crutches next to her.

"You've been in your head more and we want to know what's goin' on. We can't help you work through shit if we don't know what's goin' on," I tell her, sitting down behind her and taking the brush from her hands.

Darcy looks down at her hands in her lap for a second as she thinks about how she wants to word the thoughts in her mind. I use the time to brush through the silky strands of her hair. Crash and I have been taking turns brushing her hair out for her. I love the intimacy and feeling of helping with something that may seem so simple, but only brings us closer. Out of the corner of my eye, I notice my brother standing in the doorway waiting to hear the answer.

"What's going to happen when the baby is born? I mean it's either yours or Crash's. I don't want either one of you to feel a certain way if the baby isn't yours. Does that even make sense?" she asks, rushing her words together in her nervousness.

"Is that what's been makin' you so quiet and reserved around us lately?" Crash asks, walking in the bedroom and squatting down in front of our girl. "If the baby is Trojans, he or she is still my baby. The same goes for him. Maybe the next baby will be whoever didn't get you pregnant this time. I'm good with whoever the dad is because I don't see it that way."

"I agree baby," I tell her, placing a gentle kiss to the back of her neck after pushing her hair to the side. "We're all in this together and the baby is an addition to the family that we're makin'. Now, Crash, get the box down for our girl. It's time for part one of today."

Crash gets the box down and walks toward the bed. Darcy looks between us and tears into the box. As she pulls the tissue paper out of the way, I see the tears in her eyes. Pulling it out of the box as if it's the most precious thing in the world to her, Darcy looks the rag over before finally sliding her arms into it.

"Do you fully understand what puttin' that on means, firecracker?" Crash asks, circling around her to see the back with our names on it.

"I think I do," she answers hesitantly. "Tell me, please?"

"It means that in the eyes of the club, you're our wife, our old lady. This rag proclaims to anyone that sees you that you belong to Crash and me. Eventually we'll make you our wife in the eyes of the rest of the world, but for now, the club is more important. You ready for all that?" I ask her, placing a kiss on her lips before she answers.

"I am more than ready for that. I love you both and I only want nothing but the best for us," she tells us, wrapping her arms around both of us. Which is how Grace finds us as she walks in the room telling us that we need to get moving.

Grace sees Darcy's rag and unshed tears fill her eyes. She knows the importance of it and what it signifies. Just like she knows what we're about to do later on tonight. Crash's mom helped, along with Riley, to make sure tonight is perfect for our girl. I can't wait to see the look on her face as she figures out what's happening.

We help Darcy up and make sure she's steady on her crutches before moving away from her. There may have been an instance or two in which Darcy has almost face planted, and we've had to move quick to catch her. She just gets moving so fast and her center of balance is shifting with our growing baby starting to become known to the world. Darcy has more than a baby bump now that Grace keeps saying is bigger than it should be for one baby. Lord help us if there's more than one baby in there!

Loading up into the truck, I sit in back with Grace while Crash drives. It's doesn't take us long to make our way to the building where the orthopedist surgeon is located. He's in a separate building from the hospital and has everything in house that he needs to make sure our girl's leg is completely healed before removing the cast from her. I'm glad that Grace is going with us to keep us in check when they take Darcy back. We don't go with her because she has to have the x-rays done first. Since we can't go in the room, and Darcy insisted that she is more than capable of going through this appointment by herself, we are stuck sitting in uncomfortable as fuck plastic chairs that want to fall apart under our weight. Plus, there was no way in hell that Grace was missing the ultrasound that's going to tell us what her grandbaby is.

After waiting for what seems like hours instead of about twenty minutes, Darcy appears in the doorway that leads back to the rooms and x-ray. Looking up and down her delectable body, she's still using the crutches, but her leg is not hindered by the enormous cast that once encased it. We all stand up so we can head out to the truck and to her next appointment. I take the paperwork from the doctor and make sure that she doesn't need another appointment. Unless her therapist thinks she needs to have further testing done on her leg, she's good to go.

"Are you ready to go see our baby?" I ask, climbing in the front seat with her and heading toward the next office, excitement roaring through my veins at seeing our baby again.

"I am. I don't care what we're having. The only thing that's important to me is that there's no lasting effects from what was done to me," she tells us, settling her hands over mine on her baby bump.

"Agreed," Crash pipes up from the backseat. We both know that this has been weighing heavily on Darcy's mind. The next four months are going to drag by until we can see for ourselves that the baby is indeed fine.

Darcy

Excitement is coursing through my body, along with the overwhelming need to go to the bathroom. But, wanting to see our baby is more important to me in this moment. I'm laying on the table after having everything checked and speaking to Doctor Sanchez briefly, waiting for the tech to come in. My guys sit by my head while Grace is sitting in a chair next to the wall. There's no way in hell that's where she's going to be sitting when we get to see the baby on the small screen. I'll make sure that she's right next to us, so she can be involved in the moment with us.

The technician finally makes her way in the room and goes over my information quickly before pulling my dress up and covering my lower body with a sheet, so my panties aren't on full display for everyone in the room. I look up at Crash and nod my head in the direction of his mom. He tells her to come stand with us and she hesitates briefly before coming over.

"You're not intruding on anything, Grace," I tell her, reaching for her hand and pulling her closer to the bed so she can see. "This may be our baby, but your it's grandma and you deserve to be here. With us, not sitting off to the side."

Grace nods her head with unshed tears in her eyes. Crash is her only child and I know this means the world to her. It means the world to all of us that she's here with us. We've been talking about everything and we're trying to convince her to move to Dander Falls to be with us. To see her son and grandchild constantly instead of once in a while. Slowly, we're shedding her defenses and making the idea seem good to her. My hope is that seeing the heartbeat and finding out what we're having will push her over the edge and help her decide to move here.

"Are we finding out the sex of the baby today?" the technician asks, squeezing the gel out onto my stomach before placing the wand there to see everything she needs to.

"Yes!" we all answer in unison, smiles forming on our faces as our little peanut comes into view on the screen.

"Alright. Let's see if he, or she, will cooperate with us," she replies, moving the wand around and pressing down lightly when she gets in the area she needs to be in. "You're going to have a baby boy."

I look at my men and Grace to see that we all have tears in our eyes. In the next four months, we're going to have a precious baby boy to teach, help grow and learn, and make sure he turns into the kind of man his dads are. As the technician does her measurements and what else she has to look at, I keep my eyes glued to the screen, but baby names run through my mind. One name in particular gets stuck there and I can't wait to talk to Crash and Trojan about it. It will have to wait though. We have the rest of the day to get through and going to the clubhouse to let everyone know the baby's gender is part of that.

As soon as we have the pictures in our hands, at least one for each of us, I use the sheet to wipe the gel off my body and pull my dress back down. Crash helps me up and Trojan hands me the crutches I still have to use until my leg strengthens. I can start using them less and less soon, but for now, I'm going to take every precaution that I can.

Pulling into the clubhouse parking lot, I see a ton of people here. It's not just the guys from this charter, there's too many bikes here for that. Hobbling into the main room, I see my girls, Wilma, all the guys, Shy, and all of the kids running all over the place. Keira is the only one sitting since she's pregnant too. While she's not as far along as I am, she's still tired. So, she's sitting close to the table holding a pink balloon and a blue balloon. Not wanting to wait, Trojan picks me up and carries me over to the table before setting me back down and standing behind me so I don't need my crutches in this moment. Crash is standing right next to us and their warmth surrounds me as I pick the needle up and pop the pink balloon leaving the blue one standing in its place.

Every single guy in the room erupts into cheers while the girls rush over to me and pull me into their embraces. There's a party atmosphere surrounding us, and I don't understand why everyone is here. I could've called the girls to let them know what we were having instead of them making the trip back here. Before too long, my curiosity gets the better of me and I ask the question I'm dying to know the answer to.

"Why are you guys all here?" I ask Bailey, sitting down next to her at one of the tables.

"Well, we didn't want some phone call or video chat to find out what the baby was. So, we talked the guys into coming back down. It's only a few hours and we're planning on staying the weekend," she answers me, not quite meeting my eyes. This tells me that something more is going on. It's only going to be a matter of time before I get one of them to spill the beans. Maybe Sami will tell me.

"Get it out of your head," Skylar tells me, sitting down next to me and handing me a bottled water. "No one is going to tell you anything because there isn't anything to tell. We don't have anything going on at home and this is an important day for you. Not only did you get your cast off, but you got to find out that you're having a precious little boy. Stop reading anything more into it."

"Okay. I'll let it go. For now," I tell them, sitting back and relaxing.

It's nice to enjoy spending time with my family without having something else to worry about in the background. No one is after anyone and no one is suffering from anything. Well, with the exception of Riley. None of us still know what is going on with her, but one day she'll tell us. And we'll all be there for her like we are every other time one of is in need. I just hope that day is sooner rather than later.

Crash

We've been at the clubhouse for a few hours now. I'm ready to get the rest of our night under way, but Darcy has been having a good time with the girls and I don't want to interrupt her. However, I don't want her to be exhausted when we get to the final thing planned for the night either. She needs to be alert and ready for us.

My mom disappeared with Gage and Riley a little while ago to finish setting everything up. So, we need to start making our way to the back of the clubhouse property. There are woods out back with a clearing not long after you enter. A few years ago, we put some picnic tables out there under a pavilion that we built, and we keep it well taken care of. It's nice to party out there when it's just the club without any hang arounds or club girls. We can relax, eat, and do whatever else we want to.

Tonight, it's being transformed once again to suit our needs with everyone's blessing. The guys from the club were all on board with our plan and I can't wait until Darcy sees it. Hell, I can't wait to see it with all the finishing touches added on. Now, it's time to get our girl so we can get to one of the last highpoints of the day. Nothing will beat finding out that we're having a little boy though. I'm happy as fuck that our first born will be a son. Because if we have daughters that look like their mama, we're gonna need all the help we can get to keep the boys away from her. Yeah, I'm already planning that far ahead.

"Baby, we wanna go for a walk. You ready?" I ask her, holding out my hand for her to take, a fine sweat starting to cover my body as my nerves ratchet up another notch. I've never been more nervous of anything in my life. Well, until our son gets here. Then it's a whole new ballgame.

"Yeah. Are we coming back in before we go home?" she asks, looking at the girls surrounding the table.

"We'll stop back in. I promise," I tell her, letting her pull herself up by my hand and get steady on her feet before we leave the clubhouse.

"Where are we going?" she asks, once we step outside and find Trojan standing there waiting for us, his hands shoved in his pockets and a nervous grin on his face.

"See those woods back there? We're goin' out there. There's a clearin' in the woods and I thought we could walk out there, sit under the stars with you for a little bit, and then walk back. Are you up for that?" Trojan asks her, standing next to her and grabbing the wheelchair in case she needs it.

"That sounds really nice," she answers, using her crutches to help her make her way out into the grass.

Watching Darcy out of the corner of my eye, I can tell that she has no clue about what's going to happen when we make it to the clearing. This is just what we wanted, her to have no clue about what's about to go down. Hopefully everyone is gone from there and we can do what we have planned. I'm already nervous and I can't wait to see her when we both say our peace to her.

We continue at a slow pace until we finally make it to the clearing. Looking around, I don't see Gage, Riley, or my mom. I'm glad that they took a different path back to the clubhouse, so Darcy didn't see them and begin to have even more questions than she already has. She's talked the whole way out here, mainly about nothing at all. We're not going to complain one bit though. It's part of her being open and not afraid to say anything to us that she wants to. I love it and am glad that she hasn't reverted back to being shy and untrusting.

Darcy makes her way over to the picnic table, not looking around at all until she finally sits down at the closest table to us. Surrounding her are candles lit on the table that's covered in rose petals. Directly behind her on a small raised platform are candles spelling out one phrase and one phrase only. As she looks at the candles and tries to figure out what it says for her vantage point, we bend down on our knees and hold a small box in both of our hands out for her to see.

Turning back around toward us, she glances down at the box that's containing the ring we had specially made for her. It's two bands woven into one. The thicker band looks as if it's the tread of a bike tire with the thinner band wrapping around the band as if it's a vine, delicate and pure. At the very center is a black diamond instead of the normal one. Surrounding the diamond are smaller clear diamonds mixed with emeralds. I'm not sure what made us decide to put emeralds in it, but now I'm glad that we did. Our baby boy is due in May and she'll always have his birthstone with her.

"We don't have a lot of pretty words or anythin' like that. What we do know is that we want to spend the rest of our lives with you as a unit. I love you more than I ever thought would be possible, and I can't even begin to express the way that you have changed our world. You bring the light to our dark and the peace to our turmoil. I feel a calm I have never felt before and you are our home. It's wherever you are," I tell her, looking at Trojan to let him know that it's his turn to speak.

"We both know that there's nothin' in this world we won't do to protect you and give you everythin' you could ever want. You have made us happy by agreein' to be ours, you continue to make us happier than we've ever been by becomin' the mother to our first-born son. Then you accepted our rag and everythin' that it means to us and the club. Now, we ask that you make us even happier by becomin' ours in the eyes of the rest of the world," Trojan says before taking a small break. "Crash and I love you more than anythin' in this world.

"Will you marry us?" Trojan and I ask at the same time, holding our breath as we wait for her answer. The wait is killing us and making our nerves climb higher and higher as we pray that she says yes.

"I love you both so much. If I could legally marry you both, I would. But, I can only marry one of you. How am I supposed to decide who that's going to be?" she asks, tears shining in her eyes and a pain in her soul.

"You don't have to decide anythin' baby," I tell her, meaning that. "No matter what, you're goin' to carry both our last names, and we'll all wear rings. So, it's up to you which one you want to marry and which one you want to be committed to. We don't care who is your husband and who is committed to you."

"Then, yes, I will accept your ring and marry you," she tells us, waiting for us to slide the ring on her finger before she wraps her arms around me and then around Trojan. Plastering both of us with kisses that steal our breath away and make us speechless.

"You're sure?" I ask, just to be sure that this is truly what she wants. "We can have a long engagement if you want."

"I want to get married as soon as we can. When our son is born, he will have the same last name as me and his dads. Are you two up for that?" she asks, setting our world on fire at wanting to truly become ours in every sense of the word quicker than we ever dreamed.

"I'm more than good with it. You and the girls get together and figure this shit out. Once you have everythin' in place, we'll get married. We'll do whatever you need us to," Trojan tells her, sliding closer and giving her another kiss before I can do the same and we head back to the clubhouse to let everyone know.

"I agree. Let us know when, how much money is needed, and whatever else you want us to do. You want us in monkey suits, then you tell us so that we can go get some," I tell her, meaning every last word even though wearing a tux is the last thing that I want to do.

"Nope. I want you guys in jeans and what makes you comfortable. This is our day and it can be however we want it to be. I'm choosing you both and if you want to wear jeans, then that's what you're going to wear," she tells us, flooring us even more and letting this be as much about us as it is about her.

We place her in the wheelchair to get back to the clubhouse. She just got her cast off earlier today and we've been on the go since. I know she's getting tired and it's going to be a while before we can make it out of here once everyone finds out that we're getting married. I'm going to say that more than likely we'll be staying at the clubhouse tonight and heading home in the morning. Darcy is going to be ready for bed soon and it will just be easier to stay here with her. I'll make sure that my mom has a room and is comfortable before I head to bed.

Walking back into the clubhouse, everything going on stops and all eyes turn toward us. They're waiting to hear what's going on and if we're going to be celebrating or not. We have a lot to celebrate already with the baby and our girl being home where she belongs. Now, we have one more reason to celebrate and they're all waiting and wondering about it.

"She said 'yes'!" Trojan and I yell out at the same time, finally letting smiles cover our faces and the celebrating begins now.

Everyone surrounds us, and we're greeted with hugs, kisses, and back slaps. The girls are going crazy over the ring.

No one got to see it before we gave it to her and I'm glad that she was the first one to see it. My mom even drove me crazy trying to see the ring before Darcy had it placed on her finger. We kept that shit under lock and key so that our girl laid eyes on it before anyone else. Now, the fun begins, and we get to plan a day that Darcy will be proud of and we'll make her as happy as humanly possible.

Chapter Thirteen
Darcy

THE LAST MONTH HAS BEEN SO BUSY WITH all the planning and shopping. I've had appointments to go to and therapy to attend. There has even been another stylist hired at the salon so that Riley isn't getting overwhelmed. I don't want her to quit and then I have to close up shop because I can't be there as much as I once was. Even with the pregnancy advancing, I can't be there as much. I'm tired more often than not and my feet and back are always killing me. If I didn't remind myself that this is going to end with a blue bundle of joy in our arms, I'd be sick as fuck of feeling this way.

"Baby, where you at?" Trojan yells, heading back toward the bedroom I'm currently sitting in.

"In here. I'm supposed to be getting ready for tonight, but I just needed a minute before I got in the shower," I respond, telling him as I start to push myself up off the bed. It's harder and harder to do these days.

"Sit down baby. You've got time and we can just relax for the time bein'," He tells me, putting his hand on my chest and keeping me in place for now. "I can help relax you."

Immediately, I know what's on his mind and I'm not going to stop him at all. I'll take Trojan and Crash every second of the day if I could. I don't know if it has to do with being pregnant or knowing that for the rest of my life they're going to be mine. What I do know is that they both give into me almost every single time I want to have some fun. Today is no different. Originally, I did come in the bedroom to escape the wedding madness, but now, I want my man. Crash isn't here, or he'd be in the room with us. He had to go get some things for the parties that are going to happen today. The first one is going to be a baby shower at the clubhouse. We're treating it more like a cookout than anything so that the guys would stay and spend the day with us. Other than opening presents, there won't be any games or anything like that. I wanted it done this way. What happens tonight is another story altogether. From what I understand the girls went all out and they closed the Kitty Kat for us.

Trojan stops all thoughts that aren't about him the second he kisses my neck. He spends time there licking, nipping, and soothing the sting away. My body is trembling and on fire for his touch, I can't wait to get his hands on other parts of my body as I push my ass into his groin and start to grind against him. I know this is going to push him over the edge and take me how I really want to be taken; hard and fast.

I can feel him undoing his jeans as I pull my panties down, leaving my dress in place. All he has to do is pull it up so that he can reach where I want him most. I'm already wet and aching for him, he discovers this when he reaches his hand between my legs and feels how wet I am. Tilting my head back so that I can reach his mouth, I desperately want to kiss him. To make him as breathless as he makes me every time we kiss. Whether it's Crash or Trojan, I'm always left breathless and wanting just from a simple touch of their lips.

"Please, Dom, I need you now," I beg of him, using his real name instead of his road name.

This accomplishes exactly what I want and with one swift thrust, Trojan is inside me and we both groan out in unison. He pistons in and out of me while I push my ass back against him just as hard as he's going after me. We're both competing to finish, only I know he'll make sure that I find my release before he does. No matter, both men make sure I get mine before them. Usually it's more than once, but today, that's not going to be the case.

I reach down and begin to play with my tits as Trojan watches over my shoulder. It's driving him crazy and I know that's it's going to push him harder. He reaches between my legs and begins to circle my clit as I continue squeezing and kneading my overly sensitive tits. Trojan is starting to lose control of his movements and moving faster. Arching my back, I let him continue to thrust in and out of my willing body while I push back and make him lose control even more.

Reaching behind my head with one hand, I grab a handful of Trojan's hair to pull him closer to me. I need to feel his mouth on me again. That's what's going to push me over the edge right now. He can sense what I need and gives it to me immediately and without hesitation. I start chanting that I'm close and it continues to spur him on and make sure that I get mine.

"Give. It. To. Me!" He growls out to me, twisting his hips and becoming even more erratic in his movements.

His words throw me over the edge, and I feel myself letting go. Wave after wave of my release washes over me and I can't help but cry out no matter who hears me. within a few thrusts, Trojan follows me over the edge and moans out my name as he kisses me full of every bit of passion and love he has in his body. He pulls out of me and rubs his hands up and down my sides. This is what they usually do when we're done having sex. I roll into him and wrap my arms around him. Giving him the same treatment, I rub my hands up and down his back.

Trojan gets up first and I can hear the shower turn on before he returns and picks me up off the bed and carries me into the bathroom. Setting me down on the toilet seat, I let him pull my dress off my head while I use my hands and finish pushing his jeans down his muscular thighs. We make our way into the shower and I stand under the shower while he washes me from my head down to my toes. Once he's done, I give him the same treatment before getting out and drying one another off.

We finish getting ready while Crash finishes up what he's working on. The four of us are going to the clubhouse together and I have a few things that I'm taking with us. I've been baking and cooking up a storm with Grace's help. None of them want me to do too much and I can't help but be going a little bit crazy right now.

"Everybody here?" Crash asks, walking through the front door and meeting us in the kitchen. "You show her yet?"

"Nope. I was waitin' on you to get here," Trojan tells him, standing behind me and putting his hands on my shoulders. "You ready to show her now?"

Crash nods his head and they each grab one of my hands before leading me to the hallway where Grace is standing. The door where all the guns sit is slightly ajar and I don't want to go in here, but it seems to be important to the guys, so I'll walk in there with him. Instead of being filled with the guns, the entire room is cleaned out and it's been painted a light shade of blues and greens. The room is spacious, and I can't wait to see what it's going to look like when we get it decorated and all the furniture in here.

"You guys are amazing! I can't believe that you guys did this for us," I tell them, wrapping them both in hugs and placing kisses on their lips before turning to Grace and wrapping my arms around her too.

"We knew you didn't want them to be in here and that we're goin' to need a nursery. This room is the closest to ours, so we thought it would be perfect," Crash tells me, pulling me back against his body as I imagine the room filled with furniture, clothes, toys, and everything else our son will need.

"I love it! Now, I have another thought about a name," I tell them, pulling them in close and whispering my idea of the perfect name to them. The rest of you will just have to wait!

We've been at the clubhouse for a little while and I am parked in one of the more comfortable chairs brought out from inside. These days, I can't get comfortable. At six months pregnant, I suddenly popped and now carry around a beachball in my stomach. It's not huge, but enough to make me uncomfortable as all get out. I can't imagine what's going to happen when I get even bigger. And I have no doubt that I will get bigger than what I currently am.

I'm surrounded by our family and friends. There's kids running all over the place and Bailey is the only one that isn't sitting with us right this second. She's farther out in the yard where they set up a memorial for the child that Gage and she lost a while back. Whenever they come to Dander Falls, she always spends a few minutes up there. Gage does the same thing when he goes to Clifton Falls.

"How are you feelin'?" Trojan asks, pulling up a chair next to me and sitting down with a beer in his hand.

"I'm okay. A little uncomfortable, but when aren't I lately?" I ask, uncapping the bottled water and taking a long pull. "You guys okay?"

"Yeah. We're catchin' up with everyone and talkin' about a run that we want to put on for the domestic violence program. I think when Bailey gets back here, they're goin' to do presents and shit," he tells me, looking out over everyone that's here to celebrate with us. "You sure you're ready to be tied to us in a few days?"

"Trojan, I want nothing more than to be your wife. Well, to one of you. I'm still figuring that shit out," I tell him, placing my hand on his arm and trying to take away his second-guessing himself about what I want. "If I didn't want to be with you, I never would've accepted the rag. And I sure as fuck wouldn't have said yes to marrying you."

This seems to take away some of the fear running through him. He's been like this since I got kidnapped. For the most part he's fine and tells me what to and how to do it like the alpha asshole they are. Then he has moments where he's so unsure of himself and what I'm doing with them. These moments are the ones that I love them even more. Crash makes his way over to us and I know that he's waiting to get on with the day. While I'm excited to go out tonight, even looking like a beached whale, they're just as excited to go out and spend the night with the boys to do what they do. Well, as long as they keep their cocks firmly in their pants.

"You need anythin' baby?" Crash asks, taking a long pull from the beer he's drinking.

"Nope. I'm getting hungry, but I know Gage and Grim are working on it. I can wait until everything is ready to go and the kids are fed," I tell them as my stomach grumbles to showcase my hunger. I'm always hungry these days too.

Skylar approaches us from behind, laughing at hearing my stomach. She hands me a plate with some pasta salad on it. I try to argue with her about waiting and letting the kids eat first, but she won't hear it. Instead she tells me that this bowl was put aside for later on when we go to the Kitty Kat. Yeah, we'll have other food there, but she knows that over the past week I've been craving pasta salad.

I dig in to my salad and continue to watch everyone around us. The kids are having a ball running around and playing games with one another. Jameson, Anthony, and little Zander are keeping an eye on all the younger kids. Tank's three sons, Chance, Brax, and Shawn, are starting to follow in their footsteps so they're trying to follow the three older boys around. I can't wait until our little one can begin to follow them around when we're all together and lead any other little boys that join him here. This is what makes life worth living and going through all the shit to get to the good.

I see Bailey making her way back down to the rest of us. Instead of seeing her face covered in tears and sad, there's a serene smile covering her face and her eyes are shimmering. I'm not sure exactly what's going on, but we'll find out when she's ready for us to know. Maybe it's just my overactive imagination running wild and there's nothing there to tell. She just had a good visit with her son before spending the rest of the day with her family making memories to last a lifetime.

"Burgers will be ready in five is you want to start makin' plates," Grim hollers out, taking the platter of hot dogs to the table while the old ladies line up to make plates for the kids.

"What do you want, firecracker?" Trojan asks, standing up and turning to face me.

"I want to go make my own. I need exercise and walking through the food line isn't going to hurt me at all. You can stay right on my ass the whole time," I tell them, holding out my hands for him to pull me up.

"I was already on your ass this mornin," he retorts with a smile lighting up his entire face.

"Is that so?" Crash asks, joining our conversation. "Well, you can bet your ass I'll be on it later tonight."

"No, you won't. You two are staying at the clubhouse with the rest of the guys. She's staying at Riley's with us. Tomorrow morning is when you'll lay eyes on your girl again. Not one second before she walks down the aisle to marry you two asshats," Bailey tells us, planting her hands on her hips and tilting her head slightly, just daring us to say one word to the contrary.

"What the fuck are you talkin' about?" Trojan asks, rising to his full height with a confused and slightly pissed off look on his face.

"You can't see the bride before the wedding," Bailey answers like it makes all the sense in the world. "We already talked to Gage and have Shadow and Mike with us for the night. Not sure how they're going to like watching male strippers, but they got babysitting duty. "Plus, Addison is going to meet us at the Kitty Kat later and she's bringing the normal bouncers in to keep an eye on us."

"You got everythin' figured out, don't ya?" Crash asks her, not happy in the least and letting it be known with the attitude in his voice.

I place a hand on each of my men in an attempt to calm them down. They center me just as much as I center them and calm them down when it's needed. This is also news to me and I don't know what to tell them that's going to satisfy their need to keep me in their sight at all times. What I do know is that I'm not going to argue with Bailey. I can see the hard glint in her eyes and I know that no one is going to win this argument.

"I'll spend the entire day with you guys, enjoying the time we have with our family. We'll open our son's gifts, have some dinner, and then I'll go out with the girls," I tell them, looking between the two alpha cavemen standing before me. "When it's time to leave, I'll have protection on me and I know they'll let you know if anything happens to me. Tomorrow morning, we'll all be back under the roof of the clubhouse and in no time at all, I'll be your wife."

"Do you know which one of us you're goin' to marry yet?" Crash asks, grabbing my hand and lacing his fingers with mine.

"Yeah. I'm goin' to marry Trojan. This wasn't an easy decision for me to make. Please don't be upset," I tell him, holding the side of his face in my hand and staring in his eyes.

"Why would I be upset?" he asks, leaning into my touch. "We told you from the beginnin' that it didn't matter to us. You're already wearin' my name on your rag, my ring on your finger, and you'll still carry my last name."

"Now that everything is settled, you better feed your girl. I know if it were me, I'd be ready to chop your balls off for making me wait when I was pregnant," Bailey tells them, putting her hand on the small of my back and directing me towards the tables filled to capacity with food.

Crash and Trojan both cringe and grab their balls They lead me over to the food line and follow me through making sure that I get enough to eat. I know the plates that they have loaded up will end up coming to me too. Yeah, I've been eating a lot the last few weeks. After loading up our plates and making our way to a table, we're joined by several couples from Clifton Falls, Gage, and Riley. Throughout dinner we make small talk and I can see the prospects and one or two club girls cleaning off the tables laden with food.

While everyone has me busy talking, laughing, and trying to get the baby's name out of me, people are working tirelessly bringing new things out of the clubhouse and setting it up. There's already a table filled with gifts that spill on the ground surrounding it. I'm surprised that the table is still standing with everything on it. It fills my heart to see how everyone pulled together to make sure that the baby has a ton of new things. And I know that the love and support will be shown from every person sitting and standing with us now.

"Are you done baby?" Crash asks me, standing up with his plates to take care of.

"Yeah. I don't think I could eat another bit without blowing up," I tell him, getting everyone around us to laugh while I rub my belly in satisfaction.

"Why don't you go take a nap and we'll wake you up in like an hour," Maddie tells me, sitting back down in front of Tank. "I know when I was pregnant, I was tired all the time."

"You were also cookin' three kids," Tank tells her affectionately. "And my boys would run anyone ragged."

We all laugh, but a nap does sound good right about now. I nod my head and Trojan helps me stand up before going to follow me into the clubhouse. Telling him that I don't need them to come with me and they should stay with their brothers, I make my way into the couch and lay down. It takes a little bit to get comfortable, but once I do, I can't help but pass right out.

Waking up with a jolt, I feel the baby moving around and tears form in my eyes. I see Crash and Trojan sitting in the chairs next to the couch I'm lying on and I tell them to come to me quickly. Grabbing a hand from each of them, I place it on my stomach and tell them to wait for a second. When they feel the slight movement on my stomach, they look at one another before looking at me. Crash is the first to lean down and kiss me senseless. It's quickly followed by Trojan doing the same thing.

"Everyday we get to see you grow round with our baby is a gift," Crash tells me, standing back up and helping me off the couch.

Trojan and him lead me to the bathroom before we make our way back outside. There's a chair sitting front and center for me to sit in with two more on the sides of it. All the kids are lined up at the table with the gifts on it. I guess we're getting to the baby shower part of the day. It suits me just fine so that I can possibly take another nap before going out tonight. Or maybe have some fun with my men before we leave for the night. Anything is possible.

"Now, I know the guys don't necessarily want to be here for this part, but they're going to suck it up and stick around. They know that once this is done, the night is theirs and they're going to party," Bailey says, getting everyone's attention. "The kids all wanted to help and be a part of this, so they're going to be in charge of handing out the gifts for the three of you to open."

They come up to us one by one and hand us a gift before making their way back to the table. Jameson stays close to Zoey while Anthony is close to Kasey. It's cute to watch them help the girls out and I can only hope that our baby will be the same way with any little girls that are born into this club.

We spend over an hour opening every last gift that was on the table. Pops comes up to us last and hands us an envelope. Inside is a picture of a nursery set that is hand carved. There's a motorcycle on the ends of the crib and the top of the toy box that goes with it. Surrounding the motorcycle is 'Wild Kings MC'. I can't stop the tears that flow freely from my eyes at the love and care that was put into this furniture set.

"Thank you so much," I tell him, grabbing his hands so that I can give him a hug of appreciation. "It's so beautiful."

"You're welcome sweetie," he tells me, returning the hug before Crash and Trojan let out a growl of anger at another man touching me. "It will be delivered to the clubhouse in a few days. That way you can pick it up and take it home to set up."

By the time we're done with opening gifts and eating cake, yes, I ate more, dusk is beginning, and I know it's only a matter of time before we leave to go to the strip club. There's not enough time to take a nap or have any fun with my guys before we head out. So, I guess we'll just have to make up for it tomorrow after we're married.

I have another piece of cake while the guys load everything up in the truck so that we can take it home at some point soon. There's so much that I wonder how it's all going to fit in the truck in one load. But, miraculously it does. There's everything from diapers and wipes to clothes, blankets, booties, toys, and baby wash and lotion. I can't even begin to list everything that we got from everyone today. I'm amazed that there's still things we're going to have to buy before the baby gets here.

"Are you about ready to head out to the Kitty Kat?" Skylar asks me, bringing me a bottled water and sitting down in the chair that Trojan vacated.

"Yeah. In all honesty, I'm ready to head to bed, but I know that's not an option right now," I tell her, knowing that we're going to have fun tonight.

"I know you are. We'll head out in a few minutes so that you can have some fun before you pass out," she tells me, standing up and helping me stand up so that we can leave.

Walking into the main room of the clubhouse, I see my men sitting in chairs with a beer in their hand. They stand up when I walk in and wait for me to get close to them. Each one of them hug and kiss me before wrapping their arms around my body. I snuggle in close and let them hold me close.

"I know things tend to get crazy with these women, behave yourself tonight," Crash tells me, slapping me on the ass before walking to the bar to get rid of his empty bottle.

"We'll know if you have any moments like you usually do with Wood. Remember Shadow and Mike will be with you guys if you need anythin' at all," Trojan tells me, placing a sweet and lingering kiss on my lips before both men walk me out to the SUV we'll be taking tonight. After each one of them give me a kiss to make sure that I remember them and only them, they stand back and watch as we all pile in and get ready to leave.

The girls all pile in with me next to Bailey in the front seat. I'm not sure who the designated driver will be when we get out of there tonight, but it's probably going to be one of the prospects. At least that's what I'm hoping because I know these girls like to drink when they get the chance to. Since Alice and Pops are watching the kids here I know they're going to live it up tonight. The same way the guys will at the clubhouse.

The strip club was closed for the night so that we can have fun watching men get naked. Well, almost naked. I can guarantee that if they stripped down to nothing, our men would be here in a heartbeat, beating the shit out of them. Just because we got to see the goods and they can't stand anyone touching us, looking at us, us looking at them, or anything else involving the opposite sex. Honestly, I'm surprised we get to watch strippers at all. Bailey and Skylar must have pulled some major strings to get this to happen.

We're sitting right at the end of the stage and I'm sitting dead center and a little bit above everyone else. The reason for this is beyond me and I'm sure that I don't want to even begin to know what's going to happen at any given time. Bailey, Skylar, and Riley are sitting the closest to me and I can tell that nothing good is going to end up coming from this.

"So, I hear that we have a bride to be in the house tonight," one of the strippers announces. "Why don't you come up on stage for your last night as a single woman?"

The rest of the strippers come out on the stage and the girls surrounding me are chanting for me to get up on stage. How they expect me to easily get on stage at six months pregnant is beyond me, but I'm game to try. Looking over my shoulders, I find Shadow and Mike and point my finger at them, so they know not to blab to Crash and Trojan about me getting up on stage. I know they won't unless my men ask specific questions about it. Then, I'm royally fucked, and I won't be enjoying it. At all.

Bailey points to the side of the stage and I see steps leading up that I can climb. One of the strippers walks over to meet me and grabs my hand to help me. He leads me to a chair that's been placed center stage and stands next to me until I'm comfortable. Then, all hell breaks loose as *Anywhere* by *112* starts playing. I have men surrounding me, grinding and dancing away like their lives depend on it. I've never really been to a strip club before and I can't stop laughing. I'm laughing so hard that I feel like I'm going to pee my pants. Unfortunately, I'm stuck on stage and I can't leave right now. Looks like I better calm myself down.

All of a sudden, one man does some move on the floor in front of me and I absolutely lose it. Somehow, I manage to slide out of the chair and onto the floor with my pussy practically in his face. He stares up at me and both of our faces are turning red. Why does this shit happen to me all the time? There's no graceful way to get up, so I scoot myself across the stage until I'm at the edge and my dress is up around my chest. The girls are hooting and hollering, and the strippers are surrounding me. Shadow is the only one to come to my rescue.

I catch him running towards me from a few feet away. Grabbing my hands, he slowly and carefully helps me off the stage while trying to cover my stomach and ass from anyone else seeing it. It's obviously too late for that, but I'm thankful that he's at least trying to protect my modesty. Bailey and Whitney sober immediately when they see my dilemma and help me sit back down in the chair I vacated earlier.

Tears are running down my face from embarrassment and shame and all I want to do is go to Riley's apartment. Melody hands me a bottle of water while Keira hands me some napkins to wipe my nose and clean my face up a little bit.

While I'm thankful that they're trying to help me, I'm ready to go.

"Riley, do you mind if I head over to your house now? You guys can enjoy the rest of the show, but I'm ready for bed," I ask her, turning to face her and showing her that I really don't want to be here anymore.

"Are you sure?" she asks, leaning forward to put her hand on my arm and so I can hear her better. "I can go with you so you're not alone."

"No, please stay. If you don't mind, I'll just go to the second bedroom and go to bed," I tell her, standing and wiping myself off. "I'll see if Shadow can go with me while Mike stays with you guys."

Riley nods her head and I begin to make my way to the exit. Shadow and Mike are standing there watching us and avoiding all eye contact with the men on stage. Before I can tell them that I'm ready to go, I'm surrounded by the rest of the girls. I guess that they're ready to leave now too. This isn't what I wanted, and I hate that they're all leaving because I want to go now instead of enjoying the rest of the show.

"I'm sure that you guys can stay and watch the show," I tell them, turning to face them and placing my hand on my belly for comfort.

"No. We didn't think this all the way through and you got hurt because of it. I'm so sorry," Bailey tells me. "So, now we're going to go back to Riley's and have some girl time. We need to make sure that everything is ready for tomorrow morning anyway."

I can tell that at least half the girls are pretty buzzed, and I don't know how they plan on doing anything before they pass out. I'm glad they were enjoying themselves though. Next time, I'll be able to join in and have a good time. This will become a distant memory and we'll laugh about it soon enough.

The ride to Riley's is thankfully uneventful and I'm more exhausted than ever before. I'm not sure if it's all the events from today that finally caught up to me, or just what happened a little while ago on stage. But, I'm ready for bed and nothing is going to keep me out of it. Hopefully they all understand. Especially since my eyes are already starting to droop and I don't know if I am going to make it the next few minutes to her house.

Riley and Keira wake me up as Bailey shuts the SUV off. Shadow is already at my door to help me in the room while the rest of the girls do what they have to. I'm told to go in Riley's room and get in bed while she helps get the rest of the girls whatever they need for the rest of the night and then she'll be in. That's the last thing I remember before my eyes close and I fall into a dreamless sleep.

Chapter Fourteen
Crash

TODAY IS THE DAY I'VE BEEN waiting for. Darcy is going to become ours officially and I have been counting down the hours until we get to see her. Trojan and I sat off to the side most of the night while the rest of the guys partied and watched the strippers. We drank ourselves as drunk as we dared to get while naked women and club girls surrounded us. To the outsider, it would look like a normal party. Unfortunately, those haven't held any appeal for my brother and I since Darcy came into our lives.

Hearing a knock on my door, I drag my tired ass to it and fling it open without making sure I'm even halfway decent. Red is standing at my door as I answer it naked as the day I was born. What the fuck? She knows she's not supposed to be here right now and I'm not going to deal with her shit an hour or so before I get married to the girl of my dreams.

"What the fuck do you want? You know you're not supposed to be here today," I ask her, letting the annoyance and anger come out fully in my voice.

"I thought you could use some relief before you tie yourself to one pussy for the rest of your life," she tells me, going to run her hand down my naked chest.

"Not in your dreams bitch!" I holler out. "Gage, Grim, someone get the fuck up here!"

Gage, Grim, and countless other men come pounding up the stairs. They take one look at me and then Red. Some of them are thinking the worst, but those that know me, know that I wouldn't touch this bitch with a twenty-foot pole and some other guy's cock. I take a minute to calm down before I explain the situation. Red stands there, shifting from one foot to the other while she tries to figure out how she's going to get out of the mess she currently finds herself in. I'm done with this bitch and I know that Gage has had more than one complaint about her as of late.

"I was just wakin' up when there was a knock on my door. I figured it was Trojan comin' to make sure that I was up and startin' to get ready. When I opened the door, this bitch stood there. Wantin' to give me some 'relief' before I got married today," I tell the men surrounding me, not sparing the cum guzzler in front of me a glance. She doesn't deserve anything from a single one of us.

"Red, this is not the first time I've had to fuckin' talk to you about this shit!" Gage yells at her, taking one slow step after another toward her. "You are no longer welcome at any of the Wild Kings clubhouses! Not only did you know you weren't supposed to be here today, you have once again tried to get a brother that is claimed to fuck you. We don't condone cheatin' and you're not that fuckin' good to begin with. Get your shit and get the fuck out of my clubhouse!"

Gage tells Wayne to follow this bitch and make sure that she leaves in less than five minutes. If she can't manage to get all her shit, and just the shit she came in with, then it's no longer hers. Wayne quickly follows the bitch and I walk back into my room. Trojan follows me with a bag. He sits down on my bed and starts taking shit out of it, laying it all out beside him.

There's a new pair of jeans for both of us with black button down long sleeve shirts. We may not be wearing tuxedos or suits, but we are going to make sure that we look good for Darcy. This day is about the three of us and I know that we want it to be special for her. I know the men have something planned for today too, but Trojan and I have no clue what it is. They're being tight lipped about it.

I jump in the shower as quick as I can so that Trojan can jump in after me. There's guys in every available room getting ready, so we decided that he'd just shower in here and we'd get ready together. It's easier and I know that he'll calm me down and I'll calm him down. We're both nervous wrecks about Darcy meeting us at the end of the makeshift aisle. For some reason, we both believe that she's going to pull a runner and not meet us there.

"You're up," I tell him, walking back into my room with a towel wrapped around my waist.

Trojan walks into the bathroom and shuts the door behind him. There's already towels and everything in there for him, so I get dressed while he's washing up. As soon as I have my jeans and boots on, I make sure that my hair looks good and slather some gel in it to stay in place. By the time I'm done with that, Trojan is walking back out the same way I did. He grabs his jeans and throws them on before putting his socks and boots on. After he makes sure his hair is good, we put our shirts on and make our way down to the bar.

Tank and Glock are the first two that we see sitting enjoying a beer before the ceremony begins. We order our own and sit down next to the two men. For the next twenty minutes or so we shoot the shit and try to keep our minds off the wedding and everything about it. That's the only way that we're going to get through the next little while without getting completely smashed. More of our brothers come down and once we're all here, Gage stands up and makes a toast.

"Crash and Trojan are the first in this charter to get an old lady and get married to her. They have found a woman that accepts them for who they are and loves them regardless of their cavemen tendencies and boneheaded ideas," he pauses as the men surrounding us laugh at the accuracy of his statement. "May we all be lucky enough to find what they have and find the ones that we're meant to be with."

We all raise our drinks and salute one another. Even though none of us will willingly admit it, we want to find the girl we're supposed to spend the rest of our lives with. Darcy is truly the one that's meant for us and she takes our shit and gives it back when she can. She knows when to give it back and when not to. Darcy truly was made for us.

Darcy

Waking up, I go to the bathroom and hop in the shower. I'm not sure if anyone else is up, but I'm in a hurry to get ready. The quicker that I get ready, the sooner I can get back to the clubhouse where my men are. That's not to say that I don't have an immense case of nerves right now. A million and one questions play on a constant loop in my head with no stopping them. Are Crash and Trojan going to be waiting for me at the end of the aisle? Will I truly make them happy for the rest of our lives? Will they get bored and cheat on me with club girls or whatever other female sparks their interest? Even feeling the baby move doesn't stop the barrage of questions.

Once I'm out of the shower, I wrap myself in the robe I brought from home. As soon as I got further along in my pregnancy, I knew that I wanted to have a robe for when I wanted to walk around without a lot of clothes on. Crash and Trojan ran out and got me a soft, fuzzy white robe covered in hearts. It goes down to my knees and I love the feeling of it against my skin. When I'm not with my men and missing them, I feel like they're close to me. It may sound weird, but that's how it is with me.

"You up and okay in there?" Riley asks me from the other side of the door.

"Yeah," I answer, opening the door and seeing Riley and the rest of the girls standing on the other side in various forms of dress, hair, and make-up. "You've all already taken showers and stuff?"

"Yep. We've been up for a while. While you were getting your beauty sleep, we were making sure everything was set up at the clubhouse and started getting dressed," Bailey tells me. "Now, we're all about getting you ready and making sure today is a day nothing less than you and the guys deserve. It's going to be the best day yet. At least until the little one is born."

"Do we have a name picked out yet?" Melody asks, trying to get the name out of me. Again.

"Not happening. Nice try though," I tell them, letting the laughter flow freely and feeling my nerves lessen a little bit.

For the next hour, I'm dressed, my hair is done by Riley, and Maddie does my makeup. The girls finish getting ready and we all pile into the SUV and make our way to the clubhouse. With every mile we drive, my nerves begin to climb higher and higher again. It's to the point that I can feel my hands shaking and my leg begins tapping on the floor in front of me.

Bailey and Skylar run in and make sure that everything is set up the way it's supposed to be. Maddie and Keira go in ahead of us to make sure that Crash and Trojan aren't in the main room so that I can go in and hide in the game room downstairs until it's time to walk down the aisle to my men.

As soon as we make our way into the room I'll be waiting in, Tank knocks on the door with one of the triplets. It's Brax, I think. He walks in, holding two different bags and makes his way first to his wife, giving her a hug and kiss with a few whispered words. Once he's done with her, he makes his way over to me, handing me the bags and waiting for me to open them. The first bag contains a dainty bracelet in the same design as my engagement ring. It's platinum and I instantly fall in love with it. The same way that I did with my ring. It fits the three of us perfectly and I can't wait to see what the other bag contains. Before I can move on though, Tank tells me to look at the inside of the bracelet. Carefully turning it over in my hands, I see our three names engraved with our wedding date. Below that it says, 'You are our world, our sunshine, our home'.

Setting the first bag to the side, with Whitney helping me put the bracelet on, I open the second bag to see a hair clip with diamonds and emeralds sprinkled throughout it. The part where the gems rest is in the shape of three hearts contacted to one another. I can't help the tears that start to fill my eyes knowing that I'm not going to let one single tear slip down my cheek and ruin all the hard work that these girls have done today. Riley takes the clip from my hand and places it in my hair so that everyone can see it when they're behind me.

"Tank, please tell them that I love the gifts. Can you take Maddie up with these for them please?" I ask him, picking up the two bags that I brought with us.

I found them matching leather bands holding a small platinum plate that I had engraved with our son's initials. That way, they could show them off and no one would know what it stood for. We're keeping this secret until our son makes his entrance into this world. I hope that they love them as much as I love the gifts that they got me. I'll never be able to thank them for everything they've given to me.

Maddie and Tank leave the room as I sit in the chair and wring my hands together. Looking at the clock on the wall, I see that we have about ten more minutes before it's time to head on out to meet my men at the end of the aisle. I'm getting excited and I am ready to head out there now.

"You doing okay?" Skylar asks me, sitting down next to me with Reagan next to her.

Reagan is going to be our flower girl while Jameson is the ring bearer. We wanted to have more of the kids involved, so Anthony helped sit everyone while the younger kids are going to stand in the aisle and help Reagan throw flowers from where they're standing. It's the best that we could come up with and the girls fell in love with the idea.

"I'm ready to go now," I tell her honestly, standing up and beginning to pace the floor. "But, before I head out there, I guess I better head to the bathroom one more time, so I don't have to go halfway through the ceremony."

She helps me in the bathroom and holds the back up my dress up while I do my business. I should be embarrassed that someone else is in here helping me go to the bathroom, but I can't. Skylar isn't even looking in my direction, but she's looking in the mirror above the sink farther down the wall from where I am. It's high enough that she can't see me. Finally finished, I stand up and wash my hands before we head back out to the game room.

Pops is standing there waiting for us. I'm not sure what he wants from me, but we're about to find out. As soon as he sees us, he stops talking to Bailey and makes his way over to me. he looks me up and down, not in a creepy way, but in a proud father kind of way that makes my eyes begin to tear up again. I guess today is the day for me to be an emotional wreck as everything makes me want to start crying.

"You look beautiful Darcy. I have a question for you before you make your way out to your men," he says, before turning to look at his daughter who nods her head. "Would you like me to walk you down the aisle? It would be my honor to do this for you."

Taking a minute to look back and forth between the man standing before me and his daughter, I mull over the question and think of my own father. He's missing this day with me and I can't help but let one tear fall at my loss. "I would be honored to have you walk me down the aisle Pops," I tell him honestly.

A smile brighter than the sun breaks out on his face and he holds his arm out for me to hang on to. Finally, I take in the way he's dressed and see that he's wearing a nice pair of jeans with a grey button-down shirt on under his cut. He looks amazing and now I really can't wait to see my men.

As we get to the back door of the clubhouse, I hear the song *Marry Me* by *Thomas Rhett* start to play. I've played this song a few times since getting engaged to Crash and Trojan and they must have chosen this song without my knowledge. Tears form, again, at knowing they were paying attention to everything I have done or said since we started planning today. It shouldn't come as any surprise though since they pay attention to me every single day and anticipate what I want, and need, the best that they can.

We finally get to walk through the door and my eyes land on the bikes lined up on the outside of the chairs, the kids standing tall and proud on the inside of the aisle, the green flower petals lining the aisle, and all of the guests standing and looking at me. My focus finds Crash and Trojan standing up front, tall, sexy as fuck, and dressed up in a way. They're wearing black long sleeve shirts tucked into their jeans with their cuts resting on top of it. There's my world standing there with love shining from their faces as they look back at me. A peacefulness comes over me and I know that I'm walking towards home and the rest of my life.

Trojan

Standing in front of my family and our friends, I take a deep breath as the song we chose for Darcy to walk down the aisle begins to play. Everyone turns their attention to the door, waiting for a glimpse at the woman that brings our entire world into focus. The woman that has given us more than we could have ever hoped for, and the woman that makes us want to be the best men we can be.

On my first glimpse of her, I see her hair piled on top of her head, the clip that we bought shining bright while tucked into her hair, while little ringlets frame her face and down her back. The dress that she chose emphasizes where our son lies safe. It's white with small straps going over her shoulders and a thin green ribbon circles right under her full tits. Beginning under the ribbon, the dress flows down around her ankles and sways with her steps toward us. The smile lighting up her face shines bright enough to light a biggest area on the darkest day. Darcy is absolutely radiant and I'm glad that we get to call her ours. There is nothing but love pouring from her and it's amazing to witness the purity of it.

Pops brought the idea to us that he would ask if she wanted him to walk her down the aisle. He's done this before and I know that it would mean the world to our girl. So, we gave him our blessing and he disappeared before anything else could be said about it. It looks like he went to talk to her and she fell in love with the idea like we knew she would. But, there's just a hint of sadness in her eyes and I'm sure that she's missing her dad right about now. This is supposed to be him holding her arm and leading her toward us.

As soon as they get to us, I grab our girl's small, delicate hand and hold it in mine. She stares into my eyes and the rest of the world surrounding us disappears in an instant. Other than the first few words, I don't hear anything that the preacher we found says. In fact, Crash has to nudge me when it comes time for us to say our vows.

"Darcy, when we first saw you, we knew that you would be the perfect woman for us. You are strong, feisty, full of fire, and you love with your whole heart. You know when to give us hell for somethin' we've done to piss you off and when to hold that shit in for a little while. We're full of darkness and you're the light that we want to run toward. Crash and I aren't the most vocal, but we know that we want every single piece of you and we'll do anythin' in our power to make sure that the light never fades away. I love you with everythin' I am and will do so for the rest of my life and beyond," I tell her, letting every emotion shine through with no care in the world of who's watching me right now.

"Darcy, you may say what you want to the two men standing before you. Then I will let Crash say his," the preacher tells her before stepping back a little bit.

"Crash and Trojan, I pushed and pushed until you made sure that you filled every single part of me. When I needed someone the most, you were there. Even when I didn't want it to be you two coming to my rescue. As soon as I see you, I feel like I am coming home. Every single time. You have made me feel complete and have given me the best thing, besides the two of you, in the little boy that will be here in a few short months. Every day is a battle, but I wouldn't want to wage war with anyone other than either one of you. I love you forever and beyond," she tells us, letting a few tears slip from her eyes while glancing back and forth between my brother and me.

Crash steps forward and replaces my hand with his. He does nothing but look at our girl for a minute. "Darcy, firecracker, I'm definitely a man of few words. You have shown me that no matter what, there are good and innocent people in this world. We have found the best part of ourselves when we found you. I would have chased you until the end of time if it meant that you would agree to be ours. I love you more than anythin' in this world. And I will always, only placin' our son before you. Thank you for everythin' you have given us and continue to give us. But most of all, thank you for givin' us your love."

The preacher finishes the ceremony and I don't hear another word. Darcy consumes Crash and I to the point of distraction. Within a few minutes, the preacher is pronouncing us husband and wife after we slip our rings on one another's finger. Crash and I have the same rings while Darcy has a wedding band that goes along with her engagement ring perfectly. I can't wait any longer to get a taste of our girl. Holding her face gently between my hands, I stare into her eyes before I place the sweetest and softest kiss against her lips. For a minute, nothing exists except her lips on mine. Breaking apart, Crash takes his turn and gives her the same treatment as I did. This is the sweetest moment in our lives.

We've been at the reception for a few hours and I know that Darcy is getting ready to crash. She's been sitting in the same spot for a little while now, her eyes getting heavy. Before she can go upstairs to our room, we need to do two more things; have our first dance and have cake. Those are things that she would regret missing out on and I'm not going to let it happen. Looking at Crash over top of her head, I nod to let him know we need to move forward with these two events now.

I stand up and hold out my hand to her as Crash goes and tells the DJ what song we want to play. Once we're on the makeshift dancefloor, *You Make It Easy* by *Jason Aldean* begins to play. Holding her in my arms, I slowly move so she doesn't trip up or anything. Moving her slow and steady is what I want as I hold her close to me. About half way through the song, Crash steps in and takes my spot. He slowly spins her on the floor as I stand and watch them. There's no jealousy or bad feelings. I feel nothing but love watching my brother and our girl dancing.

Skylar gets the cake ready as the song comes to an end so that we can cut it once the song is done. Darcy is dead on her feet and the only thing I'm worried about right now is getting her into bed. Not for sex or anything else, I want her in bed so that she can go to sleep and not do any harm to herself or the baby.

"You ready for cake baby?" I ask, as they make their way toward me. "I know you're ready for bed and we're goin' to get there in just a few minutes. Let's get the cake done and we'll head inside."

"No, you guys can party with your brothers and everyone else her," she tries to tell us, knowing that she's not going to win this one. "You shouldn't have to go to bed just because I'm tired."

"Not happenin' baby. We're not goin' to be anywhere other than right next to you," Crash tells her, taking the words out of my mouth. "This is our night and we're goin' to be sleepin' with you so that we can begin the rest of our lives together when we open our eyes."

Darcy nods her head and we make our way over to Skylar and the table holding the exact cake that she fell in love with. Together, the three of us cut through the cake and place four small pieces on a plate. We're not planning on smashing the cake in her face, but that all depends on what she does to us. Crash and her go first. They gently feed one another the cake and smile at one another. Darcy then turns to me and I see the devilish glint in her eyes a second too late. Before I can blink, cake is smashed in my face and she spreads it around, covering half of my face with the cake and frosting. Laughing, I take the piece in my hand and go to give her the same treatment. She manages to duck out of the way, so that only a little frosting swipes up the side of her face.

"I want to thank everyone for comin' to help us celebrate our marriage to this amazin' girl that stole our hearts with one look," I tell everyone. "It's time for us to disappear for the night while the rest of you party."

Amongst hoots and hollers, Crash, Darcy, and I enter the clubhouse and make our way to our room. Once the door is shut, we help get her out of the dress and hang it on the back of the door. Underneath she had on a strapless white corset with a green lacy overlay at the top. There's a matching pair of white and green panties covering her pussy while garters hold up thigh high white stockings. If we knew she was wearing this the whole day, we would've made our way up here a hell of a lot sooner.

"Climb in bed baby," Crash tells her as he begins to strip down to nothing. I copy him and we both climb into bed on either side of our girl.

She's already passed out cold and doesn't realize we're even in bed with her. "Best day ever!" I whisper to Crash. He agrees and we both lay our heads down to let sleep claim us for now. As soon as we wake up, we won't be leaving this room for a very long time.

Chapter Fifteen
Darcy

EVERY DAY FOR THE LAST THREE MONTHS I have put in a few hours at the salon, mainly doing paperwork. Riley and Crystal, the new stylist, won't let me do much else. I'm actually grateful since it means I can sit on my ever-expanding ass. I thought I was tired before, but it's nothing like it is now. Any day now our little guy could come into this world and it won't come soon enough for me.

I'm already almost a week overdue and I'm getting picked up in a minute to head to Doctor Sanchez's office. We've already discussed being induced and today is the day that it's going to happen. I don't care what anyone else says about it, I can't go one more day carrying this baby. I'm miserable and biting everyone's head off. Crash and Trojan are being amazing considering how much shit I give them. Most days, I'm surprised they don't hide out at the clubhouse to get away from me.

"You ready to go baby?" Trojan asks, walking in the salon.

Nodding my head, I close the computer out, make sure the girls don't need anything else, and let my man help me out of the chair I've been sitting in for the past hour. As we make our way out of the door, I can't help but feel elated that today is the day our son makes his first appearance into the world. Part of me wants to keep him safe and sound in my belly, but another part of me will be happy when he's born.

"Are you nervous?" Crash asks me, as I get helped up into the front of the truck.

"No. I'm ready for this to be over with. Besides, I know the two of you are nervous enough for all of us," I respond with a smile on my face at the conversations we've been having lately regarding the baby and what's going to happen when he's finally in our arms.

My guys laugh along with me and we begin the short drive to the doctor's office. Within minutes, I'm in an exam room and lying on a table waiting for Doctor Sanchez to come in. We don't have to wait very long as she appears and does her exam before really uttering a word to us.

"I think that today, we need to induce you. You're already over four centimeters dilated and having contractions. I fear that you're too tired and in too much pain to feel the contractions that you've been having. I'll meet you at the hospital in an hour to check your progress and see what our next step is. Sound good?" she asks, helping me sit up before getting the paperwork I need to take over with me.

"You have made my day, Doc," I tell her, gingerly getting off the table and standing between my guys. "We'll see you soon."

True to her word, Doctor Sanchez arrived at the hospital shortly after I got a room and the nurse finished hooking me up to everything. I'm laying in bed as she comes through the door. After checking me, she tells me that she's going to break my water and see if that speeds anything up. I turn my attention to the TV as she does what she has to. Well, until I feel the gush of liquid pouring from my body. Fuck! I never thought it would be like this.

A nurse is already standing by with a clean gown, new bedding, and an extra pillow. I gladly get up and remove the soiled gown before replacing it with a fresh one. The only thing I have to say is that I'm glad I wasn't out in public or home when my water broke. Crash and Trojan probably would've flipped the fuck out while I made the situation worse by laughing or crying my ass off.

Within an hour, the contractions are coming fast and hard. "I hate both of you so much! You'll never get within a hundred yards of my body ever again!" I scream at them in pain.

"You don't mean that firecracker," Trojan tells me, taking the washcloth and wiping my sweat drenched forehead yet again while Crash goes to get me more ice chips.

"I do mean that with every fiber of my being. You go through this fucking pain and tell me you'd let me touch you again motherfucker!" I yell out as another contraction takes hold.

Trojan and Crash are taking turns letting me know where I am with my contractions, which helps a little bit. They've been patient and kind as I do nothing more than cuss them out and tell them how much I hate them both. In reality, I could never hate them, but it helps me take away from thinking of all the pain racking my body as our son makes his way in the world.

Finally, a little after nine at night, our son entered the world crying and screaming his anger out. I'm exhausted and completely hooked around his little finger already. Crash and Trojan will kill me if I tell anyone, but they both had tears rolling down their faces and a look of pure awe as they got their first glimpse of him.

"Are you ready to let people in?" Crash asks me, once he sees my eyes open again.

"Yes. I know they've been waiting to see him and we can't hold them much longer," I tell them, holding my arms out for my son.

Within ten minutes, my room is filled to capacity. They're all crowding around the baby cradled in my arms. I know they're waiting to hear what his name is, so I look at the guys and give them a nod. Crash addresses the room while Trojan sits on the bed next to me, wrapping his arm around our son and me.

"We'd like for you to meet Axle Blake Evans-Martin," he announces, beaming down at us with a proud smile on his face.

Everyone tells us how much they love his name and spend the next hour taking turns coddling him while I relax. Trojan and Crash are watching everyone with eagle eyes considering they are holding their entire world in their arms. If I thought they were bad and overprotective with me, that's nothing compared to how they're already being with Axle. This is not going to go good for anyone if they don't relax a little bit. I can already see the fights going down in the coming months and years.

Crash

We're finally home with Axle and I am glad that we're getting into a routine that's manageable for all of us. Darcy has gotten on our asses more than once in the last few days about keeping such a close eye on him. No one can get around him without one of us hovering. This includes Darcy. It's crazy and I don't know why we're even begin like this, but it has to do with not wanting anything to happen to our son. If he cries, we want to be there in that second to help him.

Right now, he's sleeping peacefully in his room and we've got the monitors on to hear any little noise that comes from him. Darcy is taking a nap while the baby does so she's ready to feed and change him when he wakes up again. Trojan is laying down with her while I am watching TV. Well, I'm pretending to watch TV. Nothing can hold my interest for more than a few minutes. Maybe I need to go out for a ride to clear my head.

Leaving a note on the stand beside the bed, I tell them that I've gone for a ride to clear my head and check on things at the clubhouse for a little bit. I'll be back soon, knowing that I can't stay away from the house for very long. My entire world is under one roof and that's where I always want to be. I'll never go far from them, and I'll always return to them. My life, my love, and my son mean more to me than anything else ever has. Well, anything other than the Wild Kings. The club will forever be my family.

Trojan

The last month has truly opened my eyes to how strong and amazing Darcy is. She's been taking care of a newborn, put up with our crazy as fuck asses, and been doing things around the house. I know she's been thinking about going back to the salon even though she doesn't want to leave the baby. If anything, I see her going back part time in the beginning and then deciding from there.

Axle is growing like a weed and getting stronger every day. I'm in awe of the things that he learns daily. Already he has a look reserved for his mama. All he has to do is hear her voice and a little look comes over his adorable face. It's the same when Crash and I start talking to him. I swear that he turns his little head toward us and waits for us to pick him up. I'm probably being biased and none of this really happens, but it's what I tell myself and what I'll continue to tell myself.

Our routine is simple. We get up early in the morning when Axle wants to eat. As soon as he's taken care of, Darcy takes a nap while Crash and I get ready for the day. He goes to work for a few hours and comes home to let me go to work for a few hours. We go to the clubhouse regularly and whenever we're needed. The three of us cook dinner together before Darcy feeds Axle again. Once he's done eating, Crash and I take turns bathing him and getting him ready for bed. Then, the three of us spend a few minutes putting him down before heading to bed ourselves.

I hate that we still have at least two more weeks until we can properly touch our girl again, but she's been pushing already. So, we give in enough to get her off and let her give us a hand job or blow job. You can bet your ass that as soon as we get the green light, Darcy won't be moving from the bed other than when our son needs her. We will keep her busy as fuck.

Never once did I think that I'd want to be tied down to one woman for the rest of my life. I was wrong. Darcy is our true love and has blessed us with the most incredible little boy we could ever ask for. The only thing that would make it better would be a daughter. But, that's not going to happen right now. As soon as possible we will have her pregnant again.

Epilogue

Gage

AFTER BAILEY AND THE LOSS OF MY BABY, I never thought I'd give anyone a chance at getting close to me again. Bailey broke my heart when I realized that she would never truly be over Grim. It shattered into a million pieces when I found out that my baby never had his chance to live. Ryan, as Bailey decided we would name him, should've been given the chance to live his life and it was taken from him for some unknown reason.

All of that shit flew out the window the second I laid eyes on Riley for the first time. I could see the pain, regret, and torture marring her face. Only then did I take in her beauty and realize that there was more to her than met the eye. I got her phone number before leaving Clifton Falls and we've talked ever since. Not too many know her backstory, but she has entrusted me with it. I am taking it on and doing everything in my power to make sure the wrong that was done to her is righted.

"Crash, I need your help," I tell him, as he enters my office and takes a seat opposite me.

"What's up Prez?" he asks, leaning forward to pay close attention to what I'm about to tell him.

"This goes no farther than right here. Trojan and Darcy cannot know what I'm about to tell you. This is not my story to tell and the only reason you're hearin' it is for the help you can give me," I tell him, letting this information sink in.

"Whatever you need Prez," he tells me, fully facing me so that I know he's not going to spill the beans.

I let him in on the bare minimum details about Riley's time with Sam and her daughter Shelby. I've called in markers, promised markers to friendly clubs, and done as much searching on my own as I could with no luck. Now, I need to pull in the big guns and have Crash help me find Riley's daughter and bring her home. Riley is fading away to nothing knowing that her daughter is out there in the world and she has no clue where. I can't imagine the pain she's going through. All I know is that I want to be the one there to wipe her tears, make it through the day, and bring her daughter back to her. I'll stop at nothing to get Shelby back where she belongs; in the arms of her loving mother.

"I got you. You have my word I'll do whatever I can to help you bring her daughter home. You claimin' her Prez?" he asks, staring at me and trying to gauge how much I'm vested in this.

"I don't know yet. What I do know is I want to heal this amazin' woman and make her whole again. I love spendin' time with her and she's on my mind more than she should be. We both come with a ton of baggage and it's not going to go away," I tell him honestly.

Crash nods and leaves the office. Leaving me alone with my thoughts when all I really want to do is make my way over to Riley's house and spend the night with her. I'm there more than I'm here these days. Hell, I can't even tell you when I was at my apartment the last time for more than grabbing a few more clothes.

Riley

I don't know what is going through Gage's head anymore. He spends all of his free time with me doing absolutely nothing at all. We usually sit in my quiet little house and watch TV or movies. There's no touching or kissing, nothing more than friends spending time with one another.

He's been there when I've needed to vent about my day, missing my daughter, and anything else. I'm there for him to vent to, as much as he can without giving any club business away. And, he's determined to help me find my daughter and bring her home. I will do anything I have to in order to bring her home. No matter how long it takes. I just want my baby girl back in my arms where she belongs. I never signed my rights away, she was stolen from me right after I gave birth to her.

 Every day I struggle to make it through without grabbing a bottle or the nearest painkiller. Right after she was taken from me, I drank like a fish and popped any pain pill I could get my hands on. I'm not proud of my reaction to her being taken from me, but it was where my head was at then. That's why I couldn't betray my best friend, Keira. She meant the world to me and I couldn't let that monster get his hands on her.

 Some of you may hate me for even contemplating going through with betraying her, but in the end, it's my story and my life. I knew I'd never forgive myself for hurting her more than she already was, so I kept my mouth shut and never once uttered a word about where she was or what was done to me.

 Gage is worming his way into my heart and putting one piece back at a time. I'm not sure that I'll ever be good enough for him, and that's why I think I have to push him away. I need to limit my time with him before he completely destroys any defense I have against him. It won't take much honestly. Not for him. But, I'm going to do everything in my power to keep my wall firmly intact and up where it belongs!

The End

Darcy's Downfall Playlist

The Sound Of Silence – Disturbed

Simple Man – Shinedown

I'll Follow You – Shinedown

If You Only Knew – Shinedown

Bad Company – Five Finger Death Punch

Will You Still Love Me Tomorrow – Sweet Talk Radio

My Faith In You – Brantley Gilbert

Tuesday's Gone – Lynyrd Skynyrd

But We Lost It – Pink

Through Glass – Stone Sour

Marry Me – Thomas Rhett

You Make It Easy – Jason Aldean

Heaven – Kane Brown

The Ones That Like Me – Brantley Gilbert

You Promised – Brantley Gilbert

What Ifs – Kane Brown

Country Girl (Shake It For Me) – Luke Bryan

That's My Kind Of Night – Luke Bryan

Anywhere – 112

Acknowledgments

First, I would like to thank the readers. If it weren't for you, your continued support, and taking a chance so long ago (it feels like it) on a new author, I wouldn't have made it as far as I have. You guys continue to make me want to get my stories out to you, see what new things I can do such as collaborating with other authors, and eventually go to a signing.

My kids and family mean the world to me and have given me nothing but unwavering support and encouragement. They let me work when I have a deadline looming and do what they can to help me do everything else. Even though my kids may not understand everything I have to do when I'm working, they continue to encourage me to follow my dreams and reach for the stars.

My amazing PA, Michelle. You have been a tremendous part of my support system since the very beginning. I'm lucky to call you one of my best friends and to have you in my corner. Since you became my PA, you keep my butt on track and hold me accountable for when I write and how much work I put in. You have gotten my name out there with everything you do behind the scenes and I'll never be able to thank you enough. Love you!!

Jenni, my adopted mama, you have been a show of support with everything. Thank you for taking the time to read through my words and point out anything that's wrong with the story, timelines, and the dreaded comma. You have helped me talk through story lines I get stuck on and when I can't figure things out. This is in a professional and personal manner. Thank you for being there for myself and my kids when you didn't have to be. Love you!!

Kim. You have become and amazing friend from a million miles away. I love your ability to pick things out that I overlook, including the smallest details that I forget. When I need someone, you have always been there for me and my kids. Thank you for being a friend, a member of my family, a beta reader, and someone that takes a minute out of your day to check on me when you know things are crazy and I'm way past my boiling point. We love you!!

Darlene, you have been with me since the very beginning. You have become an amazing friend, an awesome beta reader, and someone that has had my back no matter what. My kids love you and you have become a member of our family. When I have wanted to throw in the towel and give up on my dream, you talked me down and talked me into continuing on with this journey. Thank you for everything. Love you!!

Shelly, from Graphics by Shelly. You create some amazing covers and put up with me when I can't make up my mind, if I want to change something, and when I don't know exactly what I'm looking for. Thank you for creating some amazing covers for me that help bring my stories to life!!

There are a few people that have been with me from the start and become friends and a part of my family. You know who you are, and I am thankful that you are there for me. When things go crazy in my personal life, you're the ones I turn to and the ones that have my back. Even though we're thousands of miles apart, you have been there for me when I haven't had anyone else. Thank you for everything you have done for me!!

I'm sure that there are people I'm forgetting. For that, I'm truly sorry. Please know that everyone is important to me and I will never be able to thank you enough for everything!!

About the Author

I am a single mom of three amazing children, living in Upstate New York. We have lived in New York forever and I can't wait to start showing my kids other states.

I developed a love for reading at a young age from my grandma. My kids are following in my footsteps and read almost as much as I do. I read anything I can get my hands on. Now, I get to live my dream and put my own stories out in the world. If I can help just one person know that someone else out there is going through something they are, I'll consider myself successful.

If I'm not writing, or reading, you can find me hanging out with my kids, watching NASCAR, listening to music, and teaching my kids how to bake and cook. We love to bake and learn how to make new things. I also love to rearrange my house every so often. It tends to drive some people around me crazy!

One fact about me is that I'm extremely shy. But, I love meeting new people and hearing stories about their lives. You can meet so many amazing and interesting people by just taking a few minutes to listen!

Here are some links to follow me:

Facebook:
https://www.facebook.com/ErinOsborneAuthor/
Twitter:
https://twitter.com/author_osborne
My website:
http://erinosborne1013.wix.com/authorerinosborne
Spotify:
https://open.spotify.com/user/emgriff07

Other Books

Wild Kings MC
Skylar's Saviors
Bailey's Saving Grace
Tank's Salvation
Melody's Temptation
Blade's Awakening
Irish's Destiny
Rage's Redemption

Wild Kings MC: Dander Falls
Darcy's Downfall

Alpha Demons MC
Tempted By Demons' – Coming soon

Old Ladies Club
Old Ladies Club Book 1: Wild Kings MC
Old Ladies Club Book 2: Soul Shifterz MC

Coming Soon

ALPHA DEMONS MC

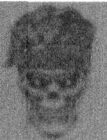

Tempted By
Demons

ERIN OSBORNE & KAYCE KYLE

Brantley "Lucifer" Black

Since I was fourteen years old I've been this town's worst nightmare, becoming a ward of the state alongside my brother, my partner in crime, and VP. I've done many horrible things in my life. You see, I'm the President of the Alpha Demons MC. When I was younger, I was burned by the women in my life including my mother. So, I vowed never to give my heart to anyone else. Now, most people run from me when I come walking down the street. The only ones that truly know me are the brothers in my club. Can one chance encounter change my life? Will I take a gamble with the heart most claim I don't even have and open up again? Or, will I lose everything before it has a chance to begin?

Preslee Collins

I'm down on my luck other than meeting two amazing men in a short period of time. I have a boss that is disgusting and run into some issues with him. When I think things are going to continue on a path leading nowhere, I find a sign that may just save me. Can I take a chance on love in an unconventional manner? Is someone out to get me and ruin my happiness, and if so, will my savior's turn out to be spawned from hell itself?

Xavier "Duke" Cassle

As Vice President of the Alpha Demons MC, my job is to stand by my brother's side and support my best friend. The two of us are all we've ever had since we were teens. We may not always see eye to eye, but we have one another's back no matter what. Will one person come between my best friend and brother? Can we overcome every obstacle put in our way and find the happiness in life that's always eluded us?

** Intended for mature audiences, 18+

Cover Designer: Graphics by Shelly

https://www.amazon.com/Tempted-Demons-Alpha-MC-ebook/dp/B07D3YZD3X/ref=sr_1_2?ie=UTF8&qid=1527629156&sr=8-2&keywords=tempted+by+demons

Made in the USA
Coppell, TX
09 May 2021